# Cuttle

*a novel*

by

Chelsea Britain

ISBN 978-1-951796-00-6 (hardcover)
ISBN 978-1-951796-01-3 (paperback)
ISBN 978-1-951796-03-7 (ebook: mobi)
ISBN 978-1-951796-04-4 (ebook: epub)


Cover design by Tom Anderson
Interior illustrations by David North

# Cuttle

# Chapter 1

*Cuttlefish only get together socially to mate.*

This isn't where I want to be. I could be running now along the Cuyahoga, the sun warming my shoulders as yellow leaves drift down to the water in lazy waves. I think of the mud caking on my tennis shoes, the white noise of the river rushing through the locks, the sweet sense of security I get there like a just-fed boxer crab nestling down into an anemone.

Instead, I'm in the den of the football-watching, more like a skipjack tuna hooked on a long line. This is my great fall break transition period—involuntary, unavoidable, an untimely end to a comfortable way of life.

"Actually, Cam's not with me," I say as I take a seat on the sofa.

My dad leans forward in his armchair. "But Sunday," he says. "We're matched in Fantasy. What, is he at one of the restaurants? I guess. It's Friday." But not the first Friday of the month, so not a specials night at the steakhouse. Live music at the inn, maybe?

I look at the TV as my dad winds down his list of potential

Cam locations. Sports get him this way, and we've entered that crucial pre-game period when the pizza or wings can be delivered but the phone can't be answered.

I turn up the volume on two men engaging in the sweaty football speculation. Dad finds these noises comforting, familiar, like the prayers he's repeated a thousand times, the smell of mesquite, or the crunch of stale Doritos.

"Actually, Dad, Cam and I separated."

My father's eyes bug out of his head like a ratfish.

"Cam," he sputters, then, "Sunday!"

Dad charts his life in a parade of these Sundays, Browns wins and Browns losses, spicy wing-induced gastrointestinal distress and gradual hearing loss. The Sundays will just keep coming. Followed by the holidays. Followed by the basketball. There's no good time for a breakup or a Browns loss.

Then he turns blotchy, few-hours-after-leftover-wings-style. "You and Cam," he says. "What do you mean, *separated*? When?"

"Six months ago." Eight for me. Apparently separation's subjective; it doesn't just happen when you make a decision or crawl out a window.

"Separated meaning...separated for how long?"

I try to think of something more pacifying than "permanently." I used to have a stack of note cards with phrases for all these occasions. "In a better place" seems promising.

But Dad rebounds before I can choose one, bursting out of his easy chair and muttering at a constant rate like a farting herring. This quickly devolves into something that sounds a little Latin, maybe that he picked up as an altar boy. Like his holy spirit's moving him, finally.

I should have seen this coming. Mom warned me he and Cam have bonded. She traces this back to about six years ago, when they committed to join forces for a complex March bracket-making contest while I was in the shower. There's no way to know what inspired this level of commitment. When I was a teenager, Dad couldn't even commit to picking up my tampons when he went into Stow.

But that basketball year turned into another, and then another. Now they're in an imaginary football league, too, the Marion Motley Crew, and they go out tailgating and eating spicy meat products together. They're a *team* that yells and sweats and mourns the decline of reffing standards.

Here in their football-watching space, I think I can still smell Cam, his spearmint and sandalwood that always used to stay in my nose through a few saline rinses.

After Dad and I make it through the *how's*—Cam and I are separated like megaladons and rainbow trout, separated like Dad's red meat and Mom's asparagus, separated like the Browns and the Ravens—we move on to the *why's.*

*Why* is more difficult. Cam and I maintained a symbiotic relationship for almost a decade. I think of Cam, with his MBA and his restaurants in Fairlawn. Of Fairlawn, with its Earthfare, a sprawling suburban dream. Of me climbing out of his bathroom window with my rat's travel cage wedged under my elbow.

It's not like I planned to separate. It happened last February, high flu season, when I was putting one of my triclosan-free hand sanitizers in my bag and Cam asked why I didn't just leave it at his house. I told him I didn't want to leave a triclosan-free hand sanitizer at his house, and he said if I didn't want to leave a triclosan-free hand sanitizer at his house at that point in our relationship, then I must not care about him very much.

We hadn't been arguing. Competition for the resources that mattered to us was low. We were similar in size and shape, but genetically disparate. I collected a vial of his saliva and compared our DNA through an appropriate web-based service about six months into our relationship. We're not distant cousins or anything; all markers pointed to success.

My dad makes a beeline for the hallway and yells for my mom.

This should have gone differently. There's a pattern for breakup response: disbelief, followed by *that bastarding,* followed by ice cream. I was looking forward to the ice cream. I guess I didn't take into account that Dad's bonded, full of the right neurotransmitters that work the same way for Cam as they do for the Browns—unconditional acceptance, unquestioned allegiance, a forever kind of bond.

He reappears in the doorway. "Who's going to drive you to the fish conference?" he demands.

I start to say it's not a fish conference but stop when I see he's almost the color of my favorite acai sorbet. And I know, suddenly, that this is just the first of many of those important, rest-of-my-life occasions a Cam might have made easier.

"You can't drive yourself," Dad says. "Cincinnati. The fish...*traffic!*"

*Molluscs.* Cuttlefish are *molluscs,* I remind him. But he thinks this is some kind of conspiracy. So I tell him about the GPS on my phone, instead. Not having a GPS was how I found

Cam to begin with, lost at the end of what I thought was a shortcut to the highway but that was actually a jogging path. Now I have an app, so there's no risk of a repeat relationship.

I'm like a *mollusc*, I assure my dad. I learn from my mistakes.

He starts to pace, tripping over the pizza box before launching into his go-to spiel about flat tires. In the universe my dad inhabits, there are at any given time more flat tires on highway 77 than romance novels in the Cleveland airport.

But this is a pattern I know, at least, one I can handle. I respond, as always, with my advanced degree spiel that suggests I'm car-savvy, because my dad's been led to believe doctorates confer things like parallel parking competency.

He pauses and raises his arms, palm up. I assume he's appealing to his Catholic heavens rather than trying to appeal to my own rationality.

"What about the hamster?" he asks. "What's going to happen to him? Did you even think about what this…"

I remind him Scribbles is a rat. Dad thinks "hamster" is a euphemism.

And then, just like that, it's over, like the Cretaceous period with the asteroid that ushered in the Palogene. Dad falls back into his recliner, and his jaw goes slack like a gulper eel.

I sit through a couple commercials and watch for movement that doesn't come. I guess he's in a transition period, too.

A couple hours later, I'm buckling Scribbles' travel cage

into my passenger seat when my mom's Subaru comes careening into the driveway, almost sideswiping the Meyers' rose bushes.

She yells for me to wait. She's discovered a new kind of blush. My mom discovers new cosmetics with the same enthusiasm van Leeuwenhoek must have felt the first time he looked into his microscope and saw bacteria. Blush is an advantage, to her, a kind of evolutionary adaptation like the ability to camouflage or flash an eyespot to confuse a predator. Bright colors are good for mating, and this new shade's called "orgasm."

"For your conference," she tells me as she hands it over. Then she starts talking about blending again. *Blend with the little sponges. Apply the eye liner liberally. Use the freaking mascara.* There's a process to this, an order.

"And don't apologize," she adds.

I make the semi-affirmative, pulsed grunt like a humpback I perfected sometime between my First Communion and the sixth grade Valentine's dance.

My mom takes this as an invitation to segue into her traditional pep talk about self-confidence and unexpected opportunities and good posture. She's been expanding this speech roughly since my sixth grade Valentine's dance, actually, long before I knew I had anything to be less than confident about.

I nod along as I survey the yard. The leaves are evenly distributed over the grass now, the patches where I used to rake them back and forth grown over with fescue a shade lighter than the rest. We're a week away from peak foliage here, another week at home, along the shoreline. Most of the trees will have lost their leaves by my cousin's orchestra concert next month, and then Mom will have hidden them away in the big pumpkin composting bag in the garage by Thanksgiving. I like these patterns, like knowing what's coming.

"Remember," she says, "your paper was published."

I continue the nod. It was in a small journal, though, which is like having bioluminescence without an oil-filled swim bladder in the Mariana trench of academia. At interdisciplinary conferences, survival's really only guaranteed to the Kraken.

But during this transition period, I'm embracing...things, my mom reminds me. Myself. My differences. My bosom. (This speech is expanding.) But *good* things, anyway, because I'm letting go of my preconceived notions, of my self-consciousness, of my kiddie bras and my soft ponytail holders.

"You have time, don't you?" she asks. "You can go by the market on your way home?"

"The market?"

She nods. "There's a guy in the café."

This is part of a larger pattern I'm not ready for. A few months ago, my mom found social media and the #FOMO—fear of missing out. Currently, she's afraid that she's missing out on grandkids and that I'm missing out on all the single men in the greater Cleveland metro area.

And of course my career stalling out is the perfect opportunity for me to embrace the #FOMO, to seize the day, to run like someone's left the gate open, and etc. Because I have plenty of time to do these things now.

In my mom's imagination, #FOMOing will go like this: I'll collect makeup and emergency hoop earrings, and then, one day, I'll enter a public building and emerge attached to an attractive man like some kind of rouged lamprey. She used to practice sending me into the post office and the grocery store in preparation for this day.

She keeps talking, identifying markers of the cafe man's likely reproductive fitness—his shoulder width, his healthy BMI, and his only slightly receding hairline.

I identify a Blanding's turtle in the creek at the edge of the lawn.

Maybe it's a timing thing, I tell her, my body recognizing falling leaves and the stench of death that heralds the soon-to-be Ohio tundra. Maybe I should wait until February to make evaluations of reproductive fitness, a year since my breakup with Cam, like the 22 years I was single before him. Maybe I'm on a 22 year cycle.

Cycles are important. October's the time for endings, for months of dormancy, of stability. I didn't choose October to start a new life pattern.

"No ring," Mom adds, ignoring me. In addition to those for color and depth, my mother's evolved with a third ocular structure dedicated to identifying bare ring fingers. Success always comes down to this, of course, to some little evolutionary advantage that shines through all the drift.

"And I heard his coffee order. *Almond milk.*" The big oak rustles overhead, dropping a leaf into her hair. "He seemed like a really nice guy."

I think of Cam, the definition of *really nice guy*, and decide to engage this alternative fantasy for now. Theoretically, the cafe man's also single, with a healthy microbiome and a just-right IQ. He's probably a dessert chef, too, and his parents are dead.

"No," Mom interrupts me here. "His parents could live far away. Not like Cam's. You're going to want in-laws who are alive." She says this like she's never encouraged her mother-in-law to eat past-due chicken soup.

"In New Zealand," I decide, "and he makes annual visits to the Galapagos."

"See what you could be missing out on?"

"Or he lives with his parents and is allergic to the Galapagos."

"That's ridiculous," Mom says. "What would he be allergic to in the Galapagos?"

I let her have this point, because this is how you date, how you #FOMO, by exhausting all available options.

"You have to put yourself *out there*," she says. This is the woman who, shortly after Cam and I broke up, asked why I hadn't established closer relations with my colleagues—men who come out of their labs only to urinate and to collect pretzels from the vending machine. And not always to urinate.

And when I think about the great *out there* beyond my lab, suddenly, I'd like to focus on anything else—the Blanding's turtle, the stranger in the market cafe, even the imminent Browns loss.

"You have time," Mom tells me. "He was just sitting down with his laptop when I left. A *mac*."

I make my humpback sound.

She doesn't accept this—because I might be missing out

on something wonderful, and it might be because she didn't squeeze me enough as a baby. What if she'd hugged me more? Would I be happier? Would there be grandkids? Maternal guilt runs deep. And she knows all the baby-squeezing research. My mom studies humans like I study cuttlefish and my dad studies football—methodically, passionately, comprehensively.

When I'm pulling out of the driveway, I see her flapping in my rearview mirror like a puffin taking flight. I stop and roll down my window.

"Your blush," she says when she catches up to me. "Put on your blush first."


I bypass the café on my way home, instead giving into the magnetic pull of my lab like a loggerhead sea turtle returning to its natal beach.

The hallway at the back of the biology building's quiet, a sweet haven of terrazzo and shiny concrete that's been my primary habitat these last eight years. I know all its rhythms now, its pipe knocks and its buzzy fluorescents, its orange-scented cleaner wafting from the bathrooms. The women's is all mine here, with a bottle of Eucerin by the sink and a lawn chair for journal-reading by the little window.

I look in Milner's office as I pass by. He's left his light on again and forgotten to put out his trash. This is usual, known, like the off-kilter bubbler in his sea shrimp tank and the stench of Chinese takeout wafting from Kyle's lab next door.

Kyle is Milner's other advisee and studies clownfish. Clownfish are a lot like sea shrimp—easy, manageable, of Cam-like predictability. They school and choose mating pairs in an ordered way; the largest in a school is female, the second largest, male. They change genders to suit, much like Kyle changes projects. This year, he's using mirrors to try to confuse the measurement process, making the fish appear larger or smaller. It's like academia in microcosm, an irony that's probably wasted on him.

I straighten my *N.A. Novak* card in its holder and use the fob to get into my lab. Then lamps I've collected over the years switch on instead of the overhead fluorescents. The protein skimmer hums. Things are right here, normal. There's no indication all of this is about to be defunct.

My cuttles greet me at the front of their tank like usual. Bitty, the smallest, flutters her tentacles at the cabinet with the mazes, then at the freezer with her new mussels.

Just a few weeks ago, Bitty secured her place as the fastest maze-navigating mollusc in history. Now she's retired, also in transition as she prepares for her big, end-of-life move to the Eerie Aquarium.

I think she looks bored. Does she have regrets, I wonder, or question her purpose? Could she even be in crisis already, considering doing something rash, maybe even something like mating to herald the end of her little cuttle cardiovascular system? Cuttles have patterns, too, like careers and breakups are supposed to—they hatch, live, mate, and die of heart failure.

I want to think my cuttles are different, safe from these crippling biological imperatives that destroy their non maze-navigating cousins in the wild.

I look at my whiteboard, where maze times usually make a smelly dry erase rainbow. *Days until cuttle relocation: 56* is all that's there now, in a blue box at the top.

I sit down at my desk and consider other lists.

*Things I can do with the rest of the semester:*
    *-Two papers (already edited)*
    *-Conference presentation next week (already memorized)*
    *-Self- actualize*

*Things I can do after that:*

*Things I can do now:*

I tell myself this is just part of my career transition, like my post-Cam Saturday nights, like the reintroduction of flax seeds into my morning oatmeal. Not like the beginning of the Palogene period.

I should be able to handle this process. I'm at the point in my career when most women take a breather anyway, consider birthing things or applying for teaching jobs, going on cruise vacations or developing obsessions with amateur photography.

I consider what I do, how *I* self-actualize. I add *(re) Evaluate Eerie Aquarium staff* to the list of things I can do. Then I change the *56* on the white board to *55*, drop the cuttles a little crab, and pick up Milner's trash on my way out.

It's almost dark when I get to the house, the orange pendant lights casting their happy glow out the front windows. Heather got rid of the fluorescents when I moved in at the beginning of my dissertation a little over six years ago.

I think often now about those sweet, transition-free days, all the research funding in the world ahead of me, my Saturday nights occupied by a Cam I didn't have to think about.

From the driveway, I can see the contours of the city skyline, a little halo of light through the university sports complex that turns into trendy lofts that turns into an outlet mall that turns into the shotgun houses that rush towards downtown. Cleveland's in transition, too, always spreading out or sucking in like a swim bladder.

Lillie, our other roommate, is waiting for me in the kitchen. She's already folded into her listening lotus on a barstool when I come in.

Over the last several years, I've found the listening lotus to be the most threatening of all Lillie's positions. She's like an Indonesian flower urchin—you think she's just sitting there, inert but interesting, until her stillness gets you.

At first, she feigns passivity, concealing her listening agenda as she greets me and invites Scribbles to crawl up her arm and sit on her shoulder like a furry, obese cockatoo.

"Did you have a good trip home?" she asks.

I tell her it was fine, that *I'm* fine, you know, seizing the day and wearing orgasmic blush.

Scribbles clicks his teeth, and Lillie hands him one of the cakes she bakes for him in her rice cooker. Then she refolds into her lotus, and I take a seat on the edge of the sofa and prepare to emotionally offgass like a cheap mattress.

She starts with questions she knows the answers to, about my lab and when the cuttles move, if I did a lot of running over the weekend and how my mom's liking her new bridge group.

Lillie's patient like this, like that deep-sea octopus that brooded for four and a half years.

"And your dad?" she asks. "How's he?"

I watch as Scribbles finishes his cake and starts nibbling at her hemp necklace.

"Fine. It's football season."

"And Cam?"

"Will be there tomorrow," I tell her, "for football."

Lillie flexes her calves like she's thinking about transitioning into springing lotus. "Cam changed his status," she offers after a minute.

"His status?"

Lillie's an expert on statuses. With the same efficiency she can decipher computer code, she can translate human emotion, can identify how any person indicates distress, interest, and attachment. And detachment, obviously.

Her own dating life's simple, limited to fellow computer programmers. She's been dating the same one for the last couple years—Ned, of the regular movie nights. Lillie's steadfast like this, predictable, incorruptible like the blockchain.

"Cam's Social status doesn't say 'in a relationship' anymore," she explains.

"Oh." I've never thought about Cam's Social status before. Does this mean he was right that I didn't care about him? I feel selfish thinking about my own status, instead. What is it? Pre-empty tank syndrome? Existential void? Does Social know what's happening to my career the same way it knows how much I stalk the International Marine Research Institute or when I need more of my salt deodorant?

But Lillie doesn't need Social to answer this. Lillie can read my face better than html. "You never had a status," she offers.

"Oh."

"So your dad's okay?"

I tell her Dad's transitioning, like me, like Cleveland twenty years ago. He'll catch up. It's just that his attachment to Cam was stronger than mine. He's grieving a loss. And me? I'm not grieving. I'm embracing...well, you know, things in memes—uncertainty, purposelessness, freedom. That's it, *freedom*.

"This is a *streeessful* time for you," Lillie says, with the drawn-out vowel sounds she usually reserves for my rat.

I deny this and try to tell her this is a stressful time for my *cuttles*, late in their lifespans, their careers ended with no warning. Patterns are important. Change causes stress, which causes mineral depletion, which causes heart failure. Cuttles are like humans this way, just a couple missed sleeps away from total self-destruction.

The way Lillie's looking at me, I wonder how close to self-destruction I look now. There's a fine line between the start of a #FOMO and a mental breakdown.

So I try to imagine proceeding as normal from here. I look past Lillie, through the window to the sports complex, and think about running my easy loops around the tennis courts and soccer fields, listing the shark species in my head and pretending this semester, this life stage, is like any other.

"I was thinking maybe Scribbles should stay in my room for now," Lillie says after a minute. "At least through your conference. He's always on his wheel, and you haven't been sleeping well."

I look back at her. Lillie's known me through dozens of paper deadlines, funding crises, and data losses. Usually, she just loads a good *Frasier* DVD. Is this my breakdown, I wonder, the moment I snap like a captive orca and go work for a pharmaceutical company or have dinner with a member of the philosophy department? Is this the line I cross whereafter I'm no longer considered a suitable guardian for my rat?

She remains lotused. I don't move for a while, either.

In the end, I agree to these temporary rat care arrangements, for Scribbles' sake, and thank her. It takes her a few more minutes to unfold, and I retreat to my bedroom.

When I get inside, I notice Scribbles' corner is empty. Lillie's already moved his larger cage with his tunnel sets. She must have known this was coming. I guess I should have, too.

When I'm about to collapse onto my bed, something on the comforter catches my attention. It's shrink-wrapped and purple. I pick it up, then set it back down. I think it's a sea creature, probably one I should know, but it has a power switch.

I open the door. "Lillie?"

She pokes her head around the corner. Scribbles is still on her shoulder.

"Did you tell Heather about Cam's Social status?" I ask.

Lillie glances at the thing on my bed, then over at Scribbles. Scribbles avoids eye contact.

"I think I mentioned it," she says. Then she uses her slow voice to tell me about online dating and new species that are out there just waiting to be discovered.

The purple sea creature rolls towards the weight of my purse, and I wonder if this is when the breakdown starts.

# Chapter 2

A November kind of wind pushes in late Monday afternoon, sending soccer balls soaring over the walking paths and frisbees zipping around the stadium.

Lillie, Heather, and I dodge a baby stroller as we discuss the features of my new vibrator.

"So it's a...bunny?"

"Bunny *supreme*," Heather corrects.

When I picture the thing on my bed, I see that bloated giant squid that washed up in Wellington last year, except in magenta. But maybe they all look like that. Since it didn't fit into the designed-to-be-inserted-into-my-body drawer with the tampons and thermometer and extra epipens, the bunny supreme is currently serving as abstract art on my nightstand.

"It's good," Heather assures me. Heather runs the

university's equine science breeding program and knows penises better than I know squid. She mentioned earlier that she almost chose the pickle instead of the bunny.

Apparently sex has changed a lot since I last tried it. There are apps now, and vegetables and furry animal likenesses are being used as pleasure aids. And I was probably already behind when I started dating Cam a decade ago.

We pick up our pace, imitating the walk the old ladies at the mall do, all the intensity of the running of the bulls in Barcelona but with extra hip swaying. This walk is for confidence, Heather says, for strutting into my conference on Saturday, for facing potential future employers, for telling Kyle to shove it. It's all about posture. Like stingrays. Stingrays are confident. Stingrays are sexy. I just need to sway like a stingray.

When I attempt the sway she's demonstrating, my knees hyperextend. But of course this awkward period is an integral part of the #FOMOing process, just like getting used to my free Saturday nights, flax seeds in my morning oatmeal, and the gradual but involuntary expansion of my closet.

Heather's kick-started my post-lab wardrobe with a new skirted legging to replace the polyester-shorts-over-leggings arrangement I've relied on since middle school gym class. Skirted leggings inspire confidence, she said. And Heather, handler of the horse penises, wearer of the spandex riding breeches, power-dater extraordinaire, knows confidence.

The butt-flap leggings look good on me, Lillie points out, adding that they *streeetch* and *breeeathe* and make me more comfortable.

The skirt flaps harder in a gust, and it occurs to me that

not all of my body needs to breathe. I'm not a bloody sea slug.

We face the wind head on as we round the turn to the soccer field, where a bustling Sunday game's just picking up. Leaves rattle around on the trees. A cloud bank rolls in from the West, casting a long shadow over the locker rooms. The last time I went running on a Sunday, a stray soccer ball knocked me into the water fountains.

I watch the players clump, then disperse again. They're like schooling sardines—always shifting, always changing, but somehow they stay together. These are patterns you can count on, if you know what to look for, the same way you can count on my gait not attracting any potential mates at this weekend's interdisciplinary conference.

But Heather's playing a long game. Maybe there won't be dateable men at the conference, she concedes, but what about, say, the post office? What about these soccer players or my new dentist? You never know when you'll run into a suitable male and be wearing the wrong kind of gym shorts.

Maybe it's my joints, she says, that are holding me back. Or maybe it's my quads. So we do that awkward hobble-around-on-one-foot-while-you-pull-the-other-to-your-butt exercise.

Maybe I need to open my heart chakra, Lillie suggests. I could try yoga. The skirted leggings would fit right in at her vinyasa class.

I guess this is how #FOMOing looks for a self-actualizing thirty-two-year-old. There are a lot of concerns about my heart chakra.

When we're by the water fountains, the soccer players all scream, bouncing down the field and batting at each other.

Normally, this would get Heather's attention; she can identify reproductive fitness in body odor and primal grunts like I can identify chord progressions. But today, her mind's on Matt, Lillie's colleague, rather than on any of the sweaty males nearby.

Heather's patterns are changing, too. Until recently, she hadn't found anyone who could outperform her own bunny supreme. But tonight's her fourth date with Matt (a first for Heather in at least as many years), on a Monday (not a casual sex night), to a late seating at Amero's (Italian food that's widely accepted to be greater Cleveland's benchmark of serious relationshiphood).

She repeats a joke Matt told her about code-writing. At least I think it's a joke. There aren't any transition periods for Heather, any gradual separation or linking periods; Heather dives after what she wants like a thick-billed murre, seven hundred feet under water before she even notices she's out of air.

Matt talk inevitably morphs into wedding talk, into plus ones at her twin sister's wedding next month, into the usual drama. But this is how weddings always go. One minute, you're snuggling on a railroad track exchanging eskimo kisses as a photographer snaps your save-the-date pictures, and the next, you're out tens of thousands of dollars and there's a state-wide prime rib shortage. And your maid of honor isn't sure whether she's bringing a plus-one.

"But that's going to be fine," Heather tells me when I ask about her plane ticket. "We'll probably both be dating someone new by then, anyway. Having *fun*."

"*Fuuun*," Lillie echoes.

*          *

I wear my new blush the next morning as I scope out the Eerie Aquarium, sneaking like a cuttle, swaying like a stingray.

I'm playing the human game today, the one my mom invented when I was five and we'd pretend we were undercover aliens visiting Earth to study its life forms—for research, of course, underfunded like all important projects. She had to recharacterize it when I started wearing gloves around the other children to prevent contamination.

I get my first points for dodging a horde of children in the Amazon room. They're everywhere today, incubating early winter viruses, shrieking at the penguins, and sneezing into the horseshoe crabs.

I pull my hair forward over my earplugs as I enter the shark tunnel. This morning, it's like the bottleneck at 77 and 20 just outside Fairlawn. I end up stalled between a woman who's trying to take a selfie with a moray eel and a blue-vested aquarium employee who asks me if I need help.

Engaging a stranger's worth ten points, and I don't have a choice. So I look at my map, then at a horn shark drifting by. I tell her I was just admiring him. What a horn shark, and all that. Stately, you know, very spotted. These complements are worth five points each.

I've chosen the right ones. The woman's face erupts into a smile as she tells me about George, who's the first horn shark ever born at the aquarium.

I nod along, pressed up against the glass to create some distance. George is seven this year and loves crabs. Yes, how quickly he grew. No, I didn't notice his mouth. Very attractive. And *two* dorsal fins. Wow. There are a few other sharks in the tank with George, a lemon and a bull and a sandbar shark the woman says likes to hide. But George, he has the best personality. Such exuberance, such healthy digestion. Somewhere nearby, a baby shrieks like a masturbating Atlantic bottlenose.

I continue nodding. This is how you win the human game, with nods and agreement. All humans are irrationally proud of something, parenting something they can't see clearly. You just have to figure out what it is and say the right words about it.

Around the time I'm starting to run out of good words for George, the crowd parts, and I feign a pressing interest in the penguins.

I follow my map through the Arctic to the Caribbean waters where my cuttles will retire—wrongly, of course; there aren't any cuttlefish in the Caribbean. But correcting a human is minus a hundred points. And I think this room's good for them otherwise, quiet and soothing. Little rays swim around the petting tank in the center, and the walls are flanked by parrotfish, eels, and angels.

The cuttles' future home is at the back of the room with a wide access platform overhead. There's already a "coming soon" sign for their exhibit. I ignore the "temporary" before it and tell myself this is just in the way that everything's temporary. And they've been so vibrant lately, doing really well with their food transition. They probably don't even know how old they are.

The tank's bigger than promised, much deeper than their

current one and sparsely populated with some anemone and a spattering of coral nestled in the sandy substrate. It takes me a while to locate the protein skimmer. I can't see it well enough from the floor, and there's a blue-vested employee guarding the "staff only" staircase.

So I focus on blending in for a while. I make a cursory circle around the room, wash my hands at the little station, pet a stingray, then wash my hands again. Eventually, a toddler goes head-first for the baby nurse sharks, distracting the staff member long enough for me sneak through the stairwell door.

A couple minutes later, the toddler-chaser's looking at me like he's just encountered a bunny supreme on the platform instead of a normal, skirted legging-clad biologist.

He's mostly unintelligible, but I make out "danger" and "staff." Saliva goes flying with the *p*'s and *f*'s, at risk of contaminating the water.

He doesn't stop until the door opens behind him and a taller blue-vested employee walks out. His face shows shock, too, like you'd think I were doing something more exciting than checking a protein skimmer.

At least this one recovers quickly. "It's okay," he tells "Steve." Steve doesn't move.

I consider my options, fighting or fleeing, or maybe feigning being lost, looking for the horn shark—*Where are you, George? Not in here, then?*—and then making a mad dash for the spotted turtles.

It takes me a minute to recognize the taller employee from his pictures online, but then I'm sure he's David

Williams, with the MS and the internship several years ago at Shedd. His hair's different than in the pictures I found of him running high school track in California. It's a uniform sandy color now, no more white tips like a reef shark.

"I think you're Nora?" he asks me when Steve finally elects to flee.

It doesn't matter how many points you have in the human game; if you're exposed, you lose.

I think first about what Heather would do. David's symmetrical, wide-shouldered, I guess less differentiated than he was with his highlights in California. Probably still more sexually appealing than a vaginal squid, though. I have nothing to compare to the upper end of this spectrum.

"We talked on the phone," he says. "I'm Dave."

I sit up and shake his hand, apologizing in the way I've trained, because this is my cuttles' future caretaker, with access to exclusive aquarium feed catalogues, probably fresher mussels than I can get and more species of crab. I bare my teeth, touch my hair, and make eye-to-forehead contact. I was just checking the protein skimmer, I tell him. I didn't mean to upset Steve.

Dave understands, of course, and assures me he's ready for the cuttles' arrival. How excited I must feel to be at the end of my research with them, and so on.

Yes, I parrot, exciting, majestic—no, that's wrong, better suited to George. There are so many ways this could go wrong, more ways even than I have time to consider, so I just ask to see the protein skimmer.

Dave uses a long metal pole to retrieve it and hands it over for my inspection.

I note the model number and capacity. It's a brand I've had my eye on since cuttle batch #2, much better than the one at my lab.

Dave takes a seat beside me on the platform. I suck in a deep breath. He's at least unscented.

"Do you think I need to move any of that coral?" His voice is low and tolerably quiet. "I wasn't sure what their tank environment was like at home."

I remind him the cuttles prefer a constant 70 degrees, 30% salinity, lights 12 hours a day with a fade in and fade out of 45 minutes on either side. They need to avoid copper in their equipment and all under-gravel filters. They could use an extra bubbler for oxygen. And of course no tankmates. I wouldn't want them to encounter anything more exciting in their golden months than a sea sponge.

"How long have you had them?" he asks.

"Almost seventeen months." The generally-accepted upper limit of their lifespans. But that doesn't take into account their diet and all their mental stimulation.

"And they did mazes, is that right? That must have been really interesting. I'd love to hear about it."

"I'll send you a paper."

"Sweet," he says. "Do you live close?"

Not *close*. I've mapped out four routes here based on traffic patterns, and it takes almost fifteen minutes at rush hour. "Close to UC," I tell him.

"I'll get you a pass," he says, "so you can visit them whenever you want."

"Thanks. Sweet," I add, trying to mirror. But I was never very good at mirroring, and now the overhead fluorescents are burning down into my eyes like the bloody asteroid that ended the Cretaceous period.

And maybe this is it, what loss feels like after you've bonded. Maybe this is what I should have felt with Cam. I can't stop thinking about all the too-bright lights and all the people the cuttles don't know, all the sounds they haven't heard before and all the children that might run into the glass and surprise them while I'm fifteen minutes away.

"Are those anemones all right for them?" Dave asks, gesturing to the water.

I nod and try to focus on the anemones, on anything but what's going to happen in 53 days.

I scan the other exhibits. The room's just at murmur-level up here. One blue-vested staff member's helping some kids pet a baby nurse shark. In the opposite corner, Steve's telling a pair of harassed-looking parents about a snowflake eel. Whatever you can say about a snowflake eel.

"I'll take good care of your cuttlefish," Dave says.

"And you're staying? You'll be here?"

"Long after they are."

I look at him.

"I mean I'm not going anywhere. I'll be able to keep an eye on them. And I can let you know if anything...if they're...eating differently or anything."

Before I go, I give Dave my phone number, the house number, and Lillie's cell, just in case, and add his number to my speed dial.

"And you'll have to watch for a dorsal stripe," I tell him.

"If they start to get malnour…" I can't finish this.

"Daily," he promises. "If there's anything wrong, anything at all, I'll know right away."


An hour later, I'm sitting in the quiet of my car in the Denny's parking lot just off 77, doing what I guess you do in major transitions, re-checking my email and reconsidering my life choices. There's nothing else to do now. My presentation for the conference on Saturday's already memorized. The cuttles' food transition is progressing on schedule. I've disinfected their carrying cases twice.

I read over Milner's last email again. Someone from alumni relations wants to photograph me with the cuttles next Thursday. There's a link to her email so I can tell her about the warm and stimulating environment here at UC and how people I've never even heard of have most definitely furthered my career ambitions.

I guess they know I don't have anything else to do next Thursday. And this is the traditional job of the department's token female, posing for brochures and producing quotes about the value of research and soaring like an albatross and etc. The postdoc token female is important, a marker of diversity, something to show off like a big Pacific octopus.

I think of my-life-eight-months-ago, when Cam would have managed this for me. He was good at transition periods, at dealing with advisers and alumni relations. He knew all these answers without having to think about them.

I read a new paper on Atlantic squid on my phone before driving back to the lab.

When I get in, there's Chinese takeout in the trash bin. I sniff. It's fresh; Kyle's here.

I hurry by his office window and don't switch on my lamps when I get to my lab. Kyle and I aren't especially symbiotic even though we share the hallway; we don't share things like research, conference presentations, or snack foods. I tried giving him an excel format once, at my mom's insistence, but he wasn't interested in improving his data organization or pattern recognition. Kyle's an academic bottom-feeder, scavenging like a lobster.

When I set down my purse, the cuttles flutter forward, ready to hear my presentation again. This is how I learn the rhythm, like how I learned all the other rhythms, practicing them over and over with different words. It's not just what you say or how valid your research is, but the order that matters, familiar speech patterns their brains accept. The humans, I mean, not the cuttlefish.

*The Se-pi-a officinalis RESPONDS CON-SIST-ENTLY to variations in both the TEX-TURE of the cues and subtle changes in their POS-ITIONING, PAUSE!* I suck in a breath to the beat of three in my favorite Sousa march.

*All subjects navigated new mazes at STATISTICALLY SIG-NIF-I-CANT-LY DE-CREASED times when these cues were placed in DIS-SIMILAR mazes-BREATHE!*

The door to my office opens. Kyle doesn't respond to cues like lights, so maybe he's playing odds; I'm here often enough that he might just pop over and try the door handle randomly. Kyles thrive on intermittent rewards.

I've heard this is a generational thing and can't help but wonder if Kyles are all I can reasonably expect to encounter in my great thirty-two-year-old #FOMO. Is this my romantic future? Is the great *out there* populated by purposeless Kyles? Do I really want to find out?

In a show of rare intellectual prowess, he greets me with, "What are you working on?"

I tell him I'm getting ready for my presentation. (*PRES-EN-TAT-ION. Con-fer-ence. Talk, read PA-PER, PAUSE!*)

Kyle doesn't move from my doorway. There's nothing for him to do here; he's listed as a lab assistant to give him funding, but a competent grad assistant feeds the cuttles. Not that Kyle's offered. Recently, Milner's been calling him lab *supervisor* (-unworthy-of-real-funding) to assuage his ego.

"You're not applying?" he asks.

"Applying?"

He glares, maybe. It's hard to distinguish Kyle's glare from Kyle's smile, from the everyday facial expression of the common gerbil. Kyle's why I have a lawn chair in the women's restroom. For a while, before he found something to do—clownfish and mirrors were actually a breakthrough—Milner gave him a desk in my lab and thought we might work "together."

He scratches at his receding hairline. "You're not applying for anything? Are you gonna teach or..."

I maintain eye-to-high-forehead contact. *Exude confidence,* Heather's voice in my head says. *Where's your blush?* asks my head-mother.

I change the subject before I can think too much about all the things I'm not doing next. "Do you know where Milner is?" I ask.

"Tim?" Kyle shrugs. He knows. He's become to Milner—

to *Tim*—something of a tongue-eating sea louse. They play ping-pong every Thursday in the rec room by the engineering department.

"Yeah," he says, then, "I don't know."

"Is he still working on his paper?"

"No. Yeah. Probably."

Milner's paper should be quick now that I've found the pattern for him. He didn't realize there was more than one variable affecting his shrimp's reproduction. When protein and ammonia went up and salinity went down, mating behaviors decreased. Shrimp habits are dependent on a series of conditions rather than just one. I don't know how Milner missed it. Until about a month ago, when I compared all of his data together, all he had to report was, as he put it, "sometimes shrimp aren't horny."

Eventually, Kyle's face returns to gerbil-neutral, and he slinks out of my office, trailing Chinese food smell. I crack open a window.

My mind's stuck on shrimp then, on salinity accidents, and I make a note to write up a comprehensive care guide for Dave before dropping the cuttles their afternoon snack.

# Chapter 3

*When threatened, a cuttlefish can release ink to confuse its attacker. Sometimes, it will also create a mucous decoy that mimics its own body. These pseudomorphs can distract a predator while the cuttlefish goes on its merry way.*

Heather was right. There *is* a dateable-looking male at the conference. He was even at my presentation, eating hummus with what I'm pretty sure were multigrain crackers. It was so distracting—either him or the hummus, it's hard to tell—that I almost misspoke when someone asked whether I'd used different stimuli in the mazes for forward and backward than for left and right. It was the dumbest question in the room with just one exception.

That exception took up the last six minutes of my ten-minute question time. That exception, now eight minutes *past* my allotted question time, is blocking my way out the door. The door leading to the vending machines, which I'm pretty sure have Reese's cups.

He's large, visibly dangerous, stonefish-style, and aggressive in his eye-to-*my*-forehead contact.

"My concern," he repeats, "is that you're not employing the right language to describe the phenomena."

*Phenomena.* And there's the cue, the downfall of any interdisciplinary conference; the philosophers come. Then they call things *phenomena*, and all of a sudden, everything we do becomes subject to their laws. Once they get to grad school, they start to make up and alter these laws like science is a long game of mau.

I try to repeat my findings using shorter, less contentious phrases. *Cuttlefish smart. See cues. Go through maze.* This time, I return eye-to-forehead contact and tell myself I'm a confident, sexy-or-maybe-not-so-sexy stingray.

"But cognition," stonefish-man continues, as though my paper wasn't accepted to present at a conference on animal cognition. "Surely *that's* not what you mean."

I know how this goes. If you can't circle it on a readout from an electron microscope, it's the job of the philosophy faculty to speculate on whether it exists until, one by one, they exhaust, dropping out of the debate and thus forfeiting. It's a lot like sea slug penis fencing. The last one talking gets to rename the thing that may or may not exist and suggest an ontological scheme in which it may or may not do so.

I squint at a mole on his forehead and wish I had a good evolutionary inking response.

"You said the cuttlefish, it *believes* the seaweed means the path to the right, but..."

"Right." There was exactly one smiling, friendly-looking in this room—with a skintone indicative of a healthy liver function and good-looking hummus. And I'm talking to the stonefish.

"As though it *knows* things," he continues. "You seem to be suggesting it has higher-order thoughts."

I consider my options, realize fighting's useless and fleeing's not possible. So I decide to play dead. I freeze my face and suppress any signs of movement. This is relatively easy, having missed lunch.

"Real intentional states," the philosopher continues.

I suppose he means as opposed to imaginary, unintentional ones. I remain frozen like a Livingston's cichlid, hunting for peace.

"Is that *content*, though?" he demands. "I mean, would you say the cuttlefish is processing semantic *content* when it's doing that? That there's some meaning conferred over and above the processing of stimuli?"

I suppress the urge to blink and notice as his hand catches the light that he's wearing a wedding band. And people have expressed concern *I'm* going to scare off potential mates with molluscs.

He waits for a response this time. He must have encountered presenters playing dead before.

"It...uh huh. Meaning conferred. Everywhere," I add, in case this helps the conversation end more quickly. My stomach growls. "I'm just going to run and..."

"So you don't think the cuttlefish is just manipulating syntax?"

I shake my head. I'm pretty sure my cuttlefish don't know what syntax is.

He crosses his arms. "How do you know *that*?"

I explain again, only more succinctly, the scope of my research and its conclusions—cuttlefish can find their way through mazes with the help of a complex series of learned stimuli from their immediate environments.

The philosopher sighs. My stomach gurgles.

When I turn to look at the clock, something on a table in the front row catches my eye. There, just where the lone healthy-acting male in the room was sitting, are his hummus and crackers. Abandoned. Unfinished. There's no briefcase in sight. *Hallelujah*, my stomach belts like the woman who sits behind my dad in church.

I scuttle sideways like a fiddler crab—how the female typically indicates mating interest—and move in on the snack, begging stonefish-man to excuse me.

It's immediately apparent the hummus is creamy perfection, just the right texture, no lumps. I unwrap the crackers.

"So, you say the cuttlefish is thinking." He follows me and positions himself in front of the desk so I have to look at him.

I use a cracker to shovel some hummus into my mouth and make a noise between my usual humpback affirmation and an orgasming walrus.

"*Thinking*?" he demands.

I remember from elementary school that stuffing food into your mouth and then talking to show your conversant the partially-masticated "seafood" was meant to deter further conversation.

"Yes," I say widely. "That's what I said."

But he's unaffected. He must be a good philosopher, one

of the more resilient ones.

"And does the cuttlefish *know* it's thinking?"

"Mmm," I respond. Even without having taken it off my nightstand, I don't think the bunny supreme could compete with this hummus.

"So my concern, again, Ms. Novak, is that you're misusing the term."

I swallow. "Cufflefiff?"

He raises his hands, then drops them, palms down. But philosophers can get aggressive about anything.

"*Think*," he says, obviously unexhausted. "*I* don't think it's thinking. *I* think it's just manipulating syntax."

I shovel some more crackers into my mouth. They're multigrain like I thought, just a different brand than I'm used to.

The door opens and people start shuffling in for the next session. I try to swallow some dry cracker, my face hot with impending interpersonal disaster, as I lock eyes with the hummus-eater.

The owner of the heavenly hummus now balled up somewhere near my larynx takes his seat, and I freeze, a cracker poised at my chin. When Heather was explaining the fine art of accepting food from strange men, this probably isn't what she meant.

I turn, make eye contact, remember I'm not a shark challenging him over a dead seal, and refocus on his forehead. There's no protocol for this. So I lower my cracker hand and start to explain why I thought it was okay to eat his snack. You know, he looked so *gone*, it looked so *creamy*.

"There was a philosopher," I add, turning, but the philosopher's vanished. A line of bored-looking cognitive scientists have taken over his row. "I was…"

Hummus hunk smiles—a genuine xygomatic smile, with crinkled eyes and everything. He gestures to the seat next to him. "No problem," he says.

I consider my options. There aren't options. So I sit.

When he meets my eyes again, my mitral valve musters a half-hearted flutter. This is quick, reflexive, like being in a romance novel, I think—staring into smoldering gray-green eyes, experiencing uncontrollable sweating, turning my face down to my heaving bosom, and other common heart attack symptoms. It's his symmetry, his smile, his hummus. *Attraction*, finally. Or cortisol, or just adrenaline. Or maybe an underlying cardiac issue exacerbated by low blood sugar.

"I didn't have time for lunch," I say, "and it…it was really good hummus."

"Thank you."

"What brand?"

He looks surprised. I guess he's probably used to receiving these kinds of complements insincerely—"nice hummus," "what great crackers you have," and what not.

"The hummus," I prompt.

"I make it."

I feel my face morph into its own xygomatic smile. This is enough to make me reconsider the emergency hoop earrings I left in my purse and Heather's foolproof ELF flirting method: Eyes-Laugh-Fingers.

I commence eye flirting when I ask about his chickpea sourcing. I look at him, meeting his forehead before my gaze is suddenly drawn to the floor, then to the wall, then back to him. This is something I haven't practiced, since it wasn't required with Cam all those years. I'm probably getting the timing wrong.

He introduces himself as Jarod Berkland from Washington and compliments my presentation. I compliment his choice of crackers. By the third round of eye flirting, I'm feeling a little seasick.

I go for a laugh next, at his account of describing chickpeas to the cashier at a store down the street.

Then *he* laughs when I tell him my own conference food-seeking adventure, only leaving out that my end goal was Pizza Hut. I'm interrupted—thankfully, before he can ask—by the introduction of the next speaker.

This presentation's slow, on the social implications of the feces-flinging behavior of some kind of monkey. I take notes and contemplate how to finger flirt now Jarod and I have successfully exchanged laughs. Unfortunately, there's no cause to touch someone sitting next to me in this setting, and with flu season right around the corner, and who knows what he might have picked up on his plane ride here.

So, after listening to a long data set, I decide to use my toes to signal interest instead of my fingers. I inch forward in my seat and move my ankle in circles until the edge of my shoe barely brushes Jarod's briefcase. Then I pull my foot up under me like Lillie's half-lotus and feign fascination with my notes. Which currently include part of a line graph and a banana.

Jarod moves, bends, and invades my bubble. I don't move. Maybe he smells like residual hummus. Maybe it's pheromones. Maybe it doesn't matter.

He reaches into the briefcase and emerges with another sleeve of crackers and a second Pyrex tub of hummus. And when he sets these on the table in front of me, they're like Fleming's moldy petri dishes, Mendel's pea plants, the fossilized remains of Archaeopteryx—better, I think, than a pebble to a gentoo penguin or a sea sponge to a humpback dolphin ever could be.

My toes bask in the glory of flirtation victory for a while, and I tune out the presenter's research methods and eat half the tub of hummus before the question period wraps up and Jarod goes to toss the empty cracker sleeves into the trash.

Then the philosopher appears as a disembodied voice beside me. "So I was thinking, actually, *content* was what was being mistaken."

I try not to look up. I can see his shoes in front of the desk. I point to the door and tell him I have to go, but I'm too late; he's already started. And everyone knows that once they've started, all you can do is wait for one of us to collapse. Me. For me to collapse. I haven't even digested the hummus. I don't have a chance.

"It seems to me that you didn't appreciate the difference between pure syntax informational-processing-*you*-know-what-I-mean—and semantic content."

I *don't* know what he means, of course, and probably wouldn't appreciate it even if I did. So I verbally ink, throwing out everything pacifying that I can think of—I was mistaken. I must have been misusing the term. Which term? Any of them. All of them. I must have misunderstood. It might have been my ovaries.

"But response, when you say the cuttlefish is *responding*..."

Something brushes my elbow, and the philosopher pauses to take a breath as I spin around and directly into Jarod's chest.

We have a dinner reservation, Jarod tells the philosopher. He'll have to excuse us, what with the feces-flinging session going over.

I turn to stonefish-man, then back to hummus-making hunk, then to the door, suspended like a plankter in goo after an Indonesian mudslide.

Then instinct kicks in. I don't wait to listen to the rest of Jarod's lie or whatever the philosopher says next. Instead, I scuttle sideways through the rows of chairs like a very unsexy fiddler crab and make a beeline for the lobby.

It's not until I'm behind a partition overflowing with fake plants that I realize I should have waited for my rescuer to maintain the pretense of our dinner outing.

I exhale when he rounds the corner and gives me a thumbs up, signaling the philosopher's been successfully diverted. I watch him cross the lobby, this man who rescued me from an evening of botched linguistics and makes—and shares—hummus. He looks like a non-academic and smells like...Did I smell him? I should have smelled him. He must have not smelled bad, at least, or I would have noticed. He's exactly the kind of person I would try to date, I think, if I were #FOMOing at full power, on a full stomach.

And I have no way to thank him; offering a Reece's cup or even a paperback journal seems insufficient now. So I just say "thank you."

He smiles. He's really good at smiling. "Well," he says, "he's probably got a light bulb that needs changing, anyway. You know how many philosophers it takes to change a light bulb?"

I remove a strand of fake pothos from my shoulder and shake my head.

"Three," Jarod tells me. "One to suggest there's a problem with a light bulb that means it needs to be changed, one to say the problem's misnamed—it's not a bulb made of light, after all—and one to say there's no such thing as a bulb, anyway. It's just a particular grouping of atoms, or quanta or, you know, *something*, arranged bulb-wise."

I laugh—really—and tell him my favorite philosopher-crossing-the-road joke before I've had a chance to consider his unique philosopher-diffusing skill set.

"You're not a one of them, are you?"

"Worse," he says. "I'm an ecologist."

As he explains some ecology/philosophy crossover, my eyes are drawn to a sign for the breakfast buffet with a photo of juevos rancheros, and my stomach rumbles on par with a beach of mating sea lions.

"You're hungry," he says. "Come to dinner with me."

My stomach agrees. I look at Jarod, then back at the two-dimensional juevos rancheros.

"If you want," he says. "If you don't have other plans."

I *do* have other plans—room service, probably juevos rancheros in bed with my laptop and my *Frasier* DVD's. But I've found a hummus-maker at an interdisciplinary conference, and he wants to eat with me. So probably this takes precedence during a #FOMOing period.

I agree, and he suggests I wait inside the revolving door while he gets a cab. The wind's whipping around the little overhang above the sidewalk, and it's started to drizzle.

I know I should have so much more information about him before we actually eat together, but I can't think of any of it now.

"Jarod?"

He turns back, and my inferior esophageal sphincter tells me not to question this.

"You don't fish, do you?"

He shakes his head.

"Okay," I say, and hope this is enough.


The place we pick is quiet. By the time our food arrives, the sun's already gone down. I can see the lights of the bridge from our table against the window but not the water below. There's a long line of brake lights heading into Kentucky.

We talk about interdisciplinary conferences and academic politics over my sauce-free noodles. Jarod has some dish with eggplant and assures me he doesn't eat fish (parasites and etc.), with the exception of his molecularly-distilled, sustainably-sourced, responsibly-caught Norwegian cod liver oil. These are the things you need to know about someone early, what they eat and their stances on various environmental issues that no dating app would give you.

After asking after my cuttles' personalities—because of course they *think*—he tells me about his own encounter with a philosopher at a conference in California.

"...and I just kept telling him I was studying desert ecosystems and had never seen an orangutan in the desert."

My laugh's easy, real, not lubricated by alcohol or anything else.

"But nothing mattered," Jarod continues. "It was like the future of evolutionary ecology was all up to the orangutans, the armadillos and the javelinas be damned. I thought I was going to have, you know, nightmares or something afterwards, where I'd wake up screaming, 'The orangutans! The orangutans! They're killing off all the bobcats!'"

I snort, too much like Heather's Morgan horses. Some water goes up my nose.

"And you ended up at his school?" I ask. In Seattle, I note, where *Frasier* is.

Jarod raises his hands—palms up, nonthreatening. "He's retired now, but I don't think I could have even done the interview if I'd known he was there. Seriously, you handled your question much better than I did. You were really good. Didn't even roll your eyes once."

I smile. This is easy, too. Probably it's his hummus. This wasn't a variable at play in my interpersonal interactions before.

"But," he says, "your paper was already published. You had a good reason to be confident. I looked you up."

I feel my cheeks heat as I fish around for the last scraps of my noodles. "A little journal," I tell him.

"Not little. In that field, especially, it's a big deal. Are you working on something else now?"

This opens the floodgates to my current issues with "something else" and "now." I set down my fork and tell the stranger seated across from me about how my cuttles are moving and my research is ending, how I'm in a crisis—a *transition period*—with no idea what's coming next.

But Jarod surprises me by responding like this issue's a normal one, not like I'm having a mental breakdown or am a potentially dangerous noddle-eater he's just offered his eggplant-cutting knife to. He even makes this disaster of mine sound like something else—like a triumph, almost, like my little postdoc publication as a sole author can take on the world. He understands, he tells me. He's going through a transition period, too. He has a couple job offers and a tough decision to make soon.

"I actually might end up in your neck of the woods," he says. "I was planning to come scope out Case soon. It's there or Northwestern."

I tell him Case is good. Of course I've heard Northwestern's good, too. It's a tough decision, he says, between two different research focuses, which I can understand. And he's dragging his heels, which I excel at.

The rest of the conversation comes easy, and I don't realize most of the restaurant's cleared out until he's folding his napkin into a dinosaur.

"I learned that from a group of students in the origami club," he tells me. "They folded their midterms into flowers last semester."

I reach across the table to examine his work. It's a pretty objectively impressive skill set, hummus-making, ecology research, and dinosaur origami.

So it's only natural that I agree to show him my more recent paper and that he agrees to share his on desalination in estuaries, which would definitely interest Milner.

We head back to the hotel lobby for tea and some weird little cakes that taste like the strawberry eclairs my grandmother used to feed her shih-tzu, sitting in the dimly-lit bar area by the wishing fountain and almost within view of the juevos rancheros sign. We talk more about our papers and research funding, about places we'd like to see and species we'd like to study.

At some point, I bring up *Frasier*.

"I love that show," he says.

I gulp a too-hot sip of tea and feel my face flush as he tells me he's watched *Frasier* since it was live and then watched it again on Netflix, though he doesn't have any of the DVD's.

I have all the DVD's. And this is the connection I'm looking for, of course, the easy kind. Humans all need some connections, at least for our immunity and our telomeres, and *Frasier* seems like a pretty ideal basis for a healthy relationship.

So I eat too many of the little cakes as we discuss the merits of the darker seasons and the development of our favorite characters.

"But your favorite episode," he prompts. "You have to have a favorite."

My mouth's full of eclair. I mime a heart with my hands to indicate the Valentine's episode.

"The one where Niles..." he starts.

I nod and wave my arms.

"...burns a hole in his pants and lights Frasier's couch on fire!"

I swallow. "...to classical music!"

My mitral valve flutters for real as he tells me about visiting the Elliot Bay Cafe, how the towers where Frasier lived were named after the real-life cafe, how the name "Nervosa" was invented, and how the title color changed each season in the intros, which somehow I didn't notice. But I believe him right away, before even doing a basic internet search. Maybe this is love.

"It might have changed my career path," he says. "Do you remember the episode where Lillith comes back?"

"'The Show Where Lillith Comes Back?' When we first meet her?"

"That's the one. It came out when I was just finishing my doctorate. I was considering a postdoc rather than going into research right away. But I saw her, and I thought, 'She's gorgeous, she's brilliant...So witty, too! Wow. I've really been in school too long.' And so I left and took that first job in Texas."

"Grad school," I echo. Lillith came back in the first season. She was coming *back* from *Cheers*. "On Netflix?" I ask.

He laughs, a small but beautiful, non-wolfy laugh. "Wasn't a thing yet."

"Lillith was in the first season, wasn't she?" I ask like I don't know.

"That sounds right."

"I don't remember it very well," I admit, "1993." Possibly because I was eleven.

He smiles and sets down his coffee. "I miss those Thursday nights," he says. "I used to stop working on my dissertation to go next door and watch it on my neighbor's TV."

*      *

Monday morning, I wake up at home around six with a Social message from Heather. She's still at her horse show but wants to remind me to sleep in. My cuttles are fine. My career's excellent. I'm a sexy stingray, and so on.

*I want a report,* she adds when she sees that I'm online.

I look out my window, where the light of the street lamp's catching little sparks blowing sideways in the wind. The beech has dropped a bunch of soggy orange leaves over the lawn.

*It's raining.*

*U didn't text after your presentation.*

So I tell her about the good questions, then about the philosopher and my excellent eye-to-forehead contact, then about the ecologist I had dinner and tea cakes with.

She writes me back with three exclamation points before the little dots indicate she's typing again. I can imagine how this looks on her face, like how her horses get when they see a plastic bag.

*WHO?*

*Jarod Berkland. UW.*

She doesn't write back right away, and I smush my pillow against my headboard and navigate to my email.

*OMG Nora he's hot.*

I'm glad it wasn't just the hummus. Or the *Frasier.* I click through my messages, but there's still nothing from Milner.

*But 48.* Heather uses the googly-eyed emoji.

*What?*

*It's not your fault,* she says. *You can't tell.*

*What?* I repeat. I wonder if this is some sort of ranking system I'm supposed to know, if this number is out of 100.

*His age,* she says. *You can find it online.*

*I know*, I tell her. *Or at least close to that. He watched* Frasier *on TV.*

*Oh.*

My computer dings with another notification from Social.

*How much Frasier?* Heather asks.

*All of it. We have the same favorite season.*

*Oh.*

*He's funny*, I add. *He knows philosopher jokes.*

*Oh*, she repeats.

There's a little red *1* over my friend box at the top of the screen.

*I need to do some entries*, Heather says. *You're okay?*

I give her a thumbs up.

*Can we talk later?*

I give her another thumbs up.

*You're not going into the lab today?*

I ignore this. It doesn't deserve a thumbs up.

As I close the chat, a notification box asks me to confirm my friendship with someone named Wesley Anderson. I follow the link to his profile and scan it for familiarity, but we don't share any friends.

Maybe he's what Lillie calls a troll. I click his picture. His face is blurry like he's moving in it. But I probably wouldn't be able to identify them, robots and hackers and whatever other dangers are out there, just by looking at their photos.

I decide to ask Lillie. It's almost time for her morning bran. But as I pass through the living room, the mass of blankets on the sofa shifts, and a head pops out from under her blue chenille.

"Hi," it says.

I jump back as a male sits up, dark brown hair pointing to

the side of his head.

He meets my eyes. He's bowed forward, mouth drooping, eyebrows out. *Guilt.*

"Uh," he says. "I'm Matt."

# Chapter 4

*Cuttlefish tailor their responses to the type of predator they're trying to evade. They might flee or hide or make themselves appear larger, flashing makeshift eye spots to scare away their would-be attacker.*

Minutes after the Matt-on-the-sofa encounter, Lillie and I are speeding towards the aquarium, and she's speaking in the same voice she used on Scribbles last year when he got an alfalfa sprout stuck up his nose.

I get her to repeat the sequence of events. I was hiding—not hiding, *waiting* in my room for Matt to leave—when Dave called. This is a good sign, Lillie assures me; it means Dave followed the emergency call sequence I gave him. The house phone was next on the list. Because my cell phone was dead. Because it wasn't used to doing so much navigating on the drive home from the conference and my charger was still packed away in my bag. Lillie has answers for everything.

Rain's coated the roads. My heart bubbler's on full power.

Everything's *fiiine*, Lillie repeats. No, she's not sure what kind of vehicle Kyle was driving. But she *is* sure he wouldn't have put the cuttles into their carrying cases without being really confident they'd been properly disinfected first. The person who absconded with a vehicle full of someone else's cuttlefish, she means, *46 days* before their scheduled transition period was complete.

My phone yells for us to make a left turn from where it's plugged into her car charger.

When we pass under the highway, I don't see any cars overhead. I picked the midday route to the aquarium, but maybe we should have taken the nighttime one. I didn't check the internet maps first. Because I was stressed, Lillie said; this is what stress feels like, *compleeetely nooormal.*

"Dave said they were doing great," she reminds me.

I look at the clock. It's 9:22. Then I look at Lillie. This is all wrong, like my empty lab, like cuttlefish-nappers in Northeastern Ohio and warm rain in October. Lillie's schedule's usually incorruptible, from her morning bran to her midday rice dishes to her lavendery showers. She leaves for work every weekday morning at 7:35.

"Why weren't you at work?"

"Mmm?"

"This morning. You should have been at work." It's like everyone's forgotten all the rules, like Cleveland's devolving into chaos.

"Oh," she says, not taking her eyes off the road. "I've been working from home more often. I was going to..."

My phone interrupts again, telling her to make a turn. We

pull into the aquarium parking lot, and I run for the door.

A few minutes later, Dave's bending over the water, and my mitral valve's flopping around like a sailfish in a fishing boat. Below us, seventeen traumatized cuttles float around in their carrying cases. I think about their empty tank at the lab, about their bubbler and their lights that are probably still on, their protein skimmer still humming.

Dave gestures to the thermostat reading at the side of the tank. It's exactly 70, he tells me, the cuttles' home water temperature. I guess I've reached whatever level of breakdown it is when you no longer appear capable of reading a thermometer.

He tells me he's monitored the salination carefully, too; it's just right, and the ph, and everything else. He thought they might be a little stressed from transport, is all, or he would have released them already. But of course it's good that he didn't, without my permission. It's just that they're probably ready for breakfast, and...I'd know best about that, too. But they're definitely not stressed, he says. Probably excited. Definitely not *too* excited. Probably just hungry. Yes, he decides, definitely hungry.

Lillie finally gets to the top of the platform.

"They look so good!" she says, the same way she said Heather's skirted leggings looked so good on me. And, you know, what a tank. So big, so clean. What a transition. And just look how they can see the stingrays. So *sooothing*.

She maintains her Scribbles voice as she introduces herself to Dave. He agrees the cuttles are just so totally great, however unfortunate it is that sneaky lab supervisor...whatever he is, that weasely guy—Kyle, obviously—brought them early.

But it's not the timing. Or not *just* the timing. It's the trauma. They weren't prepared. I wasn't with them. *I* wasn't prepared. We were supposed to have *46 days* of transitioning left when they were kidnapped by a stranger in the dark, in a mini van, apparently, like sex trafficking victims, in the rain.

Lillie turns her cooing on the cuttles. So brave, she says, so *caalm.*

I recite shark species in time with my breaths as I monitor the cuttles' colors. You can sometimes tell their moods this way, like how Bitty gets a little purple and bumpy-looking when she's concentrating in the maze. Like with humans, like how I'm probably mostly red now.

Bitty's currently the same yellowish color she takes on during her afternoon naps. She looks up at me before turning to the bottom of her travel case expectantly.

Lillie keeps cooing. Franklin falls asleep. Eventually, I suggest we release them from their carrying cases two at a time.

"A buddy system," Dave says. "Good idea."

I reach for Bitty's tank and fiddle with the float as he takes Dot's and Lillie maintains her steady vowel sounds at the water like a Mongolian throat singer.

When we release the first pair, they flutter around the bottom for a while, apparently unbothered by the coral. Bitty does a perimeter sweep, then hovers near the middle of the tank to check out the room. Dot floats slowly back and forth at a side wall like a small blimp.

"It's because this room has such good energy," Lillie says,

"and they're so smart."

"Absolutely," Dave agrees.

Zedo and Zelly are the same, exploring the new substrate before moving around closer to the surface. It takes me a while to consent to release some of the larger males, but there's no inking, no darting, and no stress colors when we do. I watch as Franklin experiments with some coral blending, mirroring the texture of an antipathes.

Then there's nothing to do but feed them their breakfast—something bland, obviously, no crabs or pulling or added stress on their little cuttle hearts. There are so many potential sources of stress here, though, with all of their patterns changing at once, so many things that could go wrong. It doesn't matter that they haven't noticed them yet. This is how it always happens in the wild; something sneaks up on them before they even know to be on alert.

Lillie stays with me on the platform when Dave goes to fetch his most nonstimulating shrimp. What a retirement home, she says. Imagine having all this space and such a nice view, admirers visiting every day, so much entertainment and gourmet seafood. What a relief this must be for me, and so on.

I try to focus on how relieved I am, how relaxed I should be now my existence no longer serves any apparent purpose and my future's a researchless, cuttleless void.

When Dave comes back with his bucket, the cuttles flutter up to the surface and hover patiently like little alien spacecraft. He feeds them, since he's washed his hands and this is just another thing I'll have to get used to, as I count their shrimp intake.

They eat quickly before returning to their tank exploration. Bitty visits with a family down on the floor. One of the larger males surveys the empty tank behind us. There's no turning back then, no way to coax them back into their travel cases and take them home and have everything the way it was before.

After some time, Dave starts giving me the look the directors at orchestra camp used to get watching the parents who stuck around after orientation, like I might at any moment fake a family crisis or steal my child's inhaler to institute a camp-wide search ending with a long car ride home and a three day wait to see a pediatrician.

My eyes land on Franklin. Does he look bloated?

But nothing happens. I watch for crises that don't come for a while longer before Dave invites us to meet his jellyfish, and I agree in order to appease Lillie ("Jellyfish! What *sooothing* neighbors!"), and because it will buy me more time.

My knees are numb from the platform when I get up, and it takes a while for my eyes to adjust to the light when Dave leads us through a door behind some parrotfish on the main level. It's a kind of cave, the lights over the water barely bright enough for us to see our feet. This is Dave's domain, the culmination of a masters in marine biology and a lifelong passion for ulmaridae.

All around us, moon jellyfish contract and expand like glowing blue frisbees.

I look at Dave. He smiles—upper lip down, lower lip up. *Pride.* And all I can think of is how he could have cultivated the cauliflower jelly or the bloodybelly comb, the porpita porpita, the fried egg, the flower hat, or even that one from the Arctic that looks like Darth Vader. Or he could have gone for deadly, instead—the sea wasp box, the lion's mane, the tiny but lethal irukandji. But Dave chose none of these. Instead, Dave chose the common moon jellyfish, notable mainly for its blobular slowness.

He points out some smaller shapes rushing past the glass in a weak current. "Ephras," he says softly, like he doesn't want to wake the baby jellyfish. "We've been keeping this area closed the last few days. They're just leaving the stack."

Lillie mirrors his whisper with words like "amazing" and "majestic" as I walk down the hall to look at the tank's filtration system. There's a spray bar to create a current and a larger system behind some screens.

"It's like they come out of nowhere. They're microscopic," Dave tells Lillie, "propelling themselves through the water until they get in the stack, and then one day, they just sort of take off." He opens his fingers and lifts his hands, *poof*-style, like that clown my father got for my fifth birthday party after he pulled a quarter out of Susie Ansen's ear.

When Lillie catches up to me, she points out all the bubbles along the back of the tank. She knows how I like extra oxygen. And aren't they incredible, she asks, these so-small-you-almost-can't-see-them baby moon jellyfish? Extraordinary? Obviously the result of *really excellent care?*

I nod. They're the aquatic, semi-translucent version of throw pillows. But we should be getting back, I say. The cuttles could be pooping by now.

Out in the main room, Lillie wanders towards the entrance to study an informational poster. I walk to the cuttles' tank. It's easier to see them from ground level. An older man's watching them, his nose just inches from the glass. Dot flutters her tentacles at him.

"They're going to be even more popular than the stingrays," Dave says when he joins me.

I look at him, then back at the tank. Franklin digs a bit in the substrate—soft, as promised, and at least seven inches deep—as Dave talks about imported mussels and coffee.

An image of Kyle balancing a cup from Dunkin Donuts on his Chinese takeout pops into my head. *Kyle, touching my cuttles.* Acid stings the back of my throat.

"Maybe we could meet up for coffee sometime?" Dave asks.

I try to swallow and look at Dave, because Dave's *not* Kyle, and Dave feeds my cuttlefish now.

He looks back at the tank. "I'd like to know more about them," he says. "And your paper. And their histories."

I make my humpback noise to stall as I evaluate. I think of New Zealand green mussels first, but of course I can see Dave's attractive independently of his feed catalogs, in an ephra kind of way, all symmetrical and well-formed and unobtrusive. My head-mom screams about the emergency hoop earrings at the bottom of my purse.

"Yes," I tell him, and then add a "great" for good measure.

Lillie appears behind us. "Sorry," she says, "I didn't mean to surprise you. I was just thinking you might not want to go back up on the platform right now. There's a group of kids coming in for a tour. They're in the Arctic room headed this way, and if they saw you up there and one of them got the idea to go up, too…"

"They could contaminate the tank," I finish.

Lillie nods.

Dave suggests we come back at closing time so I can reevaluate how the cuttles are getting along and make any needed changes before their dinner.

I agree and let him lead us towards a side door. We turn back just in time to see Bitty flutter forward for several feet before slamming her feeding tentacles into the glass.

That evening, I watch the sun go down from the aquarium parking lot as I wait for closing time. This isn't the same as the parents who stay at a hotel near orchestra camp, the ones who say they've always wanted a week of Muncie sightseeing. This is just being responsible.

I look at the clock on my dashboard. It's only 5:28. I can't go in early without looking overeager, especially now Dave and I are planning to have coffee together. And I'm almost ovulating, probably giving off a lot of confusing pheromones right now.

*You must have been angry*, Jarod texts, about the early morning cuttle-napping. I'm sure he understands this academia-specific kind of betrayal even if he hasn't had animals in his care. It's like if he showed up at work one morning and an ecosystem were missing, the high desert there one day and then *bam!* some Kyle thought it would be fine up in the Yukon.

*You've reported Kyle?* he asks.

I assure him I have, to Milner and to the head of the department, and to the head of the engineering department next door, in case they ever leave that unlocked, and to the dean and the president. I sent a long email about the dangers of irresponsible lab assistants that even Lillie couldn't temper with her vowel sounds. But I know Milner, at least, won't do anything about it, and the others are likely to assume Kyle was somehow doing his job. Like Kyle's used to managing things. Like he's capable. Like he's worthy of providing cuttle transport and making decisions unrelated to mirrors and clownfish just because he has an office and a penis.

*But they're all right?*

*So far.* I adjust the end of the car charger. My phone hasn't seen this much action since Franklin swallowed a filter sponge last year.

*I might have found something to cheer you up,* Jarod writes after a minute.

I'm picturing a neurotoxin that's undetectable in Kyle's Chinese takeout, both faster and more deadly than MSG, when the next text comes through.

*IMRI has a call for a new fellowship. A big one.*

My heart bubbler burps at "IMRI," and when I click on the link, I get that feeling the cuttles must get on mussels day.

It's a research fellowship, up to two of them, an invitation to submit proposals. They're looking for research that might give insight into how a species or an ecosystem is affected by some change—rising water temperatures, desalination, shifting currents, new atmospheric conditions, and so on. They'll offer funding, accommodations, and eternal biologist rock star status.

*It might be a little late,* Jarod warns. *Proposals are due in November. But I thought in case there's something with cuttlefish, you might want to give it a shot.*

A surge of what I think is dopamine washes over me. My mind drifts to cool, clear water then, to IMRI funding and wild cuttles as I read through the details. When I look up from my phone, it's already 6:02.

*          *

I check on the cuttles several more times over the next day and a half, but they seem to be approaching their major life transition with even more zen than I have the reintroduction of flax seeds into my morning oatmeal.

So, Tuesday night, I agree to go with Heather and Lillie to a vintage store downtown. The place is painted like a mandarinfish and built like a maze that traps me between racks of old prom dresses, engulfed by that lingering smell of things-of-dead-people.

They insisted this was the best way to get Halloween costumes. Recycled, Lillie pointed out. Thrifty, Heather said. Also probably full of phosphates, 1-4 Dioxane, and endocrine disruptors that linger from chemical detergents through thousands of washes. And who knows what kinds of mold spores. But we have vinegar and baking soda and a UV light from Heather's labs, if it comes to that.

The last time I dressed up for Halloween, I was six and masquerading as an elm tree. But this is a different mission. Heather decided we need costumes to get into a club Friday night, because this is our year—the three of us are single-ish, collectively, which is like aligning a bunch of moons.

And who knows how long this single streak will last, with Lillie just newly-single and Heather only partly-single and me sharing warm beverages—the temperature is what matters, apparently—with no fewer than two men this month.

Heather's bolstered by my #FOMOing developments, upping her date-coaching game after stalking Jarod online and quizzing Lillie about Dave.

"There's a quieter area in a side room," she tells me, "and the strobe lights'll only be on the dance floor."

I step between some hat racks and look at Lillie—predictable, *stable* Lillie, who never let on that she was single before dinnertime yesterday. She'd been doing a trial separation from Ned, she told us, and it was a success.

"Matt said the club wasn't very crowded last year," Heather adds.

*Matt,* wearer of the blue chenille blanket and the guilty expression. Apparently he took up residence on the sofa waiting for Heather to come home Sunday night, the result of some horse show miscommunication.

This relationship isn't serious yet, she insists, in spite of their Italian food-eating and Matt's sofa-sleeping. Winter tournament season's coming, followed by foaling season. It would be a bad time for one of her relationships to get serious. She's not even sure she'll invite him to go to her sister's wedding.

It looks pretty serious to me. Heather's currently surveying a rack of vintage wedding dresses.

"You met him, didn't you?" she asks me.

I nod, stepping over a footstool that fluffs out like a baby king penguin.

"And?"

I settle on my humpback sound. I'm not sure how else to respond. I wouldn't have assumed Matt was for Heather if I'd met him in some other context. Heather's dates are usually peacock cichlid or killfish-types, royal gammas or electric blue rams meant to stand out in a crowd. Her longest relationships—which were a long time ago—were with men who pioneered laser surgeries or flew glider planes or sailed to a bunch of continents. Whereas Matt struck me as more of an Atlantic bumper.

Lillie, who must know him best since she's worked with him for so long, doesn't respond at all. She's facing away, focused on some decorative headbands now, and I wonder if she's grieving Ned. She hasn't called their post-trial separation a breakup or gorged on ice cream yet.

"I think I'll be a twenties ghost," she says after a minute of quiet, then, "You haven't seen anything you like?"

Heather holds up a prom dress that looks like a cupcake for my inspection, and I retreat deeper into the hat emporium.

Lillie suggests making a cuttlefish costume, but of course she hasn't considered their chromatophores, their disruptive patterning, their light show effect that lets them blend in with things moving in the current, their bilateral changes during mating season, or their texture-mimicking. Like how they can look like substrate or coral, or like the anemones they haven't seen before. They can change from stress, too, from feeding changes, new environments, and unfamiliar caretakers.

Heather recommends we check in at the aquarium on our way home. She's already gone this morning to make sure they were being fed at the right time. She echoes Lillie's assessment—they're so calm. Not too calm, very active. Not scared active. So *healthy*. They definitely like all the people. Not too many people.

"What about that fellowship Jarod sent?" she asks when Lillie's checking out. "Have you thought about getting some more cuttles through it? Or could you breed them, maybe?"

Given the reproductive assistance available to Heather's Morgans, I expect she could help me breed some sort of hybrid squid. Maybe we could engineer one with a longer lifespan, with fewer hearts to wear out. But even that wouldn't cut it for IMRI.

I explain the parameters of the fellowship and the gaping holes in my education regarding wild cuttles and how they might be affected by changing oceanic conditions. There are about a hundred and twenty known species of cuttles ranging in size from embryonic Scribbles to Franklin-at-a-buffet, but they're mostly only tracked by the people who eat them.

I'm speculating about the magnificent cuttlefish and the Eastern Australian Current when Heather finally decides on her Halloween costume; she's going to be a bride.

"Not a real bride," she assures me. "Like a zombie one."

Lillie pulls back a hat rack for me to step through. "Don't worry," she says, "we'll find you something perfect."

# Chapter 5

*When it's time to mate, some clever male cuttlefish imitate females to get by the larger males guarding harems. They take advantage of bilateral coloration, displaying the muted tones of the females with one side of their bodies while using the other side for courting.*

Thursday afternoon, I'm standing in front of Kyle's clownfish instead of the cuttles' empty tank and wearing unnecessary safety goggles, a lab coat, and an underwire bra.

"Good, Nora," the alumni relations woman says. She has red lipstick smeared on one of her front teeth and looks like a barracuda that's just swallowed an uncomfortably large snapper. "Now let's try some with you looking at the tank."

I turn and count clownfish stripes. *Flash.*

"And the clipboard again?" She should have a plastic bag, I think, like Heather uses to direct the Morgans' ears.

I look at the blank paper on the clipboard. *Flash.*

"And talking again?"

Kyle steps closer, his smile almost as wide as alumni

relations barracuda's, and I consider the tensile strength of the clipboard, how many blows it might take to fracture his skull.

"What's your favorite part of your work, Nora?"

I look at the woman, trying to move my arms in circles like she taught me earlier. *Gesturing* is what I'm doing. Not swinging. *Flash.* Pointing at the clownfish. *Flash.* Looking at the clipboard together.

I focus back on Kyle's forehead. "The..." *supportive...the swinging....*

*Flash.*

"That's okay," she says. "We can get that later."

Kyle's forehead crinkles.

"What about your goals? Talk to me about what you're thinking of doing next."

I start to say something about the IMRI fellowship I'd like to apply for, how there are an abundance of opportunities in my field. There are of course *not* an abundance of opportunities in my field, but I know that's the wrong answer.

"She's going to be a great teacher," Milner cuts in from behind the photographer.

*Flash.* Yes, I tell alumni relations woman, I-M-R-I is the one I'm thinking of. That's International Marine Re...something else I'll email her.

"We're very confident," Milner says, "that there are departments wanting professors with..."

Underwires, apparently. And lab coats. And goggles.

"You're getting a little stiff there, Nora," she says. "Can you and Kyle try walking with the clipboard again? In front of the tanks, maybe?"

"...her background," Milner finishes. Milner's university bullshitting skills are on par with a first string performing marine park dolphin.

*Flash.*

"That's great," she says. "This'll be great."

Once we're finished with the photos and I've switched back to my human-shaped bra in the bathroom, I hurry to catch up with Milner on his way out.

"I wanted to talk to you about the IMRI fellowship," I say, "if you have time."

"Gosh," he says, the way he says it when someone asks to design a new 300's course.

I wait. He doesn't say anything else, so we start moving towards the doors, my tennis shoes squeaking on the terrazzo. Milner's strides are longer than mine, but his shape slows him down. He's rounded in the middle like his sea shrimp, always bowing over a little.

"I'm not sure it's the right fit, though, given your work," he says.

I tell him I've been scouring journals for information about cuttlefish and their squid cousins in the wild that might be affected by salinity or ocean currents or some new species of marine algae.

"Well," he says, "you can keep looking. But did you see the posting at Penn?"

I make a half-hearted humpback noise. The position at Penn's just teaching, no research.

We push through to the doors and out into the breeze. Some leaves blow up into my shoelaces as Milner shuffles towards his car.

"Think about Penn," he says over his shoulder. "I'm pulling for you."

*　　　*

Halloween arrives with several gusts of distinctive Eerie wind and an energetic disturbance that seems to drive my roommates into a frenzy.

Lillie lays out clothes for my coffee with Dave tomorrow while Heather paints an Apple logo on my cheek with her eyeliner. Meanwhile, I recite deep sea species in my head in preparation for what will henceforth be known, Heather believes, as the great club-going of our early thirties.

I tug at the neck of my turtleneck. I'm wearing all black and am supposed to be an ipad. There's a laminated page from my published paper taped to my stomach.

I'm a *sexy* ipad, Heather reminds me, because this was her idea. She claims tonight isn't a date-shopping expedition, though, isn't a typical use case for a club. We're too old and probably too clothed for this. Tonight's something different, a celebration of our singlehood, an exercise in consequence-free flirting, a way to kick off what promises to be a positive dating streak for me—my first—a time to have *fun*.

But I know *fun* is loud and that clubs are for things beyond my training.

This is just practice, Heather says, like orcas playing with seals. No, I'm the orca. No, it's different. In this analogy, the seal doesn't mind. This is another club offering, short-term practice flirting, like all the smaller horse shows training for

Grand Nationals. I'll be so practiced that, by tomorrow, coffee with Dave will be like nothing. A *fun* nothing. Not nothing, then, just a great time. Not stressful at all, or weird. Not that *I'd* be weird. She means him.

Lillie takes over. The skirted leggings still look so *goood* on me, she says. So will her sweater tomorrow, the pink one. It won't itch like that time she tried to send me to an interdepartmental pizza party in cashmere. She's already mixed a lavender oatmeal bath for me to soak in pre-coffee. To give me glowing skin, *caaalm* skin. Not that there's anything to be *not* calm about.

"This is brilliant," Heather says as she studies her work in the mirror. The eyeliner apple on my cheek is perfect. The taper of the page accentuates my waist. I'm such a sexy ipad, and so on.

Lillie pops back to her room, emerging a few seconds later with an altered version of my noise-canceling headphones. She's attached a narrow strip of cardboard with a laminated ipad toolbar to the top.

I put on my toolbar as Heather checks the window for Matt again, adjusting her blood-spattered veil. Our plan's group driving, safety in numbers, in case a zombic bride and a twenties ghost and an ipad aren't intimidating enough on our own. The club's straight across the sports complex, so we could walk there just as quickly, but Heather thinks it might rain.

When Matt's headlights shine through the front window, Lillie hands me my coat.

Heather skips to the door. She's grinning. "*Fun,*" she repeats.

The club is a bar. You'd get a very different impression from "club"—pickle of the month or an extracurricular or a nice frequent flyer lounge. This isn't that. This is burst-your-spleen-level bass that comes up through my boots and shakes my skirted legging-clad butt like the fat jiggler my dad got from one of those 90's infomercials.

I hold my headphone-toolbar tight against my ears as Matt leads us to a side room. I think he looks different as a pirate tonight, without the blue chenille and the guilt. He has one of those simple, square faces like a pixilated video game character, one that shows everything. I must have misread it Monday morning when I saw the guilt. Maybe I'm off my game.

A man who reeks of aftershave and is wearing a cape brushes against me, and I leap into the wall like a Florida sturgeon in low water. *This* definitely isn't my game.

We follow Matt past the bar to a little booth in the far corner of the room, and I scoot around to the back. Lillie cracks a window behind me like she's trying to let the bass out.

"*Auctoritas ignis,*" Matt says, or something like that. *Authority. Fire.* He looks like he's talking to me. Maybe the necromancer guarding the doorway's affected him. He does strike me as kind of affected.

"What?" I ask.

Lillie hands me a laminated card with a list of drink specials. The card's smudged with fingerprints, probably covered in early flu. She points to the Candy Corn Cocktail and shows it to Matt.

Beside him, Heather's started head bobbing like a

Morgan that's been left in its stall too long.

"Water," I tell him. "Bottled."

"*Novem?*" he asks.

"One," I yell, holding up a finger. Then I watch as Heather, still bobbing, follows him to the bar. Their exchange with the bartender's silent, as far as I can tell, over the bass, gestures and nods that probably mean something to a secret society like the post office and the bank used to be to me.

I look from them to the corner of the dance floor, where twenty-somethings writhe and shimmy in a flamboyant mating dance. I've learned this contextually, but you wouldn't be sure otherwise, just by looking at them. They could be shedding their skins or marking their territories with scent cues in their hairsprays, laying eggs or struggling to excrete feces.

When Heather and Matt come back, she's holding a martini glass full of something that looks like blood—a Poison Apple, Lillie indicates on the card. Matt has a beer with an eyeball in it.

I watch as he scoots around by Lillie, taking the seat across from Heather. Is his jaw tight? Maybe I'm misreading him again, or maybe I started out biased against him. It's not just the guilt I thought I saw and the interruption to my Monday morning, making me miss the call from Dave; Matt's been disrupting Heather's patterns for a few weeks now. So I probably wouldn't be able to see anything right on his face even if it were there.

Lillie passes my bottled water and offers me the conciliatory dish of candy corn that came with her cocktail.

For a while, their conversation's muffled by my headphones, and I count Heather's new lateral head-bobbing as Matt waves his arms, wafting deodorant smell.

Heather's watching him, too, but it's hard to tell if this is attraction. I can't see if her eyes are dilated in this light, and it's only obvious that she wants to dance, like a cydia deshaisiana in a warmed seed pod, like a hopeful twenty-something who hasn't done all this before.

When she goes to the bathroom, I focus on an interaction a few tables down from ours between a fairy and a sasquatch. I think this place could be the Amazon of sloths, the Galapagos of little birds, an anthropologist's *Nature*-level study if someone could identify a consistent pattern in all the extra variables at play tonight—disguise and conversation-thwarting music and both feigned and real drunkenness.

The first round of drinks disappears quickly. The booth's a little quieter then thanks to Heather's stealth redirection of a speaker around the corner, and she convinces me to remove my toolbar.

The noise level starts out okay, but this is a toxicity thing, a slow buildup until I explode like an over-stressed pufferfish. We all have limits, parameters of survival; we're delicate creatures, in semi-liquid human state. And I might be a little extra delicate tonight.

When Matt goes to get us some Halloween-themed sundaes from the bar, Heather asks how I'm doing.

"Fun," I tell her, because this word is learned contextually.

Lillie frowns, pushing her water towards me.

"Are you getting too much noise?" Heather asks. When I don't respond quickly enough, she gets up to move the speaker farther away from us along the wall.

I ignore Lillie's transition into her listening lotus.

Because Lillie knows that #FOMOing takes more than practice to get right and that I'm better in an environment I know, in the life I've established so carefully over the last decade. Maybe I could stay at school and ask Milner for some other project, like taking over his sea shrimp, or I could take Kyle's position and be a lab supervisor. This little foray into the great *out there's* already more than I want.

When Matt comes back with our sundaes, a tall skeleton's trailing behind him. Matt says the skeleton's name is Zach as he hands me my bowl.

A dyed maraschino cherry's leaked all over my ice cream, and there's just chocolate sauce, no fudge. I'm considering adding candy corn to the edges—because we're all in disguise anyway, not following any other rules, and because I have no way of knowing if there's a lower rock bottom for my personal breakdown—when the skeleton removes his mask.

Lillie elbows me.

"Practice," Heather mouths.

A little while later, I look back at the dance floor, where Heather and Lillie are celebrating their reproductive fitness. I assured them I was all right here in the booth—practice flirting, you know, safe, not in the mood to learn "grinding" the hard way.

My flirting partner takes another sip of his beer, avoiding one of the dissolving candy eyeballs that's bobbing around in the foam.

"Rabbits, mainly," he tells me, "but I like squirrels sometimes."

Earlier in this conversation, when I thought we might actually have a conversation, he told me he likes cuttlefish, too. But it's possible he meant that he likes to eat them.

"Squirrels," I echo as the bass reverberates through my bones. *Boom. Boom. Boom. Shoosh. Boom.* I'm pretty sure practice flirting wasn't supposed to invoke talk of murdering furry woodland creatures. I don't know where it went wrong.

"Yeah," he says. "Not as much as bunnies, though."

I push my sundae away, the cherry juice pooling against the plastic. "You eat bunnies."

Zach laughs, but it's not a real laugh. His lower eyelids don't contract. "Almost nobody eats bunnies," he tells me. "The meat's too tough."

I look back at the dance floor. Strobe lights flash around the corner in waves of pink and orange.

It's not like I didn't try. I started by asking if the rabbit-hunting might be a facet of Zach's character tonight, like maybe he's a metaphorical skeleton starving for human companionship and driven to bunny-shooting madness by social isolation. My mom keeps telling me social isolation can do this. Maybe, I even posited, his meat-free body represents the humanity he shed with his first squirrel murder. But these assumptions, courtesy of my undergrad literature professor, were off the mark; Zach's dressed as a skeleton because of some movie he assumed I recognized. He shoots real, live rabbits. This is what comes of flirting.

He holds up a finger as he digs through his pocket, then passes me his keychain. "They're good luck," he says.

There's something furry attached. I drop the keys. They clatter onto the table.

"The feet," Zach clarifies, in case I didn't see it. "They bring you good luck."

"You shoot rabbits, and then you cut off their feet."

"For good luck," he repeats.

A few minutes later, I've sent a text to Heather and Lillie and am feeling my way along the vibrating wall behind the bar. My headphones are back in place, but they're not enough. A strobe light flashes overhead. The floor shakes with the bass. *Buzz. Buzzzz. Boom.* Over and over.

I flatten myself against the wall when a couple wobbly men pass by. One points to my midsection and asks if I'm a computer. He smells like grilled cheese and whiskey.

"I'm an ipad," I say, a muffled war cry of over-sensory vindication. *But don't touch me.*

His face contracts. *Confusion.* I look away. The longer *buzz* shakes my thighs.

The bathroom door's sticky when I finally push through it. Red flashes behind my eyelids, strobe spots bleeding out in the shape of bunny feet.

There's an open window by the last stall. I bend back my toolbar as I slide through.

I loop my purse over my chest and am already jogging past the soccer field by the time the cold air hits me. The vibrating inside me stills then, and it's just my boots on the asphalt and the pops of a tennis ball being hit back and forth on the court.

I circle around the tennis court, where it's light, and pick up my pace as I go through sharks.

*Horn, basking, whale.*

*Pop.*

*Lemon, dusky, silky.*

*Pop.*

*Spinner, sharpnose, broadnose sevengill.*

My headphones bounce softly against my collarbone. As I run, my shoulders start to let go of my neck, and my skin cools.

*Pop.*

*Zebra, bull, tiger.*

*Pop.*

*Goblin, porbeagle.*

*Pop.*

*Cookiecutter, frilled.*

By my second loop, my heart and breathing are in time. The tennis players are quiet except for the pops and the scuffling of their shoes I can hear when I'm close by. They don't miss any balls. There are some crickets singing in the grass still.

*Pop.*

*Nurse, angel.*

*Pop.*

*Pelagic thresher.*

# Chapter 6

*Cuttlefish have eight arms and two tentacles with detinculated suckers designed for grabbing and still never engage in unwanted touching.*

Lillie and Heather take me back to the sports complex the next morning for a pre-date walk. Not that I need it, Lillie assures me. I'm actually radiant with positivity.

Tonight, I'll be even more radiant in her sweater—her *lucky* sweater, which I'd believe had been knit by Gandhi and washed in the waters of the Ganges under a blue moon if she hadn't told me that it came from T.J. Maxx. She's worn this sacred pink sweater for every important life event since college.

Heather speculates that we should have tried something like this last night, at least made an effort to make me look more snuggly than an ipad. She's been studying soft fabric psychology recently in preparation to ease my transition into the dating world like that hippo midwife at the zoo.

I remind her last night's flirting partner was a rabbit

killer; had I looked any more snuggly, he might have mistaken me for prey.

"Zach," Lillie says, to humanize him, to start to recategorize the experience. "And maybe he meant in areas where they're overpopulated."

I ignore this.

"That's why flirting's important," Heather says. "To see if…" She's obviously trying not to say *your flirting target's a likely serial killer.* "…you have anything in common. Maybe if you'd gotten to know him better, you'd…"

"He eats farmed fish." This makes me think of Jarod, who doesn't eat farmed fish. Or fish on the red list, or fish at all except for his sustainable cod liver oil for his arthritis. Jarod would have been a good flirting stopping point.

Heather pauses, presumably calculating the odds fish consumption will come up over my coffee with Dave tonight. "Maybe fish are negotiable," she says. "And you can always change his diet later." She thinks this is how it goes, that men are like Morgans, eating whatever you put in their feed boxes and never sneaking any halibut behind your back. "And there are other important…"

"He ties bunnies upside down from a clothes line and saws off their back legs so the artery doesn't get blood on them once he's already cut off their front ones."

Lillie flinches.

"*And* he eats farmed fish."

Heather can't fix this. "But tonight's going to be nothing like that," she says after a couple more steps, and tells me again how coffee's benign, easy, the warm-up ring of dating. She'll be just a few doors down with Matt, at a Mexican place where she can check her phone in case there's a problem. Not that there'll be a problem. You can't mess up coffee. *He* can't mess up coffee. There won't be any fish there, any shooting sports, or any alcohol.

"And that place has good vibes," Lillie adds. "A lot of vegetarians hang out there. They have great almond cakes."

"You don't have anything to be nervous about," Heather agrees.

I nod, but I didn't know I was nervous. Maybe I should be. I haven't been on a first date in over a decade, if we don't count the dinner with Jarod. Which we don't, Heather says, because that wasn't planned. Or we do, maybe, because then tonight isn't so nerve-wrecking, so high stakes.

They assure me nothing much has changed since I dated the first time, never mind that this isn't Cam. Dave's just like Cam. All men are. Or none of them are. First dates, they mean, haven't changed in the last decade. I just have to be myself.

This is what I was the first time, of course, myself, waiting patiently for someone to come run into my car on a jogging path and start planning my Saturday nights. This way I am has only attracted one Cam.

We make another lap, dodging a loose soccer ball, before Lillie says we should get back for my unnecessarily soothing oatmeal bath.

Across from the sports complex, Indigo Dreams is bustling at eight pm, mugs clanking, steamers hissing. I can't detect Lillie's vibes, but there's mediocre jazz coming through the ceiling speakers that makes everything kind of buzzy.

I take another sip of my coffee. It's decaf and tastes like

very old milk. Not like crème brulee, like I imagined when I ordered. I actually expected it to come in crème brulee form, too—gooey, carmelized, *sweet,* at least.

I guess I should have planned for some disappointment tonight. I kept telling myself I could do this, being all *out there,* #FOMOing and blending like a leafy sea dragon.

Now Dave and I are thirty minutes into our date, and I've run out of questions to ask him. I've already filled in the gaps in his work and family histories. There's not a lot of medical information. His last remaining grandmother died a few years ago—of being old, he thought. I don't know what's supposed to happen next between us, what would mark this date as a success or a failure.

Dave points out a flyer for a band he knows, the way some people know all the bands and all the actors and you have no way of knowing how or why or if they're making it all up as they go. At least he can carry the conversation.

I catch my reflection in the window as he segues into a story about the aquarium's resident moray eel. I'm a study in puffy pink snuggliness, swaddled in Lillie's sweater like a cocooning insect ready to turn to goo.

When he suggests I finish the chocolate chip cookie on the plate between us, I wonder if it's nice to have someone to tell me about eels and share cookies with. Maybe this is enough.

He keeps talking about the moray. "...It's like he's playing peekaboo with a tour of preschoolers sometimes, and then, other times, he's sulking in the rocks, wanting octopus."

I nod and stifle a yawn. It's not the eel, though; it's just getting close to my bedtime, and the music's lulling me to sleep. It sounds like what they used to play on the weather channel.

"Would you want to stop in?" Dave asks. He gestures to the street. "See your cuttles?"

I sit up and suggest a faster alternative route bypassing the highway. Not that I've been driving around the aquarium unnecessarily from various points in town.

He understands, of course, that it's important to have a plan. He's been in aquatic care long enough to know you have to control as many variables as possible. And maybe this is all I need, all that really matters—this and sharing some cookies might be enough to constitute a really good relationship for me.

As Dave drives, I note his unsmelly front seat and how he makes smooth stops. I think he'd pass cuttle transport accreditation. So I'm convinced this date's a success before we even pull into the aquarium's parking lot.

When we get to the platform over the cuttles' tank, I regret letting Heather talk me into her heeled boots. They wobble over the little grooves in the flooring, more likely to cause me to fall in than to signal any level of reproductive fitness.

Dave rests a hand on my hip, ready for me to topple as I lean over the water. Or maybe he thinks I'm at risk of jumping. I can see how crème brulee coffee might do that to some people.

But the cuttles all seem fine, and my heart bubbler's unbothered by the caffeine. I identify Bitty hovering near the surface, obviously expecting a late night snack.

Dave assures me they enjoyed a new shipment of mussels

this evening just before he left to meet me. They ate quickly—not *too* quickly. They're not underfed or anything. There's no hint of a dorsal stripe.— with no struggling at all with the shells.

I watch them and evaluate. I'm not itchy, not boomy. The cuttles all look well-adjusted. Their tank's spotless. Dave isn't offgassing any smells, and he's close enough for me to tell. Whereas I still reek of oatmeal. Maybe the dating stage of my #FOMOing's complete now, success on the first try like with my GRE or tuberculosis test.

So I tell Dave I'd like to see his ephras. This is showing interest in his interests, pretty expert level, I think, considering his interest is moon jellyfish.

His face shows surprise. I've impressed him. He hurries down the stairs behind me as I walk purposefully towards the jellyfish tunnel. Before I left the house, I checked moon jellyfish in my *Wildlife Fact File*, and they're exactly as interesting as I remembered.

"Cool," I add when we get inside the cave, probably more convincingly in the dark.

He agrees but doesn't switch on the lights over the water, and I can't see his precious little ephras in the dim side light until my nose is almost pressed against the glass. The bubblers give off a steady hum I didn't notice Monday over the crowd in the main room. There's so much we miss through the noise, so much that can slip by us.

In the darkness, I stand in evident admiration. The jellyfish don't acknowledge our presence or provide any cues as to how I might show more interest—they're already "magnificent" and "incredible" per Lillie. So I start trying to count them.

Dave's quiet behind me, evidently mesmerized, or maybe he's also counting. But I know his pride in these sea-blobs is a positive character trait, seeing value in little specks another person might mistake for algal overgrowth. It's a trait I don't have, a complementary personality type to mine.

I watch one of the larger jellies bump against the filter. Jellyfish tentacles are full of mucous, so as they move through the water, food gets stuck in them and then is slowly drawn up to their mouths to be digested. It gives them plenty of time to decide if they want to eat whatever's stuck there. So I can relate to them this way; I also like having plenty of time to make decisions.

I think about what I should do next to indicate whatever I'm supposed to be indicating now, maybe issuing a sincere thank you or performing the butt-out hug I've perfected through years of family holidays. For me, these are learned behaviors, informed by decades of research and practiced ad nauseum, but they're probably instinct to Dave, with things like mood lighting and soft fabric psychology and oatmeal baths doing most of the work for him.

It takes me a minute to think of a jellyfish question. "Do their tentacles feel sticky?" I ask, and jump when Dave's breath hits my face, when his lips brush mine—without provocation, not like I've eye flirted or laughed or touched him at all.

I close my eyes and reevaluate. I didn't know jellyfish mucous was a turn-on. The glass of the tank's cool at my back. *I'm a sexy stingray*, Heather's voice says in my head, or at least I'm a well-mucoused jellyfish.

I consider my next words, looking for a way to compliment Dave instead of the jellyfish. That's what you're supposed to do, I think, after you kiss someone for the first time. But he's making talking difficult with his tongue bumping into my lips.

When he makes a noise like a gray whale surfacing, I open my eyes and consider how unprepared I am for this. I've only kissed two people—Cam and Franklin, my largest cuttle's namesake, in the trees after the second grade Christmas pageant before I kicked him in the shins. Maybe kissing's changed. And probably Dave's different than Cam or Franklin. He's very minty.

He lifts his head. I take a breath and am about to say something, but then he's kissing me again, and my mitral valve reminds me I'm claustrophobic. I start to walk backwards towards the door. He follows, his hand on my hip. My lips tingle, and my heart bubbler kicks into gear.

Things are starting to get unpleasantly slimy by the time we get out of the jellyfish cave. Dave's tongue feels like an octopus tentacle.

I take a shaky breath as he nudges me back towards a side entrance. "I'm not breathing right."

His face glows red under the Exit light. "Me neither," he says.

I bite my tongue. Or his tongue; I'm not sure. I taste blood.

"No. I'm nof breafing righf."

About an hour later, I'm in a little ER room teeming with beeping things when Heather rounds the corner with that look she had a few years ago when she caught a group of juniors smoking pot behind one of the Morgan barns.

As soon as he sees her, Dave slinks back against the wall, eyes protruding like a red-spotted blenny.

When she demands an explanation, I try to say "shellfish," but it comes out in a kind of garbled latin. My breathing's improved, but my tongue hasn't gotten much more agile since the epinephrine started to kick in. I reach for the bed sheet to soak up some more drool.

"Oh my god," Heather says. "You had a stroke." She draws her cell phone, where I'm sure she has the number of at least a couple neurologists she's had dinner with in the last handful of years.

"Ittfff..." I fish around for the note pad the CNA left somewhere in my covers. She seemed to think I was cold and kept adding blankets, so now I'm trapped in a cocoon ever expanding with mucous.

Dave says he's sorry again. He's on repeat, like the beeping heart monitor, like the acid that keeps trying to come back up my throat.

I kick out of my blanket and make a grab for the note pad.

Heather's nostrils flare. "You're having a *seizure*?"

Dave manages to sputter "accident" before Heather turns some kind of electric eel look on him.

I point to my throat, and Heather bends, studying my face. It feels like mucous might squirt out of my right eye socket again. It's swelling up, almost ripe.

Then she rounds on Dave. "Did he *hit* you?"

I reach for the pen and wave it around like a matador. *Shellfish. Anaphylaxis,* I scribble when I get her attention.

She reads this. "You fed her *fish*?" she demands, in a tone I'm sure she'd never use on the Morgans even when they poop in their water buckets.

Dave emits a kind of high-pitched whine like a dolphin stuck in a tuna net. This isn't his night, either. I thought he might pass out when I used the epipen, and then, for a while, he was under the impression people in anaphylaxis suffer from an urgent desire to be *held*.

I shake my head and write *accident.*

When Heather looks at the note pad, some bloody spit drips down onto the paper. Less than a minute later, she's morphed back into her Halloween zombie look and gone to track down a doctor.

I pull up the sheet and listen to another chorus of Dave's *sorries* I can't seem to stop before Bitch Nurse from triage rounds the corner. I got her title from a screaming man across the hall. Blessedly, Lillie's close behind her this time.

"Yer not supposed to have more'n one person'n here at a time," Bitch Nurse repeats. She does a lot of repeating. *But what did I eat that had shellfish in it? How did it start? When did I notice?* She just kept asking questions until I stabbed myself with the epipen. That finally got things moving before any kissing could be inferred. Not that she was doing much inferring.

"An yer her sister?" she asks Lillie.

Lillie nods, widening her stance and puffing up her midsection. She's one leg lift away from her soaring half-pretzel. I assume Lillie has some special karma to protect herself against these kinds of lies, a built-in defense like a spotted trunkfish.

Bitch Nurse squints at her. Lillie sucks in more air. We're not even in the same haplogroup. Sometimes, when Lillie's preparing for soaring half-pretzel, I'm not even sure we're the same species.

But Bitch Nurse backs down after a few seconds, flipping through my chart, and then Heather returns with a startled-looking doctor. This one has a long lab coat, so isn't another resident.

They all talk at once for a while, and the doctor talks at me, studying my face, pretending to study my vitals. Eventually, I agree to another IV drug.

Heather nods at the end of this exchange, satisfied for now. But she probably has an apple-flavored paste for allergies like the one for horse fly season that she'll be trying to administer to me in the middle of the night.

Bitch Nurse contracts her nose when sent to fetch the new medicine, and Lillie inserts herself between me and the doctor, blocking his attempt at patting me like a Morgan.

It's not long after he's left the room that the *sorries* start spilling out of Dave again, a kind of low, steady whine of apologetic vowel sounds. It was his lip balm. He had no idea it had shellfish in it. He'd really like to...

Heather makes a growl in her throat like a Morgan in heat, and Dave stops talking. There's a stare-down for a little while between them then, a kind of great-white-measuring process to decide who gets the dead seal. Me. I'm the dead seal. I look over at the beeping machine that seems to keep getting louder.

When Bitch Nurse reappears and shoots the new drug into my picc line, she informs me my ICE has been reached.

"Uth?" I ask.

"Yer I-C-E." She says *I* like a pirate *eyeee.* "Yer 'in case of emergency' number. We got it from yer cell phone."

"Neee," I protest. My dad put the ICE contact for Edie, my closest relative to the school, into my phone after one of his forwarded emails that warn about things like sociopaths throwing eggs at cars or putting razor blades in Halloween candy. I didn't think it was something real. Maybe we should have put "shellfish allergy" there, instead.

"Aan Aaa daaa," I explain.

"Aunt Eedie," Lillie translates.

"This shot is gonna make ya feel funny," Bitch Nurse warns before she goes.

*Call Edie*, I scribble. *I'm fine.*

"Fine," Lillie says as she reads, finding her Scribbles voice. *"Fiiine."*

*Don't let her come here. Going home soon anyway.*

Lillie twitches. Then the room twitches and goes dark.


When I wake up, Lillie's dabbing some drool off my face with one of her organic lavender hand wipes.

She presses the button for Bitch Nurse and informs me Heather's negotiated my release pending another dose of steroid in my picc line. Heather also escorted Dave out sometime while I was sleeping.

"He's so sweet," Lillie says. "He didn't want to leave you."

I cough. My throat feels like I've just swallowed some of the Halloween candy with razor blades.

"Don't worry," she says. "I told him you'd call him first thing tomorrow."

*     *

*Wut happenend?*

I adjust my computer glasses and re-read the last message. "Wut" is not a side effect from the drugs. There's a pattern to this, where "wut" means "what" and "tho" means "though," and so on. This is my first Social chat with someone who uses these words.

*I had to go to the hospital,* I explain, and think about how we got here. I was scrolling on my laptop a little after midnight, per the cocktail of drugs in my system. Wesley Anderson was there with a little a green dot by his name. I remembered I didn't know him when I confirmed his friend request, so I asked him why he added me. He said he "c's" me around "sumtimes."

*Shit,* he says. *U ok?*

*Yea,* I mirror, though I don't know why I'm mirroring this early in our social media friendship. I don't know anything about Wesley's fish consumption or whether his parents are alive or whether he's smelly, or even single or #FOMOing.

*I'm allergic to shellfish,* I explain.

*U eat them or sumthing?*

My throat giggles, then squeaks like a Pacific spinner. *Something,* I type. *Don't remember.*

*U drinking?*

*No. Epinephrine.*

*Sounds seriously threatening,* he responds quickly. Too quickly to have looked up how to spell the words. I don't know Wesley's patterns yet.

*I'm okay now*, I tell him, *just awake. I usually go to bed by ten.*

*Glad ur okay. Did u get the bitchy nurse?*

*Yes! U know her?* Is this mirroring for real, subconscious? I should have used "no" her. I could have won this.

This devolves, at some point, into what I think is a conversation, an easy exchange of information that's probably helped along by my drugs. Wesley tells me about how a bad tennis shot bent his pinky backwards and introduced him to Bitch Nurse. I tell him about my cuttlefish. He says they're "sick," contextually in a good way.

We keep typing. He tells me about his love of coffee. I tell him about my crème brulee misunderstanding. He says he goes to Indigo Dreams, too, "sumtimes." I tell him about my premature cuttlefish relocation, and he tells me about surfing in Australia.

I don't have a chance to ask if he eats fish before he tells me he's *from* Australia. He says he was a "shit" to his parents growing up, and I inquire casually if they're still living.

Sometime before it's light outside, Heather wakes me to ask if I'm seeing spiders on the ceiling, then demands I do long division in my head, then gives me a Benadryl.

My computer screen's dark, and I wait until she leaves to press the space bar. My Social chat's still open.

Wesley Anderson no longer has a green dot next to his name. His last line's *Ill say hey when I cu next.*

Lillie wakes me up before it's light out with a detox tea that tastes like Brussel sprouts and my mother's voice on her speakerphone.

"You sound groggy," Mom says.

I look at Lillie.

Lillie looks back into her bran mush. But I know she's watching, ready to pounce with more Benadryl even as the dandelion and milk thistle in the tea forcibly extract last night's drugs from my liver.

"Edie said she didn't know how it happened," my mom continues. "She thought you ate shellfish?"

Damn Edie's cocker spaniel and her early morning potty walks.

"Uh huh," I say.

"How?"

"It was in something."

Lillie looks up, then back at her bran.

"What?" Mom demands. "What could you have eaten that had shellfish in it?"

I turn to the living room window and feel Lillie's eyes on my back. It's raining again, the quiet kind of rain that creeps up on you.

"Lip balm," I say, and try to reassure her this was an isolated incident, not something at risk of being repeated. Dating's dangerous, obviously, more like windsurfing or eating at a cheap seafood chain than like gambling on coffee flavors. And up until the jellyfish cave, I thought it was going so well, I was about to be done with this part of my #FOMO.

When I say the word "date," my medical crisis is forgotten.

"You met someone at the bar!" Mom exclaims.

I try to correct her. I even describe my sole bar encounter

with the sawer-off-of-bunny-feet. But Mom's in #FOMO mode. Think of what I could be missing out on with *that* one, she says—a wildly different background, hand-eye coordination, a really fresh, local diet. She's heard all about the keto thing. And maybe they were overpopulated rabbits he was shooting. Maybe he was saving hundreds of sweet, fluffy bunnies from starvation and poverty.

Eventually, she pauses her story about the overpopulated Jackrabbits in a small suburb in Texas. "It wasn't Cam?" she asks.

Across the room, Lillie bites her lip. Her rice cooker dings, signaling Scribbles' new batch of cakes are finished, and she scurries across the kitchen—quietly, of course, so she can still hear everything.

"No." Cam doesn't have shellfish lip balm. That I know of, I mean. I guess he could have changed; I haven't known him for several months.

"He and your father...I was going to call you anyway. The Browns game," Mom says. "...you know."

Yes, I assure her, I do know. Not that I'd need to. I'm not at risk of going to football games all of a sudden and running into them there. *I* haven't changed.

"But then who was it?"

"Who?"

"You kissed *someone*. You didn't just switch lip balms."

My humpback noise won't come out. My throat's too sore. So I try to use words to assure my mom this incident was a cuttlefish thing, a coincidence. There were jellyfish. It was confusing. And I'm doing the #FOMO. This is one of those life stages when I'm bound to make some bad decisions.

# Chapter 7

*A female cuttlefish likes to keep her options open. While mating, she might accept sperm packets from several males into her mouth cavity. When she lays her eggs, she simply selects which she'd like to use for fertilization and spits out the rest.*

That night, Heather, Lillie, and I devolve into the age-old speculative yammering of our ancestors, eating pizza like we've never had heartburn. If Lillie hadn't sprinkled some microgreens over the cheese, this scene might be mistaken for a Sunday night gathering of young women in the university apartments just a couple blocks away. We commiserate over applications and Morgan hormone issues and talk about the men who are still causing us distress years after many of our peers have graduated to stable relationships in the suburbs.

"I think it's too soon," Heather says, re the taking of Matt to her sister's wedding, since he hasn't even met her favorite stud colt yet. She tears off another bite of breadstick and dunks it into the garlic sauce. "But maybe he'll get offended if I don't ask?"

This is a matrix of possibilities with no good outcome. If Heather takes Matt to the wedding, they must either (A) fly, or (B) take a very long, very boring road trip to New York state. It's too soon for them to fly except in the case of a last-minute beach trip, a spur-of-the-moment getaway somewhere with palm trees, and a road trip at this juncture in their relationship would reveal the character flaws they don't want to know about each other for several more months.

If Matt does go with her, he either (A) spends time with Heather's mostly deranged family while she does bridesmaid things, or (B) hides out in their hotel and takes on the role of wedding stalker, exchanging hurried texts with Heather across a crowded ballroom while she sneaks him plates of prime rib and asparagus in the hallway.

If, on the other hand, Heather doesn't invite Matt to the wedding, he will either (A) assume their relationship isn't *that* kind of a relationship (and Heather does *want* that kind of a relationship, even though it's too soon to *talk about* that kind of relationship), (B) assume she's going with someone else (same dilemma), or (C), be relieved, which would also signal relationship doom.

Will he see the pictures on Social later, she wonders, of her matched with her second cousin for the bridal party dance, and assume they're doing more than a slow foxtrot? Will her family think he's not relationship material and judge him forever for not being there, whispering and side-eyeing at their own wedding? Heather's family is widely credited with inventing the side-eye.

There are too many variables at play, too many ways this budding romance might unravel. And what about her father's poorly-concealed civil war memorabilia collection? What about the control undergarments she has to wear under her bridesmaid dress?

Heather tosses the greasy ends of her breadstick onto my plate and makes the horny Morgan noise. Then she rounds on me. "What about you?" she asks. "What are you doing about Jarod?" At least she's given up on Dave.

"She's been texting him," Lillie offers.

Heather raises her eyebrows.

And when I consider this, Jarod does sound more appealing than Dave, even 2,400 miles away. Could I be in a dating-adjacent position with him, I wonder, after a single conference?

Evidently, Lillie thinks so. She sets her pizza aside and opens her laptop, ready to type out a pros and cons list. I comply.

Jarod has many *pros*:
> -*incredible hummus*
> -*impressive publication history*
> -*hot, Heather says*
> -*a non fish-eater*
> -*easy to talk to*
> -*ecology background*
> - *parents likely near death*

Heather also notes two *cons*:
 *-age gap: roughly 16 years*
 *-based on my description, possibly too interested in javelinas*

"What about Dave?" Lillie asks, and goes through these *pros* quickly:
 *-attractive, she promises*
 *-attentive*
 *-caring*
 *-good energetic signature*
 *-nice to the cuttles*

"Could have killed her," Heather adds, a *con*. Also:
 *-didn't know there were crustaceans in his lip balm*
 *-tried to hold my hand*

"Underline that," I tell Lillie.

Lillie's cheek twitches like my dad's. As she types, her phone buzzes on the table beside her. She presses a button on the side.

"Was that Ned?" Heather asks.

Lillie shakes her head. "Another colleague," she says, her eyes still on the laptop.

Heather looks at me, then back at Lillie. Now Ned is just another colleague. This is when undergrads, possibly helped along by some wine, would use "breakup," ask Lillie how this is going and allow her to emotionally offgass like she always does for us. There's only so long after a separation before it becomes something that has to be mourned.

Except I didn't mourn Cam. That must be what I was

missing, whatever it is that would have made the end of our relationship something that needed to be mourned.

Lillie's phone buzzes again. There's no way to tell when her moment of breakup revelation will happen. Is this when she explodes, we wonder, the final unwanted buzz that does her in? We watch. We wait.

Lillie looks up from her screen, meets my eyes, and says, "Do you think Scribbles would like yogurt drops?"

"Yogurt drops?"

She turns the laptop around for me to see. "For his digestion. They're organic."

So maybe this isn't when she explodes. I admit I don't know enough to comment on my rat's bowel habits, and she orders the drops.

"Should Scribbles move back to my room?" I ask her. "Now that the conference…"

"Maybe after your applications."

I nod. This is a clear marker of my #FOMOing status, that I'm still perceived as a less fit rat guardian than someone going through an active breakup.

Before long, Lillie's managed to divert Heather's questions about Ned by turning the conversation back to Matt. Heather gets that zombie look again, but not in an about-to-attack-a-doctor way.

"You're exclusive?" Lillie asks.

Heather confirms this. But not exclusive *enough*, apparently, not at whatever relationship stage that calls for family wedding attendance. There are steps here I don't understand, tacit exchanges I've not experienced. For me, there weren't any clear stages between running into Cam on the jogging path and climbing out of his bathroom window because I didn't think he was going to get up to lock the front door if I left in the usual way.

"Maybe you should make a pros and cons list," I suggest, because we're older now, choosing mates consciously, preventing that helpless slide-into-relationships that plagued our twenty-something selves. And we have an open word processing document for just such a purpose.

Heather smiles. She doesn't need a list, she says. She can tell, *feel*.

Lillie types this while I consider. It's the *feel* I don't understand. My partner selection doesn't work this way; INTJ's *choose* rather than fall in love. Success is just a matter of how wisely you choose, whether the person you choose notices you doing more choosing than falling, and whether this offends them. Except that wasn't what ended it with Cam, was it? He wasn't offended. *I* was the one who jumped ship, when I was the one leaking.

I think of Cam as a control variable, the only one I have, that didn't enact whatever change in me he was supposed to. But Cam met all the criteria I'd expect in a successful mate. I think the problem was a neuro-chemical thing; apparently idiopathically, I lacked the vasopressin to affect a more lasting bond. I might have been dopamine-low to start. Probably I'm low on a lot of things. My mom's thought I've had an oxytocin deficiency since I was seven. I remember her having to spell the blood test for my pediatrician.

Would things be different, I wonder, with either Dave or Jarod? They're genetically dissimilar; pheromonally, one of them should work. But what if they're both inert? What if I'm the problem and they can't change *me*?

I ask Lillie what caused her breakup with Ned, and Heather flinches at my premature use of the *b* word.

Lillie doesn't look up this time. "We had incompatible life goals," she says to her laptop.

I apply this criteria to my own study. Cam was okay with my life goals, I think. Maybe we didn't talk about them enough. Maybe he wouldn't have been, and this is why we—why *I*—failed.

Dave's lip balm's incompatible with life. So that failed, too.

Wesley Anderson with a green dot next to his name pops into my head. There's insufficient data for a pros and cons list for him, but his alternative spelling and refusal to use contractions suggests incompatibility.

So that leaves Jarod. I think of a life with him, best case scenario—a life in which we continue to work towards publication, getting grants, touring the central states conferences together with hummus and noodles on the riverfronts. It's a good life. Maybe we make a trip to Seattle every now and then to visit the Elliott Bay Cafe and figure out how to spend a sabbatical in the Galapagos one day.

Lillie interrupts this fantasy by asking whether Scribbles is getting enough roughage.

Later that night, Scribbles has plenty of fiber and probiotics on the way, and Lillie's had a chia cup that I think might count as breakup ice cream for her. Heather packs for a riding instructors' clinic in Kentucky while I look up cuttlefish distribution maps for any hint of fellowship-worthy research.

Nothing new comes up, and I check Social again before I close down my laptop for the night.

*        *

By Tuesday morning, I have a proposal for the IMRI fellowship. Or something like a proposal. Maybe more of a plan. Maybe not a plan. What I have is a list of all the dozens of cuttlefish species known to frequent Australian waters and their relative distribution ranges. But this is something, is *enough*, I remind myself as I walk into the lab. Lillie's installed an affirmations app on my phone that tells me things like *I am enough.* and *My destiny is my own.* and *I am worthy of a wonderful life.*

Today, I tell myself I'm worthy of a major research fellowship. I step around a grad student napping in the hallway and note that the trash bin's Kyle food-free.

I've run through the IMRI criteria over and over and stayed up the last couple nights digging through papers on squid and snails and anything that might have changed in their environments—shifting currents and coral bleaching and desalination and rising water levels. I know almost everything we *don't* know about cuttlefish now. There aren't any publications; the scientific community hasn't ventured any theories as to how they might be affected by these changes. So I'm at least no worse a choice for investigating this than anyone else would be.

I find Milner in his office wrist deep in a bag of Cheetos. He closes his laptop when I come in and greets me with an *academicus tenuritis* salute, a wave and a stack of tests waiting for one of his TA's to come grade sliding off his desk.

"Nora!" He shows surprise, like I might have somewhere to be other than my empty lab on a Tuesday morning. Maybe he thinks I've moved on, that I've already joined a photography class or started incubating a fetus.

But he has good news, he tells me, since I'm still here. A teaching position's opened up at a little liberal arts school nearby that doubles as a music conservatory. I could probably even take on their gen ed physics class, he says, and teach freshmen how sound travels through water, in addition to some introductory biology sections.

He dangles the printout under my nose, waggling it like I do the smaller shrimp when Bitty's expecting crab. This is like a double rainbow, finding two positions opening in the same year in the greater flat plains tundra.

I look at the paper. Like Penn, this position's full time and pays enough to rent a bedroom in the country and eat not-always-ramen-noodles, assuming I don't require heat over the winter.

"No research," I say.

Milner squinches his lips into a pout like a parrotfish. "No," he acknowledges, "but it's a great opportunity."

I thank him and hand over the IMRI printout detailing what they're looking for. *Someone like me*, Lillie's taught me to repeat.

"It's a great fellowship," Milner agrees.

But his face goes back to parrotfish, then closer to blobfish as I tell him about the cuttle distribution maps and how temperatures are changing over reefs off Australia.

There are so many cuttles in that part of the world; the Eastern Australian coastline is to cuttles what the Galapagos is to freaky little birds.

"And you don't have experience, unfortunately, with wild cuttles," Milner says when I finish.

He has me there. But that's exactly what I *want*, I tell him, experience with wild cuttles. And how do you get that experience, other than by spending years studying tank-bred cuttles and applying for opportunities like this one?

I've been studying cuttlefish *cognition*, he reminds me. And there are no mazes off Australia. Whereas there's an older biologist at Penn who's probably going to retire in the next handful of years and, if I'm very lucky, I could take over his lab that teaches undergrads how to sequence fruit fly DNA.

Fruit flies. I wait for him to say something else, something more persuasive.

Milner makes one of his long sighs then, like he does when he has to keep office hours for his seminar. This is an ambition gap, he says, something he appreciates about me. That I'm ambitious. That I'm published, that this can take me so far if I just put my energy towards the right opportunities. Like replacing the fruit fly guy or teaching the musical prodigies how sound works.

I think instead about Lillian Stark discovering how sound waves from Naval sonar experiments around Hawaii was affecting the whales' echolocation, about how she led a campaign that single-handedly saved several humpback populations.

"And are cuttles the right species, do you think, for the IMRI?" Milner asks, not really asking.

I think about IMRI's other funded projects on sharks and major reefs and food sources in the Mariana trench. Probably even Lillian Stark wouldn't have had her level of success with, say, clownfish. It's the high profile species that have a shot at this kind of funding, the A-listers of the ocean, or at least something the A-listers eat.

But then I remember my affirmations app. If moon jellyfish are majestic, then yes, I tell Milner, so are cuttlefish. And they're ideal for isolating other variables. Because they're opportunistic hunters and can feed on any number of other species, anomalies in those populations won't affect them. They stick to offshore reefs, where the effects of bigger currents are minimized. They don't depend on coral, so bleaching won't directly affect their movements. Going to just one coast, I could track dozens of species of cuttles and isolate whether the temperature changes that have already been documented there have changed what we think we know about their distribution.

Milner picks up an ink pen to chew. "You've thought about this a lot," he says.

I nod. This is one arena in which INTJ's are always competitive. No one's ever accused us of under-thinking anything.

Milner leans back in his chair and looks up at the ceiling, at the stained tiles where one of the emergency showers in the chemistry labs busted a pipe last spring. "I just want you to be sure," he says. "I'd hate for you to waste your time. These programs at Mason and Penn, they could really go for you."

I consider this, and my *I am enough's* start to fade. He's right, of course. Those schools could go for my ovaries, he means, to pacify their boards, to pay less than my non-ovaried counterparts, to have a reason not to offer tenure or research opportunities to. Whereas IMRI doesn't have quotas to meet. They have enough money to pay a man for this position, with better chances of publication afterwards and no risk of the project being interrupted on the off chance he might birth something.

My eyes go to the framed photo of Milner's wife and kids lying on his desk by an empty Cheetos bag. He's told me about how she can't get tenure even with her postdoc from Yale and all her publication history. It's too much to commit to, doing what he calls life balance with their kids. Whereas Milner's praised when he skips out on boring faculty meetings to pick up these same children from basketball and when he misses STEM seminars for their school plays.

"These jobs," he says, "these are unicorns, Nora. They won't just pop up again next year. And with the IMRI fellowship, it's not just that you're a long shot, that you're young and don't have enough experience. I'd be rooting for you all the way, you know, but you said yourself that you don't have any idea what you'd find off that coast."

I muster one final #FOMOing thought. Isn't that what science is about, I ask, exploration unburdened by preconceived notions of what we'll discover?

Milner reminds me—gently, like he always does—that this is *not* what science is about. Science is about funding, and I'm interested in cephalopods, not in fudging up data on pharmaceuticals or corn.

"Either one of these teaching jobs could be everything you want," he says. "Just give them some more thought."

On the way out to my car, my phone buzzes. I fish it out of my jacket and see *Dave: two missed calls.*

By that evening, I've confirmed that the cuttles are fine and successfully diverted interaction with Dave, and Jarod and I are taking the next step in committing to an ongoing relationship. About thirty minutes ago, we became Social friends. This is a step that can go wrong quickly, the sudden awareness of someone's social media presence.

But our timelines are compatible, of course, like we should be; there aren't any surprises. Now we've progressed to active messaging about my fellowship dilemma and his school dilemma. Only his is less of a dilemma, since he likes both schools that have offered him jobs and will get tenure and good research opportunities either way. His is a choice, and the compromise he'll make is giving up one good choice in favor of the other.

I'll get these choices, too, he promises, down the road. Sooner than he did, of course, with my sole author publication and my work so far. Even sooner if these opportunities were what they were ten years ago. But academic ecosystems are always shifting, always devolving towards big bang-level chaos. Currently, almost any position anyone can afford to take—teaching, researching, camping with the Galapagos tortoises—is a unicorn.

*And you deserve a unicorn,* Jarod says.

I wonder if this is romance, a statement designed to make me shed my clothes like a freshwater stickleback.

*But I'm sorry if it's not the IMRI.*

My fingers hover over the keyboard for a few seconds. *I'm*

*still thinking of applying.*

He doesn't respond right away.

*For the experience,* I clarify. *Don't apologize,* my head-mom says.

*Will you have time to do the teaching apps at the same time?* he asks. *Mason seemed pretty last call.*

The answer's no, of course, probably not with this little time left. Both schools want teaching statements, educational philosophies, and sample syllabi for courses I've never designed before. And I know this is what's expected, that I'll make one of the academic life-compromises everyone talks about and trade my first N.A. Novak paper for a job I don't want, grasping at tenure for the next couple decades and finally seizing control of a dynasty of fruit flies.

Maybe if Jarod's not surprised by Milner's reaction, the IMRI really isn't my shot. And I'll be older, more experienced when the next one comes around.

*It couldn't hurt to keep your options open,* Jarod says. *But it'd be nice if I'd be right around the corner from you at Mason next year.*

I reach for my tea mug. It's empty. I've been chugging Lillie's detox tea without thinking about it. And maybe that says something about my current ability to make these kinds of decisions on my own.

*Milner doesn't think I have a shot,* I write before I get up.

The kitchen's dark when I go boil some more water. Heather's out with Matt, and Lillie's in her room working late from home again.

I take a sip of too-hot tea when I climb back into my bed.

*shot at?*

*The IMRI fellowship,* I write.

There's a pause, those three little dots that undulate like sipuncula.

*Fuck him.*

Hot dandelion water shoots up my nasal passages. I scan the text box. Wesley Anderson's there with his green dot. I sent the message about Milner to him. Jarod's green dot's disappeared. His faculty meeting must have started; it's only five in Washington.

I immediately explain this mistake to Wesley, apologizing for the mix-up. He'd just written me a *hey.*

*so u want the IMRI?* he asks at the end.

I explain the odds then, all the variables I can't control, the lack of experience I can't make up for. *It's complicated,* I finish.

*ur advisor wants u to apply for teaching shit?*

*Right.* That's exactly what I mean—all the shit I don't want, none of the shit I do want. Wesley Anderson has a way of simplifying things.

The undulating dots flash for just a second. *Tell him fuck off and do what u want,* he says.

I start to type, to tell him about Milner's reasoning. Then I remember I'm #FOMOing now, which isn't about being reasonable, and that Milner isn't required for a letter of recommendation. The IMRI fellowship's the kind of thing you recommend yourself for without support. You're supposed to be someone who can do that by the time you'd apply for an IRMI fellowship.

And something about Wesley Anderson's response strikes my new affirmations-based neurolinguistic programming as exactly right.

So I mirror then, all neuroplastic-like. *I think u r right.*

"You've made a decision," Lillie says from her sacred bendy-twisty when I come out for my last tea of the night. "What is it?"

I turn on the electric kettle. The water's already warm; it starts hissing right away.

"I'm going to work on the fellowship application," I tell her. "I'll get started on both it and the teaching and see how they go."

"That's great," she says, then, "Have you told Milner?"

The kettle clicks off, the blue light fading as I pour the water into my mug.

"Fuck him."

Lillie unfolds like an accordion. "Let me get you some other tea," she says.

"Why?"

"I think you might be having a detox reaction." She takes my mug. "Do you feel funny?"

"No," I say. *Yes,* I think, I *do* feel funny. Very funny. #FOMOing funny. This must be what happens to the people who go join reality TV shows.

Lillie dives into the tea cabinet and emerges a few seconds later with a bag that looks like a wasp nest. She dumps out my mug and pours hot water over the new bag, swirling it a few times before she hands it back to me like she might read the tea leaves.

I sniff. It doesn't smell anything like her dandelion detoxification or my usual rooibos.

"What is it?" I ask.

Lillie takes a deep breath and finds her Scribbles voice. "*Valeeerrian,*" she says.

When I get back to my room, Wesley Anderson's green dot's still there. Social chimes when I open my laptop.

*We should get together sometime if u want,* he says.

My fingers stall over the keyboard as I start to evaluate. Except this time, I don't have to evaluate.

# Chapter 8

*Because they're the best mimics, cuttlefish are great at sneaking up on their prey. But it's no problem if they're seen; they can also hypnotize their next meal with a dazzling show of light.*

I spend the next two days putting off Dave's attempts to get together—even as friends, with no chance of orally-transmitted anaphylaxis—and isolating myself in my lawn chair in the lab bathroom.

Wednesday and Thursday, I stay logged into the school's journal database and down a constant stream of tea and bagels from the engineering department's café next door. This is a sacred dance of good grad school juju, a grind, something that always comes before a significant victory.

I'm mostly alone in this hallway; Kyle's only stopped by once with his Chinese takeout. His clownfish seem to be doing more resting than mating these days. Milner's probably still working on his paper from home. This is how the middle of the semester always lags, these long weeks when everything seems to slow down.

There's a crisp breeze today from the bathroom window that looks out over the courtyard. Every now and then, I get a whiff of something plastic from the materials science lab over the soft smell of fallen leaves and outdoor molds.

It's past nine on Thursday night when I finish skimming the last paper authored by an IMRI fellowship winner. This one's in a top journal and is a verifiable tour de force of evolutionary adaptation in lemon sharkhood.

There's no hint of squiddiness here, of speculation. All the others seem to be along the same lines, celebrating mixed-race dolphins or leatherback sea turtles that predict earthquakes.

My proposal so far: Visit Australia. Swim around and try to identify cuttlefish species. See if any of them have moved.

My unique qualifications: No one else seems interested.

I'm about to shut down my laptop for the night when I see Wesley Anderson's glowing green dot in my Social window.

*Hows ur applications goin?* he asks when I "wave."

This is a wave of surrender, of defeat and botched ambition.

*Okay*, I answer instead. *How are you?* I mean to abbreviate *r* and *u*. I haven't been getting enough sleep.

*kinda shit day*, he says. *sprained my finger.*

I express the usual sympathies.

He doesn't respond.

*How?* I ask.

*tennis*

I'm typing out more thorough sympathies when he writes

again.

*When r we gonna have our rendezvous?*

I stop and erase. Do we have a rendezvous? Am I too old, too not French for a rendezvous? Do I even know what a rendezvous entails? I rub my eyes, take off my glasses, and close down my journal window.

*Yes,* I write, ignoring that this isn't a binary question. Because maybe a rendezvous is exactly what I need.

*coffee r something?* he asks.

*Yes.*

*U up for trying Indigo Dreams again?*

I swear I taste crème brulee coffee, but I swallow this away and agree.

*Pick u up Saturday?*

*I'll meet you there,* I say. *I walk.*

*7 sound alrite?*

"Alrite," I think, is so different than "all right." It speaks to me, to some primitive part of my brain that wants to apply for an IMRI fellowship and run like someone left the gate open, and etc. I type *yes,* then erase. *Yea,* I say. *Looking forward to it.*

The dots dance, then pause, then dance again.

*me too*

I pack up my laptop and don't bother to take out Milner's trash on my way out.

*        *

Saturday, after another day and a half of proposal drafting, I scrub the lab bathroom smells from my skin with an oatmeal bath Lillie drew to soothe whatever in my skin or my psyche needs soothing—a lot, presumably, at this point in my career.

As I'm drying off, Heather texts with dating advice. She's been saying things like "you can butt-in hug" and "don't mention sea slug penis fencing" to complement the affirmations app Lillie put on my phone. These all mix together with my mom's voice in my head now. *I am enough. No sea slug sex. Don't forget your orgasmic blush!*

*It's going to be great*, Heather writes. *3 dates in 3 weeks!* She's started to count Jarod now that she's convinced his pros outweigh our age difference and his javelina interest, and also because my only other date so far sent me to the ER. She thinks this number should help my self-confidence.

I take inventory of my self-confidence, studying the way my Heather-approved jeans squeeze my butt. My emergency hoop earrings are on my bed, ready for action. I'm not really sure what action is in this context.

*How would I know if this is a date?* I ask. This is a conversation Wesley and I haven't had. It's not something that comes up from seeing each other's profile pictures and messaging about broken fingers and long-shot fellowships. And I didn't know I was dating Cam until months into our relationship.

*You decide it is*, Heather answers.

So I straighten my hair, apply the blush and, like any self-actualizing thirty-two-year-old, pretend to know what I'm doing.

Lillie's waiting for me in the kitchen, semi-contorted on a barstool in her swaddled eagle pose.

"You look great," she says. Her phone buzzes on the counter. She bites her lip.

I know this gesture, remember the little red mark her mom's breast cancer scare left on her lower lip the year I moved in. "You're stressed," I observe.

"No," she says, but she doesn't make eye contact.

I take a seat next to her at the island and try to approximate the listening lotus.

Lillie pushes her phone away. "It's nothing. You'll text when you get there?"

"Yes."

"And I'll text you a little while after, and you'll respond with a cuttlefish fact?"

"Yes." This is the protocol Heather developed after watching a serial killer movie Sunday night. She thinks I might attract these personality types—accidentally, coincidentally. And it seems like a worthwhile precaution to take since my last date did come close to killing me.

I let go of the island, attempting to find the center of my lotus. My lotus doesn't have a center. My elbow bangs into the granite.

Lillie sighs. "My phone's work," she says. "It's just a little stressful right now."

"I'm sorry."

She shrugs. Then her face changes and she falls into her Scribbles voice, alternating with one that sounds eerily like my mother as she starts her pre-date pep talk. I can almost feel the #FOMO. I am worthy, I am *sooooothed*. I am seizing potentially wonderous opportunities and having fun. *Sooothing* fun.

"Pound FOMO," I say as I pick up my purse.

Lillie nods. "Pound FOMO," she says.

I dodge some exuberant undergrads playing frisbee as I cut across the sports complex, leaves crunching under my boots and high-pitched squeals cutting through the wind. These are the loud days, for the undergrads, the mating calls of optimal reproductive age and the wails of broken dreams, the tipsy hoots of sports-supporting and the soft whine of ennui that hums over all the other noises in their heads. These are the things I didn't hear from inside the STEM departments. Because I didn't join clubs, my mom says, and learn to make all these important noises myself. Hence here I go a #FOMOing.

I wrap my coat tighter around my chest and jog past the tennis courts, where it's quiet tonight, no rhythmic pops and scuffling shoes. I wonder if I'm nervous. I used to be distinctly not nervous when getting coffee, comfortable with all the things I might be missing out on. I start listing whale species.

*Orca, gray, humpback. Blue, beaked, beluga.*

When I turn onto Lincoln, the music from Indigo Dreams seems to waft down the street in the breeze.

*Bowhead, Eden, fin.*

The bell on the front door chimes over a saxophone solo, and I gag a little on what I swear smells like crème brulee all the way from the doorway.

*Narwhal, sei.*

I check my phone. I'm ten minutes early. At Lillie's suggestion, I order a chamomile tea, with a cookie, and claim a little booth in the corner.

*Byrde's.*

I forget Byrde's sometimes, like just now. I don't know what it is about it.

I text Lillie to tell her I'm here and then spend a couple minutes speculating on whether any of the men scattered around the room might be Wesley Anderson. I think of him as a hazy green dot, but I know from his profile picture that he has blonde hair. He was standing in the photo, moving and blurry, like an Amazon river dolphin that disappears into the darkness right as you try to catch it surfacing.

I rule out the men in groups and two sitting alone, both with dark hair. That leaves one blonde on a computer, one scrolling his phone and leaning against the bathroom wall, and two whose hair color I can't identify. One of them is wearing a hat. The other's hoodie covers what I can see of his head. The age distribution in the room probably spans about thirty years, though I can't tell with the hoodie-wearer. Should I have asked Wesley his age?

I look at my phone. Lillie's sent a thumbs up.

*Omura's, right, pilot.*

The barista calls my name, and I get up to get my tea, holding my breath by the flavor mixer and trying not to think about crème brulee.

*Sperm, minke.*

The mug warms my hands, then splashes when I turn into the hoodie-wearer. His hood's fallen back now, long blonde waves sticking out. He looks at my forehead. I look at his cheekbones. Then I segue straight into shark species.

My evaluation's quick. Wesley Anderson's more

attractive than any horn shark, more Australian than an echidna, and likely more fertile than a mola mola. I haven't trained for this.

He's also about as silent as an orca, not displacing any air when he crosses the room. I didn't feel him behind me when we walked back to my little corner booth, like that diver on the ocean floor who had a panic attack when nudged by a twenty-four foot male.

My heart bubbler's on high. I squeeze my chamomile mug. Across the booth, Wesley Anderson takes a swig of something that smells like dirt.

"Good booth, yeh?" His voice is soft, smooth, less outback-y than I expected from that show Heather watches on Tuesday nights.

"Good booth," I agree. I don't know what else to say, what we could possibly have in common other than liking quiet booths in corners.

His arm jerks out, and he points to my chamomile. "Better?" he asks. Than crème brulee coffee, I think he means.

"Better," I confirm. Though the chamomile's not doing anything for my heart bubbler. I think it might be fake chamomile, like their fake crème brulee. I take a yoga breath that Lillie taught me and swear I can feel the heart bubbles going to my brain. "How's your finger?" I ask.

He holds up his hand with the brace, then drops it back under the table. "Kay," he says. "Your application?"

I hear his "ur" now, one word. I think there won't be a way for me to stop hearing it. "Slow," I tell him. "Frustrating."

"Good time fura break," he says, picking up his coffee again.

I look around the room. More people have piled in by the door, and the weird candle-lights hung from the ceiling feel closer to us now, warmer. I let go of my chamomile mug. Wesley continues looking at his coffee.

After a while—maybe not very long—my phone buzzes in my purse, Lillie making sure my date's not going to kill me.

Wesley looks at my forehead. I look back at my phone. I'm maybe 80% sure.

"Sorry," I tell him. "It's my housemate. I need to say something about denticulated suckers." I type this into a sentence re cuttlefish hunting behavior.

*Good,* Lillie responds. *Have fun!*

"Denticulated suckers?" Wesley asks when I put my phone back into my purse.

"So she knows it's me. They're how cuttlefish grab their..." This is how it starts.

Wesley's still looking at me when I finish my wikipedia-composing account of cuttlefish hunting behaviors.

"Swheat," he says. "You got a lot from skewl."

"*Skewl?*"

"Skewl," he confirms, like that video of Germans trying to pronounce "squirrel."

"School," I guess.

"Yeh."

But I'm thinking of squirrels now. "Do you shoot squirrels?"

"No."

"Do you hunt other things? Rabbits?"

"No."

"Okay," I say.

Then there's silence. The music's stuck on a long bass

solo.

"I wasn't really into skewl," Wesley says after a minute.

"You were...doing something else?"

"Surfing," he says, "and sports."

"Sports," I echo, then realize I don't have anything to say about sports. "Loud?" I ask.

"Yeh," he says, "sometimes."

I swear I can hear the "sum" in his "sometimes." "And here in Cleveland, you do...?"

"Not much," he says. "I play...I don't do a lot. Whata you do?"

"Not much," I mirror. Now, anyway.

He takes a sip of his coffee. Then he looks at my forehead again.

"Less," I add, "since my research is finished."

"With your cuttles?"

I nod. "They're at the aquarium now, retired."

I'm looking at his forehead, too, when something flashes there, something I don't recognize. Wesley's face is one I can't read well. It's too still, I think, and too jerky when it does move.

"You miss em?" he asks.

"I miss them."

There's a pause. "Allergies," he says then.

I take another gulp of my chamomile. He doesn't say anything else. So I ask if he's allergic to molluscs.

He shakes his head. "That thing you had. Anaphylaxis?"

I nod, wait.

"What was it from?"

"Shellfish."

"But you're not allergic to your cuttles."

"No. I would be. If I ate them, I mean. Probably. I don't eat…"

"But you ate…"

"I kissed someone. The shellfish were in his lip balm."

Wesley's eyebrows go up, then back to neutral. "Your boyfriend or…?"

I don't know what the *or* is. I think tonight, in this booth, there are probably a whole new range of *or*'s I don't know.

"A bad date," I tell him after a minute.

"You go out a lot," Wesley says. It doesn't sound like a question.

I answer anyway. "No."

Some time passes, and the chamomile spreads warmth across my torso. Sweat beads under my nose.

Wesley stares into his coffee mug. "I'm not good at this," he says to his mug.

"Coffee?"

"Yeh."

"Okay," I say.

He makes eye contact. And then we keep looking at each other—at eyes, not at foreheads. I don't know why I don't look away. He's like the lure on an anglerfish, beacon and bioluminescent bacteria in one, a trap.

My phone buzzes, and I dig it out of my purse. Lillie's calling. I apologize.

He waves a hand. "'s fine," he says. "Your mate?"

I nod, but then the buzzing starts over. It's a voicemail. Lillie never leaves voicemail.

"I'm sorry," I tell him. "I need to…" I hit some buttons on

the phone and finally press "play" on the voicemail. It plays on speaker.

It's rapid-fire information that comes out then, non-Lillie sounds and rhythms. She thinks Scribbles is sick. She's taken him to an emergency vet. There's a text with this location in a pin, but I don't need to come, she tells me twice. She's handling the situation.

Wesley's leaning forward when the message clicks off.

"It's my rat," I tell him. "I'm sorry. There's a vet, a...pin."

He takes my phone and studies the screen. I suck in a breath that seems to pool in a giant bubble around my heart.

"It's close to town," he says. "I'll drive."

I pause, consider. I don't do much considering, actually. I'm up, following him towards the door before I even think to put on my coat.

As we're walking out into the cold and my right arm gets stuck in my coat sleeve, a tall blonde woman who also looks bioluminescent in metallic pants passes us, then turns around.

"Wes?" she asks as we move out onto the sidewalk. Then she waves her arms and starts bouncing along the curb towards us like a shiny frogfish.

"Wessie!" she yells louder, arms outstretched like detinculated suckers.

He doesn't turn around.

Hunting cuttle woman is only a few yards away when Wesley—Wes? *Wessie?*—stops at a black car parked on the street.

Behind us, the woman lets out a cry like a horny beluga.

I stop.

He shakes his head, unlocks the car, and says, "just get in."

And I do.

About ten minutes later, we're in a little exam room at the back of a strip mall. There's a Noah's ark wallpaper border at my waist and too-bright fluorescents overhead. A lump like a dogface puffer has settled in my throat.

Lillie's clutching Scribbles to her chest and shooting karmic death rays at the veterinary technician pressed against the far wall. This is a new Lillie behavior, a power I didn't know she'd mastered.

The vet tech's frozen in place, and Wes—am I calling him Wes now, too?—has gone hoodie-up in the other corner, glaring, I think, at the floor.

"We're fine here," Lillie says to the vet tech for the third time in the last five minutes. He was on after-hours duty and offered to hold Scribbles for her until the vet got in, which evidently blacklisted him in Lillie's books.

Then she turns to me, tugging at her scarf to reveal Scribbles' back. "Does he look puffy to you?" she asks.

I clear my throat. "About...usual puffiness," I say as confidently as possible, because I'm not qualified to evaluate puffiness in rats.

Lillie shows him to Wes. Wes looks at me.

"I think he's a little puffy," she says, stroking Scribbles' nose. "He seems uncomfortable."

The vet tech bends to take a look himself, and Lillie covers Scribbles with her scarf again.

"I want a Mycoplasma test." She says this in a distinctly

unLillielike way that brooks no opposition.

"Yeah, sure," the vet tech says. "His breathing sounds good, though, so you shouldn't have to worry too much once you've given him a round of an..."

"Thank you."

The vet tech retreats to his corner, and the room falls into silence again.

"So, you said he was, uh...sneezing?" I ask after a while.

Lillie nods, continuing to stroke Scribbles' nose. She has his eyes covered with her scarf. This wasn't the time, she decided, to be introducing him to new environments with strange men in scrubs or hoodies.

"And it's not another sprout stuck up his nose?" I ask.

Lillie shakes her head.

"You did the right thing bringing him in. Respiratory infections can get bad quickly," the vet tech tells me. *Gregg,* his name tag reads. "When a rat gets a cold, sometimes in just the course of a day, it can..."

"Actually," Lillie says, "Scribbles would feel more comfortable if you waited outside."

When Gregg leaves, she turns back to me. "He told me I was *probably overreacting* when I gave him the printout with the Mycoplasma protocol."

Scribbles peeks his head out, then starts to chew on her scarf.

I apologize to Wes for the interruption to our date-or-whatever-it-was as soon as the exam room door closes behind us. The waiting area's empty, draped in shadows. A flood light over the parking lot shines in from outside, but the overheads are all off here. I guess when someone comes in with a rat wrapped in her scarf, you expect her to bypass the waiting room.

Wes sits down on the other side of a long wooden bench, his head and shoulders a silhouette against the window.

"Sorry he's sick," he says.

"You don't have to stay."

He doesn't move.

We sit in the quiet for a while then, the vet's voice muffled through the exam room door. Lillie thought I looked stressed and worried I might transfer this energy to Scribbles if I stayed in the room too long.

I look at Wes. He's so still, I can't even see that he's breathing. I sit back against the wall, my body heavy I guess with whatever energy Lillie can see. I smell the flea collars up by the register when the heat kicks on, a kind of buzz that comes up through the floorboards like at the club.

This isn't a usual date activity, I think, rat vetting, if this was a date. Wes must have noticed. It seemed like he knew how to do everything when we were talking on Social. I think of the woman outside the coffee shop and wonder if she's his usual kind of date, if he'll go back there now.

"When we were leaving," I say. "I think you missed a...woman." Though gendering bioluminescent-beluga-with-denticulated-suckers person and me the same way is probably wrong.

"Yeh," he says.

"Was she a friend?"

"No."

"A girlfriend?"

"No," he says, then, "no" again.

I flinch when Lillie opens the exam room door. The *creak*'s loud this time, like a channel catfish equipped with a microphone.

"Nora, would you please come here for a minute?" Lillie asks in her best Scribbles voice. When I'm in the doorway, she gestures to the vet. "Could you repeat that?"

The vet, a bald, speckled man who looks like a grouper, takes a deep breath and nods at Scribbles. "It looks like just a little infection to me, but…"

"I want him to do a Mycoplasma test and give Scribbles a steroid shot," Lillie says. "I texted Heather, and she checked Myco infections with the university labs, and they don't always respond to antibiotics, even multiple rounds, and…"

"…and she said it's your rat," the vet finishes.

I look from him to Lillie.

"It doesn't look too serious," he continues. "You obviously caught it early, and while I'd always give a steroid in a more serious case, there's barely any discharge. I'm not even sure how…"

"There's a high risk of secondary infection," Lillie says.

I tell the vet to go with the shot. This pacifies Lillie, and she dismisses me with a nod. I guess my aura still hasn't settled.

My eyes take a minute to adjust as I come back out into the waiting room. Wes is a shadow on the bench. His hoodie's up, hiding the side of his face. I sit next to him this time, settling haphazardly onto my left hip like a crash-landing seagull.

"Scribbles is getting a steroid shot," I tell him, because I'm not sure what else to say.

He shifts. His knee brushes mine.

"I get those sometimes," he says after a while of us frozen like this, in the dark on the hard bench. "They're not bad."

An hour later, I'm watching Wes pull away from the kitchen window. Lillie will be here soon, full of new information about administering rat antibiotics. Wes—I must be calling him that now, too—and I came ahead as soon as the vet was finished.

The drive was quiet, the heat blowing over my face and my body heavy against the leather seat. I could hear some crickets outside even though I thought we'd already had a freeze. But Cleveland can surprise you like that.

I think of the loud crunch of gravel under his tires as we pulled into the driveway. It must have been quiet before. *We* must have been quiet. We said good night then, and I went inside.

I should text my mom, I think as I watch his tail lights flicker through the trees. I got into a car with someone I met on the internet. This is definitely on the #FOMO list.

*         *

Sunday night, Heather rushes home from her riding instructors' clinic to make sure my rat doesn't need horse drugs, and we gather in the living room to process the weekend—quietly, of course, because Scribbles is sleeping in the next room. Lillie's rearranged his cage with organic paper towels to avoid dust and added a humidifier with rat-safe essential oils. This is definitely not the time, she told me, to move him back to my room. I guess I'm kind of energetically leaking.

"I'm giving him the probiotics a few hours apart from the antibiotic," she tells us.

"Not Myco, then?" Heather asks.

"We don't know. The culture hasn't come back yet."

Heather nods sagely, then turns to me. "Of all the shit to happen in the middle of your date. And he—Wesley—stayed?"

I confirm he stayed and then drove me home, earning an appreciative noise from Heather. But we didn't hug, butt-in or out. Is that what would have made it a date, or at least one that went well? I've been evaluating, the way you do, making google searches.

"What's he like?" Heather asks.

"A Greek god," Lillie says before I have a chance to answer.

Heather's eyes bug.

"I'm not kidding," Lillie says. "Adonis in a freaking hoodie."

Heather sits forward, looking like a Morgan who's just seen the feed bucket. "Seriously?"

"With an Australian accent," Lillie adds.

"All he said to you was..." What was it? "Hey?"

She shrugs. "You could tell."

"Wow," Heather says. "What does he do?"

I think back through our conversation at the coffee place, trying to remember any talk of Wes's job. "I'm not sure."

"What do you mean?"

"It didn't come up." This was something I was supposed to ask, probably. "Not hunt," I offer.

"Uh huh," Heather says, then, "Does he eat fish?"

"That didn't come up, either."

Heather puts down her matcha. "Wow."

"You have no idea," Lillie says.

*       *

Monday morning, I look in on Scribbles before I go to the lab, knocking on Lillie's door twice before opening it. Her favorite soothing harpist's playing through her computer speakers, but there's no Lillie in sight. She must have gone to the health food store for more echinacea. It's important, she told me yesterday over her bran mash, to get echinacea into sick rats as consistently as possible.

Scribbles is snuggled down in a bed of paper towels with a heating pad under them. I'm studying his discharge-free nose when Lillie's phone dings on her desk.

I don't look at it until the third ding, and even then only accidentally, to see *Matt: four new messages.*

# Chapter 9

*A cuttlefish can be anything it wants, changing its texture, patterns, and colors at will—even though it's colorblind. One moment, it's a gently-swaying blade of seagrass. The next, it's a sandy substrate.*

Over the next few days, I can't seem to get Lillie alone. Not that I know what I'd ask her, how to broach the topic of Heather's-boyfriend-stealing.

Maybe I should have seen this coming; Matt and Lillie as a couple make sense from all but a karmic standpoint. They're of a kind, being programmers. They share a lifestyle and a similar background. They could even commute to work together. Their relationship would be congruous, logical. Not, for instance, like him and Heather or like me and Wes.

I spend the first part of the week working, switching between the IMRI and the university applications, but I've officially reached the point when I don't have time to finish both.

By Thursday morning, pretty much everyone's contributed to my pick-an-application dilemma. Jarod's sent an article about the dwindling number of tenure-track positions in major universities. Heather's shown me her 401K, and Lillie's found me a relaxing new tea blend. Wes has messaged a cuttlefish meme. The cuttles, whom I've visited each afternoon during Dave's lunch break, have approached their new lobster dinners with enthusiasm but offered no career guidance.

About half of a teaching statement and a set of bullet points for the fellowship are open on my laptop when Lillie knocks on my door around six in the morning.

"You're up early," she says. She hands me a mug of the new tea she's been making me. I think it's mostly tranquilizer. It has a lot of lavender.

"You're heading into work?" I ask.

"Later," she says. "I saw your light was on. Scribbles is doing well. Don't worry."

"Thanks."

Her knees do that *plié* bend that signals the start of the lotus. I sit up against my headboard.

"Scribbles is doing well," she repeats. "You know I switched him off the strawberry antibiotic and onto the piña colada flavor yesterday."

I wait, focused on her knees. Maybe this is a consequence of my messy aura. Maybe it was inevitable, at some point, that my rat would take to drinking.

"It's going well," she continues. "I think the piña colada's a higher quality flavoring. The Myco test came back positive, but he's eating normally, and the discharge is all gone now. He likes the applesauce more than the baby food, and he's taking a lot of yogurt drops. I think he should stay where he is for now."

"The test came back positive?"

She nods. "The vet tech called. I gave him my number."

"Thank you." I breathe. This is my chance. "Lillie," I say. "I saw your phone. Monday. I was there, in your room. To check on Scribbles. Matt was texting you."

She blinks, waits like that Pacific octopus.

"Are you...is there something going on with you and Matt?" *Heather's* Matt, I mean, the one I met wrapped up in Lillie's blue chenille blanket, probably looking just as guilty as I thought then. "I wasn't sure if he was just...giving you some...code or something for work, or..."

"No," she says. And that's it. She doesn't move, doesn't give anything else away.

I wait. I can't *plié* on the bed to even start a lotus. So I maintain eye-to-forehead contact. Her face stays frozen in that distinct Lillie placidity that can't be replicated with microexpression software.

"So you haven't decided yet on your applications?" she asks when I finally look away.

I shake my head.

She bites her lip, and I get that feeling you get right before someone's murdered in one of Heather's shows, when the killer's about to pop out.

She looks at the bunny supreme on my nightstand. "There's something else," she says. "You remember how I was getting notifications from Academic-A after your paper was published?"

"Yes."

"For your department," she says.

I nod.

"Well, I got one last night. Milner put up his paper. He's...shopping? Is that right? Shopping it?"

"Right." Milner should have been finished with his paper a month ago. I guess this means he'll be back in his office again soon.

"I thought you'd want to see it before you went in today," Lillie says.

She waits while I open a browser window, then shifts, bends, and lotuses right there on my floor. I can't imagine what about shrimp sex could be this disruptive.

*The Effects of Salinity, Protein, and NH3 in Stomatopod Reproduction* loads over my fellowship bullets.

I scroll through the methods and results, through the conclusions, but I know all of this already. It's the pattern I found looking through his data, the conclusion and discussion I drafted for him.

I scroll to the bottom, to the mentions. Kyle's there, second. There are five "thanks" in total. I'm not one of them.

Lillie's still in her listening lotus on my floor when I look away from the screen. Her face is rat-sick serious. "I'm sorry," she says.

"It's okay." I read the mentions again, then take a sip of the lavender tea. "I've made a decision."

Lillie smiles. "Congratulations," she says as she unfolds. "Your running shoes are by the door."

I'm on my third loop around the soccer stadium when the sun starts to peek over the downtown skyline. There's no one else here, just my shoes tapping on the asphalt. Rotting leaves have been blown into piles that dot the outer fence, and the fields are covered with mud puddles that are starting to freeze.

By the time I've run through all the eel species in my head, I've almost stopped imagining Milner in low ammonia, high salinity water being slowly consumed by amorous sea shrimp.

The sun casts long shadows across the locker rooms. I think it looks like a scene at the beginning of one of Heather's crime shows, or maybe something from a forwarded email from my dad. But Cleveland's not always what you'd expect—there are occasional dead bodies that turn up in the lake, but quiet sunrises, too, these little pockets of peace. You have to live here for a while to get to know its rhythms, just like the ones in fornicating shrimp.

Not that I could know Cleveland's rhythms now, with mine so off. You wouldn't have thought this is where I'd end up, throwing myself into an IMRI fellowship application without help, wanting to throw my advisor to some sea scavengers, #FOMOing.

I check my watch, then put it back under my sleeve. I'm starting to sweat under the jacket, too warm for the early morning dew. I keep going.

I'm in the middle of Ohio turtle species when someone calls my name.

I recognize him right away even though the hoodie's different. He's wearing shorts this time, a kind of pink-river-dolphin-in-the-Arctic vibe.

"You're not cold?" I ask when we meet at the trash can at the corner of the tennis court. It comes out "ur" in my head. I meant to offer a greeting, an expression of surprise, delight, *something*, that Wes Anderson is also at the tennis courts at sunrise.

He shakes his head and falls into step beside me. "You get up early," he says.

"You, too."

I see when we pass the tennis court that his bag's there. His racquet's propped up against the fence. "You can play?" I ask. "With your finger hurt?"

His hood falls back. Maybe he needs to play tennis like I need to run, and this is why he's willing to do it in the cold. Or maybe he likes the quiet, too, like the corner booth.

"It's not bad," he says.

I look down. His finger's all taped up like the Morgans' legs when they go in the trailer. He's just missing the cushy inner wrap for padding.

"It looks bad," I say.

He shrugs. "I've had em a lot. How's your IMRI?"

I exhale, long, like Lillie taught me, and try to sweep the resentment for Milner out of my voice and my heart chakra and wherever else it's building up all this pressure, probably in an important artery. "I'm applying," I tell him, "and setting aside the teaching applications for now. I decided this morning."

"And your advisor's over it?"

"Fuck him."

Wes exhales, a cloud against the dark grass. The lights are all off on this side of the court, but I can see his smile.

We keep walking, and I tell him about Milner's paper, how I found the actual pattern, how I did all the work on the data and drafted the relevant parts of the paper and still didn't get a mention. How Kyle did. How Milner doesn't think I have a chance at the fellowship and how I'm avoiding the lab now, avoiding him. I'd need a letter of recommendation from him to do the teaching apps, anyway.

"Fuck *him*," Wes says, more vehemently.

I nod. He stretches his bandaged hand, bending a long finger back towards his wrist.

"That hurts?" I ask.

He shrugs again, then drops it. "It's a thing I have."

"A thing?"

"My connective tissue," he says. "It's messed up."

When we pass the locker rooms, there are muffled voices coming from the quad, one of the university soccer teams starting to assemble, shivering, in the field.

"Tell me about it?"

"Yeh?"

"Yeh," I mirror.

So he does. It's sparse language, starts and stops and breaths in the wrong places. He has a genetic disease, he tells me, a collagen dysfunction that messes with his joints. Other things, too, he says, but it's his joints that are the problem for tennis.

He seems more easy talking when we're moving, looking ahead. He tells me how he used to play every day, how his fingers and knees are forcing him to slow down for now, how he came to Cleveland for surgery on one of his knees a year ago because of an old coach who retired here. How he thought he'd be better by now, back to where he was before. How he's not.

"So kinda retired for now," he finishes, "like your cuttles."

I tell him I'm in a transition period, too, but without physical pain. It's my career, not my connective tissue, that's breaking down and not regenerating itself.

"Sucks," he says.

"Yes," I agree, then, "yeh."

We walk a little while more, the university's soccer practice starting to send some yells our way. I take off my outer jacket. Wes leaves on his hoodie. There are goosebumps over his knees. The moisture on the grass sparkles as the sun peeks over the locker rooms.

"He's here," Wes says eventually, gesturing to the tennis courts, to his old coach who's stretching over by the fence. "I should go."

"Me, too."

"Your application?"

"Right."

He looks at the tennis court, then back at me. "You wanna play sometime?"

I think first of balls whizzing by my ears, flashes of middle school gym class. But I say "yes" before I've processed this fully.

"This weekend?" he asks.

I nod. We've stopped by the trash cans.

"I'm going home Friday for my cousin's orchestra concert," I tell him.

He doesn't move.

"I'll be back Saturday."

He nods.

Then we separate, walk off in different directions. As I'm about to turn towards home, I think back to our first Social conversation, to him seeing me "around."

"Wes?" I call.

He stops, faces me.

"Do you always play here?"

His hoodie bobs. "'s quiet here. I live close."

"This is where you'd seen me, before we met?"

He smiles then, I think. The sun's behind him, but I can see his teeth. "A few months back," he says. "You remember fallin over a football?"

Black and white, I remember, and hard in my appendix. "Soccer?"

"F*u*tball," he says, and I hear it now.

"Yes."

"I kicked it."

We stay there for a second. I give him the thumbs up sign, for no reason. He returns it. We turn again.

Then I'm smiling, xygomatic-like, at the sidewalk when Heather's riding boots suddenly appear in front of me. I look up. She's open-mouthed, quaking, forwarded-email-come-true, Morgan-delivering-twins style.

"That's Wes Anderson," she says.

I watch Heather weave like a too-long-stalled Morgan between the electric kettle and the tea leaves she's intermittently scooping into my mug. I think she's put in her matcha, rooibos, and earl gray so far. She stops, snorts, and adds some honey.

"A tennis player," I prompt. That was all she could get out before she rushed me back to the house and started making the Frankenstein tea.

She pours the water over before the kettle has a chance to kick off, then reaches for the sugar. This is starting to look worse, actually, than when the Morgan had twins.

"Lillie woke me up before she went to work," she says finally, pointing at Lillie's door. "She told me about Milner's paper, so I was coming to find you on my way in...and then, there you were..." She stabs a finger at the window.

"Walking," I supply.

Heather looks at me like you might a goblin shark on your family snorkeling trip to the Bahamas. "With...."

"Wes."

She lets out a kind of hiss. "Wes Anderson," she repeats. She says his name like you might "megaladon" if you found one of *those* while snorkeling, if you had a chance to say anything.

I wait for an explanation. He should be the same Wes we talked about this weekend, the same Wes Lillie described as a Greek god. I thought this would carry more weight with Heather.

"You don't understand," she says. "Drink your tea."

I sniff the mug and tentatively stick my tongue in. It's lukewarm with a sea of tea leaves floating on the surface that probably spell less doom than Heather's face.

"You've dated him?" I ask, because I guess this was bound to happen eventually, with her exhausting the supply of single men between about 27 and 40 in the greater Cleveland metro area.

Her face squinches. "Of course not. He's..." She does her mouthing to the count of ten like when her freshmen are learning how to put on the horse leg protectors. "He's a tennis player. A professional, or at least he was. Nobody knows why he stopped or what he's really doing in Cleveland. There's...speculation."

"Speculation," I echo.

Heather sits on the edge of the sofa, grabs a throw pillow, then sets it back down. "It's a lot of things," she says. "He doesn't give interviews, for one. Nora, you...you have to believe me when I say he's not your type."

I wonder what my type is and whether I should be aiming, ideally, for *not*-my-type.

"He has a reputation. You don't watch TV or read the paper, or..."

"No."

"He's...well, he's well known."

"Biblically?"

"Yes," Heather says, emphatically, then, "not specifically. That's not what I mean. Not *just* what I mean, I mean. He's not friendly. He's a tennis player," she repeats, maybe thinking this means something more to me now.

I tell her I know about the tennis, that it wasn't something he hid from me, like megaladon fantasies or halibut-eating. Tennis is to him what cuttles are to me, I think. Both of our things are ending—*transitioning*. It's actually something we have in common.

"You...you like him?" She's collapsed, now, into the Mariana trench of sofa cushion gaps and gone kind of viscous.

I don't know how to answer this, so I tell her instead about how we're going to play tennis this weekend when I get back from Ethan's orchestra concert.

She sits up. "Nora," she says, "you can't play tennis."

"I know."

She goes viscous again. "Oh my god."

*        *

Friday, I get to Cuyahoga Falls with two hours to spare before Ethan's concert. The sky's clouded over with that low gray haze that likes to stretch on through April. Mom's corralled the leaves from the front lawn into the pumpkin bag I can see through the open garage door. These are familiar patterns, ones I know from years of tundra living.

My parents are waiting for me in the entryway, my dad apparently having tracked me with one of his phone apps.

He greets me with, "Cam's coming Sunday."

"Is that what you're wearing?" Mom asks as she squeezes me.

I squeeze back. This is a ritual she started when she realized she hadn't squeezed me enough as a baby and instituted regular squeezes when I was twelve, like they might work retroactively.

"For the game," Dad says, "and wings."

"You look beautiful," Mom says she means. Then she looks at my face. "You're not wearing your new blush, are you?"

"No," I say, at the same time Dad says, "a nice young man. Asked about Scribbles the other day."

This goes on for a while in what I suppose is the usual way of retirees who both want grandchildren but are otherwise working at cross purposes. My mom interjects questions about my recent #FOMOing while my dad extols the many virtues of Cam and a new local sirloin he's serving at the steakhouse.

"Interesting," Mom says when she gets to the inevitable ecologist-related interrogation period.

My dad sits quietly across from us on the settee, opening and closing his mouth like a skipjack tuna gasping for water.

I agree with my mom that Jarod's interesting in the javelina-friendly, well-published way I favor.

When I move on to Wes and the coffee-Scribbles-tennis progression, my mom's eyes bug out, and my dad grunts like a Haemulon plumierii.

"A *tennis player*," Mom says, with the kind of awe most sensible people reserve for encounters with blue whales.

Dad leans forward and starts itching his knuckles. "Cam's right down the road," he says. "He's at the steakhouse tonight, if you wanted to stop by and say hello."

I nod. I know this, know Cam's schedule still. Cooler weather's the season for restaurant owners, shorter days and early dinners. It occurs to me I don't know when either javelina or tennis season are.

"You have time," Dad says. "We could meet you at the concert. Or we could all go by there on the way."

I tell him I need this time to work on my application. Which is true this weekend, not like the mythical three-month menstrual period I implied when I was sixteen that coincided with summer break/golf season.

"Application?" Dad asks. Then he goes back to skipjacking as I offer a brief description of the IMRI fellowship and the bullet points I have so far.

"*Australia*," he says at the end of this, the way he usually says "Philadelphia."

Mom asks how long I have before the IMRI deadline. When I tell her just two weeks, her face makes me want to look at my affirmations app and have it tell me this is enough. There should be one for researchers, I think, something customized to small data pools and long-shot fellowships and quick deadlines.

When we're finished talking, Mom sits back, and her eyes go kind of fuzzy. "An ecologist and a tennis player," she says, and I recognize this face right away. My mom is in *hope*.

Twenty-five minutes before the concert—because Dad's flat tire forecast was wrong again—my old high school auditorium's a cacophony of eighth grade instrumentalists warming up. Over-involved parents storm the stage with cameras. The stench of teenager permeates all the way to the third row.

Dad elbows me and points to his ears. I give him a thumbs up. This is a nude earplug occasion, evening dress earplug. Mine are the noise-attenuating kind made for listening to music but have the little stoppers in them I like to think will dampen the tubas.

My phone buzzes against my thigh. It's Jarod.

*I wanted to make sure you knew it was Thanksgiving.*

I click on my calendar. He means the IMRI deadline's the Monday after Thanksgiving. Thanksgiving being a national holiday, a post office holiday. A post office holiday meaning my application will have to be sent four days earlier than I'd planned to make sure it gets to New York in time.

I didn't know this. I wasn't thinking rationally and taking

national holidays into account when I decided to apply. That's not how #FOMOing works.

*Can it be sent online?* I ask.

*Sorry, no. I only thought about it because a colleague's applying and was talking about it today. You know Olunsen?*

My heart bubbler doesn't bother to perform, but my stomach twinges. Onstage, an oboe screeches. I twist my right earplug deeper into my ear canal.

I look for the little googly-eyed emoji. Everyone knows Olunsen. Olunsen studied sea birds in the nineties and found the first evidence of changing migration patterns around the poles. You could have been hiding under a rock for the last decade and still know Olunsen.

*Yes*, I write when I can't find the emoji. *I thought he was retired?*

*Pretty much*, Jarod says. *But he wants to go to South America. Penguins.* He sends a penguin emoji. There's a penguin emoji.

Of course Olunsen wants to study penguins. The board won't even have to read his application.

*I'm sorry*, Jarod says, then, *You could still go for Mason and Penn.*

I send a thumbs up, but I mean thumbs down. There are only ten days until IMRI's deadline, twelve until Mason's, then a little while until Penn's.

*You'll let me know if you want a second set of eyes on anything?* Jarod asks.

My mom taps me, reaching across Dad's half-hidden box of Whoppers, per movie theatre rules.

"Emergency hoops," she mouths.

I look around and see the auditorium's starting to fill up. Dad chews his Whoppers faster, and I dig my emergency hoops out of the bottom of my purse and stab one blindly at an earlobe. My phone vibrates again.

I set the other earring in my lap and unlock the phone. When I thank Jarod and close the text box, there's a little mark by my Social app. Wesley Anderson's green dot's there.

*We gonna play this weekend?* he asks.

*Yes.* I type. *I'll be home first thing tomorrow.*

*U at ur cousins concert?*

*About to start*, I tell him.

*u should give me ur mobile then?*

As I'm typing out my number, my dad elbows me again.

Then I smell it, spearmint and sandalwood. The earring in my lap falls to the floor.

Cam bends to pick it up before taking the empty seat next to mine.


Two hours later, Cam and I are together at the side door of the auditorium, sleet pelting the ceiling, the cold clouding up the little window. He's blocking the exit, facing me. I can see a long line of brake lights over his shoulder.

"Your dad said Scribbles was sick," he says.

The hallway's empty, but I can smell perfume, cookies, and fruit punch from back where people are gathering in the gallery. You can hear a laugh every now and then over the murmur of enthusiastic parenting.

"He's okay," I say. "It was last week, and he's on antibiotics. Lillie's keeping him in her room for now."

"Good," Cam says. "I'm glad he's better."

I nod and wonder if he was attached to my rat. Would I

have known? I'm not sure I've ever known what attachment looks like, really been able to evaluate this. It's not a microexpression. Maybe this was one of the things with Cam that I didn't pay enough attention to.

"How's Lillie?" he asks.

"She's fine."

"And Heather?"

"Fine."

"I'm sorry," he says. "I'm not trying to make you uncomfortable."

Isn't he? I meet his eyes, then scan the rest of his face. This is a face I've studied, one I've known for over a decade, one I've never *really* known, I guess, or I'd know whether he'd bonded with Scribbles and I'd probably have been able to stop him from bonding with my dad. Cam bonds like an anglerfish, a sweet-natured parasite attached to your underside, gradually losing himself until he's just a little bump of a sperm packet.

"I'm fine," I tell him.

Cam shifts his weight, shuffles the way he does when the sound system at the inn's on the fritz or when the cafe runs out of pickles. He shuffled a lot when we were together, too. I think he must never have been comfortable with me, either, not fully.

"I just want to talk to you. To catch up," he says. "To clear the air. It's been almost nine months, Nora."

I step to the side and look through the little window. The sleet's starting to get quieter, turning to snow. I don't know what Cam and I have to catch up on, what unclear air could still be between us.

"Would you get coffee with me tomorrow?" His voice is

quiet, one of ways he adapted to make things work between us as long as they did. He shouldn't have had to do so much adapting.

"I can't."

"You can't." His voice trails off like weekends I spent with the cuttles and all the nights I wouldn't even try to sleep in his bed.

"I'm going home," I tell him. "It's not you."

"Not in this." He gestures to the door. "It's supposed to snow all night and through the morning. You won't get out until at least afternoon."

I look out into the parking lot, where the action's stalled, frozen like me. Maybe I should make the drive now, take my chances in the dark and run down some of the egg-throwers Dad's emails are always warning me about.

"It'll be worse up by the lake," Cam says, reading my mind like he used to. "You can't go tonight."

So I say something about the lunch crowd on Saturday, how he'll be needed at the inn to oversee the butternut squash soup and mashed potatoes and hot roast beef slabs that always bring a crowd on a snowy day. Even if I never really knew Cam, at least I knew his restaurants.

He shakes his head. "They can manage," he says. "Ten? I'll pick you up?"

The tires grinding against the ice outside are loud. I flinch. So is the heating system and the laughter and the footsteps down the hallway. Is everything loud? Cam wasn't loud. How strange, I think, that being with him could make me hear so much now.

I study his face, but I can't see anything new there. I don't know what he wants from this, from me. Is it my eggs? Is he going through a biological crisis? Am I? Or maybe it's just his patterns changing. Maybe he doesn't like spending Saturday nights at the steakhouse now that we don't spend them together anymore. Or maybe Dad's right and he really has developed an attachment to my rat.

"Nora, please."

I squint at the window. I can see my parents' car a couple spots away now, Dad looking at us, Mom pretending to look at her cell phone.

"Somewhere quiet," Cam says, softly, then, "just coffee."

# Chapter 10

A text message wakes me up the next morning. My childhood bedroom's dark still, a street light barely peeking through the curtains.

*Just made it to the barn*, Heather texts. *Roads aren't good.*

I bump my elbow into the new reclaimed wood headboard when I sit up. My bedroom's gone farmhouse rustic, per my mom's HGTV addiction, but there are traces of my dad in here, too, and his late-night infomercials—special weights by the foot of the bed, unopened acne medication on the bathroom shelf, and a can opener on the nightstand.

I turn on the lamp. *I'll come this afternoon*, I tell Heather. Though I expect she'd reclassify this as a life flight emergency if she knew I were meeting Cam this morning.

She tells me I should take my time. It's still snowing heavily, maybe even threatening her dinner tonight with

Matt. We talk about this a little. They're starting to fall into a pattern with these Saturday night dinners, and Heather's doing more relationship-evaluating than she's used to. It's the same process as when she buys a new horse and does a full veterinary check first, all the x-rays and blood tests and scopes that try to predict what might go wrong down the road.

It's still dark when I pull myself out of bed and eat some of my dad's cholesterol-controlling oatmeal without flax seeds. I'm finishing the bowl when he comes out and takes a seat on the settee across from me.

"How'd you sleep?" he asks.

"Well." For being away from home, I mean, for being about to have ice cream with my only ex-boyfriend, for all my newfound career deficiencies and doubts about most of my life choices so far, most of which have hit me in the face in the last twelve hours.

Dad picks up the remote. It's college football day, main football warm-up day. The sweaty men in suits will be talking already, speculating like Heather about things they can't know.

But Dad doesn't turn on the TV. "You look nice," he says after a minute.

I look down. I'm wearing, at this important juncture in my existence, a Pepto Bismol-colored nightgown with rosettes on the sleeves. My mom plucked it out of the Walmart sale bin when I was in middle school and had a stomach virus in hopes of keeping me clothed while vomiting in case we had to go to the hospital. Since it stayed vomit-free, it stayed in the dresser in my bedroom.

"So you're having coffee with Cam."

"Ice cream," I correct. I could explain this, could tell him about how holding warm beverages makes us appear warmer and why ice cream's safer for me and Cam. But it wouldn't matter. Probably not much matters at this point. There's a sense of inevitably to this, a progression of certainties I couldn't have reversed even if I'd run out of the concert as soon as I saw him.

"The Dip?" Dad asks.

I nod. The place is a kind of local fixture by the river, undoubtedly even more iconic in the snow. There's a white haze on the horizon now as the sun starts to rise over the back lawn.

"You know they've redone it."

"No." I wasn't really thinking when I agreed to coffee or when I texted Cam last night to suggest ice cream, instead. I wasn't thinking most of the time I was with him. He must not have been thinking, either.

"This is a good step," Dad says.

I don't know what he thinks we're stepping towards, but I thought it was the *only* step I could take at the time. Because refusing to go somewhere with Cam would have suggested I wasn't really over the relationship and didn't care about him as a human. Which I wasn't good at showing when I was in the relationship. And I do care, of course. And I think I am over it. I'd know, wouldn't I?

"An opportunity to reconnect," Dad continues, oblivious. "Reconnect" is one of those words that sounds innocent, that shouldn't bother me. He means "opportunity" the same way that Milner thinks the positions at Penn and Mason are opportunities, legitimate possibilities that should be explored.

And maybe they're both right; maybe I'm bad at recognizing opportunities and still need people to point these out to me. Penn and Mason and Cam are understood, with better odds of success than, say, jumping into the dating pond intentionally for the first time or applying for a long-shot research fellowship. This is what my dad means, that Cam is safety, reason. That choosing this relationship could mean so much time saved, so many misunderstandings averted. Cam's already been vetted, tested, x-rayed.

"He *appreciates* you," Dad reminds me before I go to change.

Since my last visit, The Dip's old blue wallpaper has been replaced with pink polka dots, and the wood's been refinished along the walls. The big picture window over the river's fogged over now, water condensing and dripping down the paneling. There's no breeze like I remember from the ice cream counter, and pop music's playing that I think is even worse than the jazz at Indigo Dreams, a weird electronic beat with a high-pitched whine.

I'm holding my acai sorbet between my wrists when Cam joins me with his peanut butter fudge split. He sets it down in the middle of the table, fudge to me, out of habit.

When I look up, I can picture him aging through all the years we were together here, picking bits of Snickers off the banana that was all he ever really wanted as his hairline recedes a little with each bite.

"You look nice," he says.

I look down. I'm wearing a lumpy sweater from high

school in the shade of ivory my mom says makes me look like I have typhoid.

But I say, "you, too," because he's Cam, all Webster definitions of "nice." I can't smell him over the sorbet and the fudge, or maybe I've gotten used to his scent again. It can happen so quickly.

Being nice, he sees I'm looking at the fudge and tells me to go ahead.

I set down my spoon. But I was starting to reach for it. This is an old habit, obviously ingrained.

"You're doing well," he says, not a question.

"I'm doing well," I confirm anyway, because he can't see all the things that aren't going well for me. "And you?"

He looks at the banana, plowing off some caramel with the side of his spoon. "I'm doing okay," he says.

I nod. Maybe *okay* is good enough for today. I try my acai sorbet, but this is more blueberry than acai—a blend, an impostor.

I feel like I'm an impostor, too, out of place here now that Cam and I are separate. It's hard to see our separation, of course, because I know this well. He'll say each time we sit here that he needs to eat more produce and less roast beef and steak at the restaurants. He eats their broccoli and green beans, too, and occasionally a fruit pie from the inn, but nothing fresh. Not enough fiber, he'll say. I know his digestion, know he'll get a cantaloupe at Earthfare after one of these talks and it will sit on his counter for a couple weeks before his housekeeper throws it out because of fruit flies.

He's only eaten about a quarter of the banana when I

finish my sorbet. We used to finish our ice cream at the same time. We were always in time, in sync.

"I've been thinking about you a lot," he says then, "wondering how you're doing."

"Well," I repeat, "I'm doing well," and reiterate that I hope he's doing well, too. I don't know what's changed for him other than his peanut butter fudge split-eating time—not much about his routine, not his football-watching with my dad, not anything else that I can see. Cam's like an attractive, hard-hunting Atlantic cod; his patterns have always been predictable. He used to want to spawn, too—quietly, inverted, swimming in the circles we were used to.

"How are your cuttles?"

"Retired, at the Eerie Aquarium."

He sets down his spoon. "I'd like to come see them sometime."

"They're in the Caribbean room."

"There aren't any cuttles in the Caribbean," he says.

"No."

He pushes the fudge a little closer to me. It's started to congeal in little lumps against the ice cream.

Then he says, "I miss you," and the acai—blueberry, whatever it's trying to be—sloshes back up into my esophagus.

I drop my napkin on the floor. The music's changed to something with bass, *boom, boom, waiiiil, boom, boom, waiiiil,* and my wrists are wet from condensation on the bowl, the water climbing up my sleeves.

Cam reaches across the table, bypassing the fudge, and goes for my hand. He leaves his there between the banana split and my empty sorbet when I pull my hand away.

Then come the apologies. He says this—the breakup, the awkwardness—everything is his fault. He'd like to change things, to have an opportunity to do things over. There it is again, *opportunity*.

It was how much he was working, he tells me, all the stress that was getting to him. It must have rubbed off on our relationship. He says these things like *he* was the one who climbed out the window, the one who ended our easy, comfortable Saturday nights together.

But he took what we had for granted, he tells me. He wasn't trying the way you do when you find the person you want to spend the rest of your life with.

I try to tell him he was trying more than enough, that he was a good life partner, for probably anyone other than me, that this wasn't about him.

But when I finally meet his eyes, I run for the bathroom and let the sorbet leave me, too.

It's dark when I get home, the orange pendant lights shining through the front windows and moonlight reflecting off the fresh blanket of snow covering the lawn. The house is quiet. Lillie's out, and Heather's swapped her planned dinner with Matt for a late-night meetup at his place, instead.

"You look like Hell," she says as soon as she sees me. She can tell something's happened with Cam, can probably smell him on me. Whereas I haven't been able to smell anything for a few hours now.

So we sit on the sofa and offgass, almost like Lillie's here. I tell her about Cam's unCamlike declaration, about his slow banana-eating and how innocently all of this started, with a blizzard at a middle school orchestra concert.

When I finish, she makes a whistling sound like an oyster toadfish.

"It wasn't that bad." I explain how Cam recovered his senses while I was in the bathroom, how you'd expect him to, how he apologized and only attempted a butt-out hug when he dropped me back at my parents' house.

"You threw up?" She stands and goes to turn on the tea kettle.

My stomach gurgles in confirmation. I haven't tried to eat since the sorbet ejection.

"You told him you're seeing someone, though?"

I shake my head. Does she mean Jarod? She wouldn't mean Wes, I don't think. I wonder if I *am* seeing someone. I don't know when these thresholds are crossed, how much of someone you have to see to be seeing them. Would this have been the right thing to say to Cam, I wonder, even if it's not true? Would it at least have been better than letting my sorbet do the talking for me?

"He didn't ask."

"Bastard," Heather says. "You could be seeing whoever you wanted."

I make my humpback sound but wonder if anyone else would assume this. There's no pattern in my past to suggest I'd be #FOMOing now, much less dating. Cam probably doesn't even know the #FOMO, and he doesn't know I've changed. I'm not even sure I have.

Heather hands me a tea, this one all rooibos and hot.

"Is Cam..." she stops, then sits down. "Do you miss him, too?"

I evaluate. We INTJ's can do this, evaluate without confusing things even more. "No," I say. "I don't think so."

"So you're not regretting breaking up with him?"

"No." But maybe it looks that way. And maybe I *should* regret this breakup. Maybe human relationships are too far out of my field, one of the areas I'm not qualified to evaluate. My dad obviously thinks so. I just think there had to be a reason I crawled out of Cam's bathroom window even if the defective part of our relationship was always all me.

Heather refills our teas, and we sit for a while discussing the pitfalls of romantic entanglements before she turns on *Frasier*.

A few hours later, I still can't sleep. I'm watching one of the Christmas episodes and questioning most of my decision-making capabilities as Heather gets ready to head over to Matt's. She gives me one of her sleeping pills before she leaves.

*          *

My head's heavy when I wake up needing to go to the bathroom. It's that early kind of dark when the moon's low and barely sending a glow out through the trees. My alarm clock says it's 4:37.

I roll over, into something.

It feels like I'm in those slow-motion moments then like

in Heather's crime shows when someone pulls a trigger or is pushed from the roof of a skyscraper, the close-up just before the whirl of action, of processing, of consequence.

I see a hand first, long fingers stretched out on the pillowcase next to mine. A clean hand, I think, as though hygiene's somehow important now. But not *my* hand, or at least it's not attached to my body.

The hand's attached to something, though. It's not just sitting there. Did I think it would be there on its own, like that forearm my dad ordered from an infomercial when I was six that he used to keep sticking out of the armoire in the den?

This hand is attached—to an arm, to a bump that rises and falls under the covers. I watch it, thinking of Cam's light snores as I used to type on my laptop or read beside him, his weight on the mattress and his spearmint and sandalwood wafting out from under the covers.

My stomach lurches. I panic, flee, and trip over the cord to my alarm clock.

I land on the floor, my face pressed into the cork tile. Something makes a sound. The bump. The bump is what makes the sound.

I wait, frozen like a flounder. Then the bump flips over, and that's when it hits me that this bump isn't snoring.

When I've come back from the bathroom, my face wet with cold water and my stomach full of antacids, I see his hoodie lying across my desk chair. He opens his eyes and looks at me over the bunny supreme that sits fully erect on my nightstand.

Wes grunts. I collapse. This is not a lotus.

"You up?" he asks.

I shake my head. It wants to fall to the side like it's too heavy. But all of me leans forward, towards him.

He pushes up onto an elbow and scoots away a little. Then he lifts the corner of my duvet. For me, where I sleep. *Sleep*, by myself. My fitted sheet shimmers in the moonlight. My antacids fizzle in my stomach.

"Why aarrrru up?" He sounds like a water buffalo.

I shake my head. "Okay," I tell myself, "I'm okay."

"Mmm?"

I point at the bed, at my spot. The spot where I sleep, alone. "I was sleeping?" I ask. I *am* sleeping, I think. I must be.

"Mmm," he repeats, not very original for a character in a dream. My subconscious isn't very original, though.

"Okay," I repeat. "I'm okay. We were sleeping?"

Wes opens his eyes again. "Sleeping," he says.

This isn't possible, I try to tell him, this figment of my imagination in my bed at five am, or maybe it's not even five am. Maybe it's sometime else. But somewhere in the real world, anyway, I have doctors' notes dating all the way back to my first orchestra camp that confirm I have a sleeping disability.

"Are you comin back to bed?" Wes asks.

"Okay," I repeat. "I'm okay."

*       *

The next two days are like trying to solve a mystery on one of Heather's police shows, except I'm the only suspect. The second time I woke up on Sunday, Wes determined that I needed more sleep and whatever drug I'd taken had probably affected my reflexes, making tennis too dangerous. As though my reflexes were what were dangerous about my Sunday morning.

I crawled out of bed again at noon, alone, but I could still smell him on my pillow. I can still smell him two days later. It's not strong, like sandalwood or spearmint, or repulsive like aftershave or cologne or that creepy body spray Heather's insensible undergrads are all high on. I don't know what it *does* smell like, exactly, but I pick it up sometimes when I'm visiting the cuttles over Dave's lunch break or in the lab bathroom with the window open or walking around the sports complex early in the morning.

The hours after Wes left were panicked, taken over by efforts to account for every minute of the night-before-the-morning-I-woke-up-with-a-tennis-player.

It was a lot of things, Heather determined in the end, stress and sleeping pill side effects and my atypical day with Cam and how tired I was from all the driving and the more emotional *Frasier* Christmas episode and my long-term lack of bunny supreme usage.

I like to think it was mainly the sleeping pill, a variable that can be isolated. These kinds of things can happen with them, apparently. My pharmacist's husband once took one and drove a lawnmower through a fence and into their country club's kiddie pool.

Heather blames herself, of course, for giving me the pill. And she worries I have herpes or something worse now just by proximity, that even the fundamental nature of my composition may have changed now that I've slept in a bed with Wes Anderson. Just being *in* the bed could have done it, she thinks, just being *close to* the bed.

We went through all the available data, collecting answers as well as we could. It started with a text, Wes asking if my family was "alrite." I told him I wasn't sure if there were any cuttlefish in Guam. Flamboyant cuttlefish, I meant, only about three inches long. Did he know the ones I meant? The ones that are possibly around the Northern Mariana islands, because who would know? Who'd checked for cuttlefish of any kind except off major landmasses, and especially for the flamboyant cuttlefish, which no one eats, with its potent neurotoxin.

Wes said he wasn't sure, then asked if *I* was "alrite."

I told him I was very worried about the reefs around Rota. Had he checked the reefs around Rota for flamboyant cuttlefish in particular? Had anyone? There are all those reefs right offshore. Would the cuttlefish there—if there are any, I meant—would they be affected by the tides? Could they wind up in tidepools? Shouldn't someone *check*?

Wes said he'd been playing late at the sports complex, and maybe he should stop by.

That was the last text. He called shortly after. And then the doorbell camera caught me letting him in a little after ten. Heather had gone out already with Matt.

When Wes got here, I walked out onto the lawn, in full view of the doorbell, looking for something in the grass. We don't know how I got into my bed from there. We don't know how I slept with Wes in my bed, too.

I was fully clothed when I woke up, Heather pointed out, which is a good sign. He was clothed, too, except for the hoodie.

Three yogurts were missing from the refrigerator, two strawberries and one strawberry-banana. Some was found smeared over my desk and sheets. There was an empty container under my bed. And there were tea leaves found *inside* the electric kettle, chamomile.

A series of texts afterwards with Wes revealed little more. He could tell I was "kinda messed up" when he came over, and when I finally fell asleep, on his chest, after eating yogurt off his hoodie, he did, too. It was "prolly" the sleeping pill, he said, and I shouldn't worry about it.

No, Lillie told me, while Heather was looking up rare sexually-transmitted diseases, we're not worrying. Everything's *fiine*. Then she cleaned out the kettle and made me a giant pot of valerian tea.

# Chapter 11

*Cuttlefish have four methods of communication: color, texture, posture, and movement. They never misinterpret social cues.*

Tuesday afternoon, the snow's melted, and the tennis courts are a blinding blue against a sea of November grays. Soggy leaves are being raked into trash bins down by the soccer fields, and the breeze cuts through my jacket.

I refocus on the yellow ball and try not to flinch when Wes hits it at me. This one bounces at my feet before joining the others along the back fence, where they're starting to school like anthias.

He has a big trough of them. "Maybe come a little closer to the net," he tells me.

I look down. I'm still behind the farthest line. I'm pretty sure this is an evolutionary instinct. A tennis court seems like the right unit of distance to keep between you and someone you woke up with on a Sunday morning who's inclined to hit things at you.

Wes walks closer on his side. But he's better adapted than

I am, faster and more coordinated. Probably fewer things pose a threat to him. And I'm obviously not one of those things.

I take a step forward. He taps a ball to my racquet. I hit this one straight up into the air and duck when it falls back down.

"How's your application goin?"

"Slow," I tell him, missing the next ball. "And it probably won't be competitive."

"Just hold out your racquet," he says. He taps a ball over the net.

I close my eyes and open them again when it bounces back to him. He catches it, then repeats.

"Why not competitive?"

"I don't have enough experience." I step closer to the net.

"Yeh? What else?"

"I don't know anything about wild cuttlefish."

He hits this ball back with his racquet. It bounces off mine again. It's not the pops I recognize—I wonder if it was him playing, those sounds I heard after the club on Halloween—but I can feel the vibration back through my elbow. I keep my eyes open when the next ball comes.

"You think your advisor got in your head a little?"

"No." But when I think about Milner, I want to swing. I step out and push my racquet forward, hitting a ball to the back of Wes's court. "Maybe."

"You've done it before? Applied for stuff without his help?"

"No." I haven't applied for anything without Milner since I got into undergrad. I think back through all these years, all the Saturday mornings I put out his trash.

"Maybe you're better off without him," Wes says.

We hit the ball back and forth a few more times. He doesn't miss, wherever it lands on his side. I don't move.

"How's your knee?" I ask.

"The same. I'm goin Friday for a scan."

"It's important?" The next ball hits my racquet harder.

"To find out if it's better," he says.

"If it is?"

"I can prolly play next season."

I tap a ball back to him. He has to reach for this one. "And if it's not?"

He shrugs, but I feel like I know his shrugs now, like I'm starting to learn bits of his patterns. Wes is in a period of upheaval, too, like an Amazon river dolphin that's somehow found its way to the Atlantic.

I focus on him then instead of on the balls, watch as he hits them at my racquet and try to imagine him with different places in the background. I can see him with the palm trees in Florida, surrounded by golf courses, where he used to train. I can see him with Melbourne behind him, too...no, that's the Sydney Opera House—but Australia, anyway, distinctly un-tundralike. Is he better suited to being in those places? Usually you stay, or at least go back to wherever you've done most of your evolving. Heather thought that was Florida or Australia for him. A long way from Cleveland. Will he stay, I wonder, either way the scan goes? I don't ask this.

I'm getting good at standing still with my racquet extended when he lowers his and tells me we've gone past the hour I said I had to play.

I step back from the net and look at my watch. I thought this would go slowly, that I'd want to get back to my bullet points and cuttle distribution maps. But this was nothing like middle school gym class.

As we walk away from the court, he says this was good, and I agree. He turns with me when we get to the path that takes us towards the house. The sun's lower now, the breeze kicked up. We stop to pick up a soda can that's rattling down the sidewalk away from its trash bin.

"Your mate said you had an issue at home," he says.

I nod. "Issue" is Heather's classification for everything from her useless father to an acute skirted-legging malfunction.

"An ex-boyfriend at home," I clarify.

Wes doesn't say anything for a few steps. "You met up?"

I tell him about my ice cream as we pass the soccer fields, about how Cam wanted to get back together and the almost-decade we spent all of our Saturday evenings that way. It comes out this simple, nothing like the jumble it created in my head. Maybe it *is* this simple now, something in the past that can be cataloged, identified properly, not like when you first encounter a giant squid or a new deep sea species. Maybe Cam, all these years of Saturday nights, are finally understood now.

"You miss him?" Wes asks.

"No." My shoulder brushes against his when a biker passes us.

We walk a little more, and I count breaths between our footsteps, in time now. I don't think about sharks or eels or whales. We're quiet until we get to the meadow behind the house.

"I don't do this much," Wes says then.

I turn to look at him, but his hoodie's hiding his eyes. He's like a river dolphin that way—you rarely see more than a little bit of his face at once.

"Walk?" I ask.

"Date. I don't date a lot." His words are staccato, out of rhythm. His rhythms are like mine sometimes. Or at least he hears mine right.

He's looking at the path, dirt now between some overgrown timothy grass. He doesn't say anything else, doesn't show anything else, and I don't know what to ask him about this. He already knows I don't date a lot, either, but probably in a way that's different than him. Like he's probably inferred I don't have any bioluminescent beluga-people calling out to me on the streets.

"I liked tennis," I say, finally, when we get to the little grove of trees behind the house.

"Me, too. Do it again?"

I nod. "You'll tell me how your scan goes Friday?"

"I'll text," he says. And then, like a river dolphin in high water, he's gone.

*     *

I spend Wednesday in a state of nearly captive orca-level mental degradation looking for better IMRI bullets. None come, and I keep making different searches like I can force cuttlefish research into existence by sheer power of will.

I finally go back into the lab Thursday morning, hoping to cash in on some good lab juju, but my lab doesn't look like my lab anymore. The cuttles' tank is empty, drained. My lamps have been pushed to the corners by the janitorial staff, and the floor sparkles under the fluorescents. The food freezer's empty, unplugged and defrosted.

So I set up in the bathroom, instead, where the orange cleaner's too strong for a Thursday. I have to wrestle with the little knob on the window for a few minutes before I can convince it to open.

The IMRI application is the only document up on my computer now. I finished the preliminary paperwork yesterday and have highlights of other people's research on the Eastern Australian Current to show why that particular coastline's the one most likely to matter for cuttle populations. And other people's work on cuttle distribution ranges and margins of error. And other people's reports on what species have been tracked and where they've been caught recently.

I don't have much of anything to say for myself, any particular reason *I* should be the one to stalk the wild cuttles, if anyone should.

My application's less shiny, too, less *National Geographic*-worthy than all the other IMRI projects I've read about. There's only so much attention you can pay to the elegant, the magnificent, the starry, the flamboyant, and the striking cuttlefish when there is, for instance, the stumpy cuttlefish that might have migrated southward from Papua New Guinea and is listed as "uncertain" North of Darwin and the Tiwi Islands. These are exciting times for the stumpy cuttlefish.

I'm almost through a feature example of the stumpies

when my phone buzzes with a text from Jarod.

It's a link to a paper, Kikner's, on an Asian river dolphin that's evolving.

I think first of Wes, of Amazon river dolphins that dive back down into tannin-rich waters before you can catch their faces.

*I thought you might be interested in this*, Jarod says. The paper's tagged on Academic-A's IMRI thread.

I look out the window. It's starting to rain, the concrete courtyard turning its darker gray, the fallen leaves blown away now, ready for ice and snow and beet juice that will stain the sidewalks pink through March.

*He's applying?* Kikner, I mean, the king of estuary desalination. With freaking river dolphins that are actively, noticeably evolving. I thought before that Olunsen and his penguins were impossible to beat, but no one out-funds an evolving river dolphin.

*Looks like it*, Jarod says. *How are your applications going?*

I tell him it's just the IMRI now and scroll through the other new papers in the thread. There are projects on orcas, of course, and gray whales and manta rays. The lemon shark guy's applying again this year, too, this time with a paper he's already published about how they're affected by changes in reef conditions. There are numbers by all the author names and links to their publications. Seven. Five. *Twenty-two*. I'll only have a single unit to put next to my name.

*Good for you*, Jarod says, I imagine the way Milner says it to Kyle. I skim through the application on orcas. I can't even use the author's format for the first several pages since there aren't any relevant publications on cuttles to include.

I'm on his proposal—over twenty-five pages of proposal—

when Jarod writes again.

*I'm planning to come check out Case on the 24th,* he says. *Thought I'd spend Thanksgiving weekend looking around. I'd love to get together.*

I send a thumbs up.

He sends a dolphin—a regular one, a bottlenose, not a river dolphin.

The orca application includes a section on implications for other species, too, seals and sea lions and even great whites, which should, per some other papers, be more prevalent around British Columbia if it weren't for all the orcas.

I'm reading about the differences between resident and migrating pods in the strait of San Juan de Fuca when a new email pops up over my screen.

Milner's finally written me back. And maybe it's good, I think, that this didn't happen sooner, when I was imagining him being eaten alive by horny sea shrimp.

*Nora, apologies for not checking in about your applications. Been a little crazy here. Haven't seen you around and hope you're taking it easy. Have your letters of recommendation for Mason and Penn ready. -TM*

I minimize the orca window and write back. *Are you in right now?* I should tell him my IMRI plan and blame this decision on #FOMOing.

*Sorry,* he writes, *just left.* Then the little "active" dot next to his name disappears.

*       *

The next morning, I'm up early intentionally, dragging Heather out of bed in only-for-a-horse hours and trying to force-feed her a smoothie before I take her to the airport. This is how she gets when she has to face her dad's side of the family, forgetting meals and tying her hair up over and over and groaning a lot.

*Good luck with the scan today,* I text Wes. I look for the crossing fingers emoji as Heather tries to free the yellow tulle of her bridesmaid's dress from the zipper of her suitcase. She's looking pretty yellow this morning, too.

"I'll call him when I get there," she says. "That's right, isn't it?"

"Matt?"

"Of course Matt." She slams the suitcase lid down. Now one of her heels is too tall for it to close.

I take over, shoving her spanx inside a shoe and rearranging some makeup under her stick-on bra. Somewhere behind me, my phone dings.

I sit on the suitcase. Heather pauses, her hand on the zipper. "Who is that?" she asks. "It's barely five."

"Wes."

She makes a sound like a pilot whale surfacing before she pulls the zipper around.

I pick up the phone. *Thanks,* Wes says. *text u after, hang out this weekend?*

*Yes.*

Heather reads this over my shoulder, then turns to Lillie's door. But Lillie's pre-bran, out of play.

Heather looks at the suitcase again. "Are you okay?" she asks.

"I'm okay."

She pauses by the front door. "I mean with Wes."

"I'm okay," I repeat, and then we make a run for my car.


By the time we hit 480, Heather's fully awake and looking like a colicking Morgan, holding my phone and scrolling through my texts with Wes like a closer reading might reveal the secret to removing the plastic islands in the North Pacific.

"There's been no kissing?"

"No kissing," I confirm as a steel truck rattles by us in the darkness.

"And you know what a booty call is, right?"

"Yes." But Wes and I have never done the booty call. The only time we've made plans after eight at night was last weekend, when I was on the sleeping pill.

"I just don't understand," Heather says.

I turn down the heat and don't respond, because of course I don't understand, either.

She shifts around, fiddling with her purse. "Nora, I'm just worried that he's...smooth."

I think of river dolphins again.

"Like that guy," she says. She's started brushing her hair with the little fold-up brush she keeps in her purse. She's been doing this more lately, I think without noticing. "Sam. You remember, on..."

"Yes," I tell her, "'The Show Where Sam Comes Back.'"

"Yeah. I think, you know, that Wes might be like Sam."

I think of Sam, then of Wes, and I tell her that Wes doesn't seem like Sam at all.

"Okay," she says, after a couple seconds, "but I haven't

heard he's, like, a nice guy. I told you, didn't I, that he doesn't do interviews? And I haven't heard of him dating anybody. So I think he maybe more...hooks up."

I wait for her to say something else, to reveal some piece of Wes I don't know yet. But whatever else he's doing, with whoever else he's doing it with, there's nothing in my experience that suggests Wes is trying to hook up with *me*.

"Not that anyone wouldn't want to date *you* properly, I mean," Heather says. "But if you haven't talked about it, I'm worried..." Her voice trails off. I swear I can hear her scalp peeling with each stroke of the brush.

My head's loud, too, evaluating what Wes and I are doing, if we're not dating or having booty calls or hooking up. Should I have asked?

I listen to the little clicks as Heather reads through our text messages again and we get in the turn lane for the airport.

When we exit the highway, she pulls a clump of hair out of her brush. "So you think you want to do this...whatever it is that you're doing, with him?" she asks. "You've checked, I mean, made lists, and this is definitely what you want?"

I visualize a Wes pros and cons list in my head as I pull into the departures lane. But I don't fill it in.

"Yes."

Heather shoves the hairbrush back into her purse, closes her eyes, and exhales with one of Lillie's fire breaths. "Okay," she says. Then she alters her sexy stingray speech to include consent and makes me promise to avoid all pills and have Lillie make me something with a lot of caffeine before I see him again.

Later that afternoon, I'm back in the lab bathroom

speculating about other species that might be affected by southbound cuttle redistributions. It's one of those cold, windy days that feels like the grayness might burst. Dark clouds stretch sideways along the horizon.

The little window's barely cracked open, and the heating vent at my feet buzzes. I've turned off the fluorescents today and brought in one of the lamps from my office, an old blue and purple one Lillie found at a yard sale when I was just getting started with cuttles.

I'm in the middle of some Australian fishery lists when my phone dings.

*scans done*, Wes says.

*Do you know anything yet?*

*not till Monday*

I start to type sympathies. Maybe his having to wait on CT results feels like waiting on news from Penn or Mason would for me, a fifty-fifty chance that a lot might change. No, like something bigger, some application that could decide the entire rest of my career, like if there were oceans on another planet needing researchers and all of ours had just spontaneously drained down into middle earth.

*U still on ur imri?* he asks before I can think of the appropriate words to show I'm condoling.

*Yes. I have to send it Tuesday.* I think of Tuesday, four days away, of everything I have to do by then.

*U too busy to hang out this weekend?*

*No.*

*whens best?*

*Would tomorrow night work?* I'll be exhausted by then, at least. I'll need a break, time to unwind, to rest my brain before

I go back and try to edit everything. It only vaguely occurs to me that resting my brain around Wes Anderson was exactly what Heather advised avoiding.

*great,* he says.

*I'll be...* I stop typing. A disaster? Likely to take a sleeping pill if offered? *...a little tired,* I finish.

*u wanna stay in?*

*Yes.*

*Ill come over?*

My mitral valve flutters, and I repeat, *Yes.*

# Chapter 12

*Cuttlefish have three hearts and no tolerance for romantic nonsense.*

I finish a draft of my application—just a draft, disjointed, hanging together like a leafy sea dragon—a little after six on Saturday night, about half an hour before Wes is supposed to get here. My eyes are blurry from looking at the screen.

I catch my reflection in the window, where the lights over the soccer stadium are hazy through the trees. I look like grad school, like late nights and long papers. Like I could actually use some of that awakening BB cream my mom sent, if I knew how to use it.

Lillie appears with a giant mug of tea as I'm putting away my laptop. This tea's the anti-Lillie, not soothing at all. It's brown and swirly with a kind of film like an oil spill floating on top.

"It's yerba mate," she tells me. Lillie's fully awake and looks like a stingray in the middle of a school of hammerheads.

I'm ordering pizza tonight and wearing my old yoga pants, non-skirted, with a long sweater that's not too soft-looking. There's a formula for these non-dates-that-might-be-dates, a series of choices you have to get exactly right if you want to be trying just enough to avoid arousing suspicion.

Lillie lotuses on my desk chair. This one I recognize as her battle lotus, her Cam-breakup-or-widespread-data-breach lotus.

"I'm leaving the teapot on the counter," she tells me. "I'll go ahead and add honey, so all you have to do is pour it out."

I thank her, but she remains in her lotus. I take a tentative sniff of the new tea. It smells like the septic backup from the floods last year around the baseball diamond.

"You're ready? You're okay?" she asks, almost sans vowel sounds. Because this is serious, a maybe-a-date with a known tennis player, apparently the most dangerous #FOMOing I've attempted. I could, for instance, fall asleep with him again.

I take a sip of the tea. It tastes like that syrup she gave me right before the dissertation defense I got through in about fifteen minutes. So I probably won't fall asleep, at least.

"Heather's at the wedding," Lillie says. "The ceremony should be over soon. She wants you to text her as soon as Wes leaves."

"Okay."

"You look tired. You've been working all day. It's not too late to cancel."

"I'm okay." Then my phone dings.

It's Wes. *Heading over now*, he says.

I show the phone to Lillie, and she folds up tighter,

preparing for her springing lotus.

She stays lotused, and I choke down about half the mug of tea before we hear a knock at the door.

Twenty minutes later, I've had a full cup of yerba mate, and Wes is about six inches from me on the sofa. As is probably inevitable in our relationship-such-as-it-is, I'm talking about the weather—how it affects his knee and his tennis, because I don't know what else to ask or not to ask about his knee and the tennis career he might have to give up after he gets his CT results back.

I'm running low on facts about the great blizzard of 1899 when he asks about my IMRI application.

"What happens if you get it?"

When I think about this, my fingers tingle on my mug, and I'm temporarily plunged into biologist rock star visions— the quiet kind, for me, surrounded by cuttlefish and clear, turquoise waters. This is pure fantasy unhindered by real world practicalities, the kind of blue whale feeling that makes us do things like apply for long-shot fellowships or try to #FOMO.

"I'd go to Australia," I tell him. "They fund up to a few months onsite."

But it would be more than just a few months and wild cuttles. There's so much we could learn about climate change and other patterns, about reef species evolving to travel greater distances, about changing ecosystems. These are the kinds of projects that are usually underfunded, when there aren't big commercial interests at stake, the projects that could give us insight into the things that really matter.

Wes's hoodie's fallen back, and he's shifted on the sofa to

face me. But this isn't a challenge, I don't think, even with his eyes on my forehead.

"You'd move around a little?" he asks. "Along that coast?"

"I'd start in the Northern Territory to check for the stumpy," I tell him, "and then probably be mostly off Queensland."

"Brisbane's swheat."

I do a long exhale. It's the way he says "Brisbane" and "swheat" and something about being this caffeinated at seven forty-five at night. It washes over me like a tidal wave of heart bubbles.

"I haven't seen Melbourne?" I say, taking up his lilt at the end of his sentences, mirroring. Wes is all questions, when most people are statements.

So he tells me about his childhood there, in a suburb I don't know how to spell, and some places he thinks I'd like— the aquarium and the university and a path along the Yarra like the one I run on by the Cuyahoga.

I listen, focused on the words. He doesn't offer a lot of them, doesn't just keep adding like most people do once they've already said everything that matters.

"Do you go back much?" I ask. "To Australia?"

"Not much."

We sit for a minute in the quiet before he asks about my childhood and, like any self-aware, self-actualizing thirty-two-year-old, I divert this conversation to my rat.

I'm showing him Scribbles' new yogurt drops when the pizza arrives.

I don't realize it's after nine until my phone dings like an egg timer on the coffee table. The living room's dark with just the orange glow of the pendants behind us.

Pizza grease smears my phone screen as I swipe up. It's Lillie, from the next room.

*Is everything okay?* she asks.

I respond with a thumbs up.

*I heard you laugh,* she says. *Are you drinking?*

*The tea,* I tell her before I put down the phone.

I look at Wes, his pizza plate balanced on his knee and his tea mug still mostly full. We've been talking this whole time, but somehow I still don't know all the things I should about him. Like I know now that he doesn't eat fish and his parents aren't brunch people and he doesn't talk on the phone with them a lot, but I don't know anything about their health histories or his ancestry. And he knows about my rat's digestion and that Scribbles is staying in Lillie's room for now, but he doesn't know this is because I'm probably an unfit rat guardian in my current #FOMOing state. He probably doesn't even know this state isn't my normal one.

I look at the windows, at all the darkness around us, then back at him. Maybe I've forgotten how you get to know someone this way, and in the dark. Or I didn't know how to do this to begin with.

With Cam, this is about the time that I'd go home or read on the bed next to him if I were staying in town for an early breakfast at the inn the next morning. I don't know how we started this, how I'd go about establishing a new pattern with someone different.

"You're tired?" Wes asks.

He leans forward on the sofa. Our knees touch—barely, like clownfish in an anemone, just a kind of symbiotic brush that reminds you the other's there. I look at his face but can't tell if he notices. He doesn't move, doesn't show anything.

"I'm awake," I tell him. And this is true, probably not just because I've had almost an entire pot of Lillie's anti-date-sleep tea.

"You told me you go to bed by ten," Wes says.

I think back to the first night I was up late talking to him, on epinephrine and anti-histamines and steroids, back when he was just a hazy green dot on my Social chat. I feel about the same tonight. It has to be him; he's the only variable in common. I think talking to him works on my body like the cocktail of sleeping pills did, changing how everything else functions in the system, messing with all the other variables. This must be what dating is, why it's supposed to be so hard to adjust after a relationship ends.

"I'm awake," I repeat.

He says he is, too. So we're two awake people up late on a Saturday night with some extra pizza and a full bag of breadsticks still, because I wasn't sure if I could eat just the greasy ends in front of him yet or if this is one of those things you're supposed to hide from a new partner for a while.

I look at the TV, for some excuse to continue this. "We could watch something," I suggest.

He leans back, stretches his hands over his head in that way he does that bends his fingers backwards. "Yeh," he says.

So I get up and start to sift through the DVD's like I know what I'm looking for. I don't mention yet that I can't work the cable remote or the Netflix, because this is probably something it's too early to let him know. I wonder if there's a spreadsheet available somewhere with a timeline for revelations of all these personal inadequacies we don't share with people until we're more committed.

When I ask what he likes to watch, if he watches TV—is it too early to ask this?—he tells me he's not very fussy about television. He likes a lot of things. Stupid things, mostly, he says.

So I push aside Lillie's *Brideshead, Revisited* DVD and skim through Heather's crime shows, all too scary for night-viewing. My fingers land on my *Frasier* sets, but it's definitely too early for this. I didn't even watch all the seasons with Cam. Maybe I really was holding something back that whole relationship, probably even something more than *Frasier*, this experience of all eleven seasons that I could have shared with him but consciously chose not to.

It occurs to me then that Wes might not know about all eleven seasons. He wasn't in the country when *Frasier* was on TV, so maybe he'd assume this was just a casual thing, thoughtless, if I started it somewhere in the middle and didn't mention it was part of something bigger.

I pull out the third season and stall as I consider one of the episodes that's not part of a larger arc, one with no hint of long-term commitment.

I almost take the disc out to show him when I see Lillie's *Persuasion* on the shelf.

"Jane Austen?" I ask.

"Kay," he says.

I take the DVD from its case. This is me being romantic, I think, #FOMOing like an Atlantic bottlenose.

*Persuasion's* midway through the opening credits when the doorbell rings.

A few minutes later, Matt and Lillie are together in the

living room. When I left them there, Lillie wasn't in any variety of lotus, and Matt wasn't making eye contact with me. And I had to leave, because I wasn't sure what else to do. I didn't even have the presence of mind to take the DVD out of the player; I left Wes to get it.

I think about all the things that could be happening in the living room now, or at least some subset of the most disastrous things that could be happening between Lillie and Heather's boyfriend.

I could text Heather. Except I don't know what I'd tell her—that Lillie's in our living room with Matt, at almost ten pm on a Saturday, hopefully not having any inclination towards acting like an Atlantic bottlenose, but I'm not sure?

I jump when the door opens. It's Wes with our DVD.

"Were they talking?" I ask when he shuts the door behind him.

He scans my face as he reaches for the laptop, setting my tea on the nightstand next to the bunny supreme. "Talking," he confirms.

"Touching?"

He doesn't look up this time. "Standing." He presses some buttons, loading the DVD. Then he's sitting down, pushing my duvet to the foot of the bed—the bed I should have made, I think now. But we were supposed to stay in the living room. I went through this with Heather, who would probably burst out of her yellow bridesmaid sparklies if I texted that we were even bed-adjacent. Or about Matt and Lillie. Nothing is right in this apartment.

"Kay," Wes says, settling the laptop across his legs, because at least *he* knows what he's doing.

"Okay," I say.

The DVD makes a creaking sound in my computer before it starts humming like a plain midshipman fish. Wes changes a setting, a quick series of clicks that seem loud now.

I look at the tea, then at the bunny supreme, then at him in my bed. He looks different there this time. Maybe it's that the lights are on. Or maybe there's a difference between circumstance putting us here last week, with darkness and Cam and a sleeping pill and the plight of the flamboyant cuttlefish-possibly-in-the-Northern-Marianas at play, and choosing to be here now.

He gets to the main screen and reaches for the light switch, and then it's dark.

He waits to press the "play" button.

I evaluate. I don't actually know how to evaluate this. I wonder if he's evaluated. By the light of my computer screen, he looks settled, comfortable, like he does this regularly. Maybe he doesn't have to evaluate.

So I decide to imitate him, stretching my body out along the other side of the bed like I know what I'm doing, too. The mattress dips towards the middle, making a kind of mini Mariana trench between us.

I barely think about Matt and Lillie through the opening scenes. I only catch a murmur of their voices every once in a while through my closed bedroom door. I must be sliding, not paying attention, into the trench; I'm closer to Wes when I'm finally resting back against the headboard.

*Persuasion* this time around strikes me like the rest of my night, like I don't really know what's coming.

I pause it when the party gets to Lyme, right before the

disaster, because I think this is a good time to pause.

"Why don't you do interviews?" I ask.

I don't turn to see what his face is doing. Maybe he's looking at me. Or maybe he's about to lie, and I won't see his face to know the difference. Maybe I don't want to see. I keep looking at the screen, at the wall Louisa Musgrave's about to hurl herself from just because she wants Wentworth to catch her.

"'m bad at them," Wes says.

"Are you?" I ask. Does he have flash cards with all the phrases? Does he practice the rhythms? Does he write out his answers in a text document, like I do, and memorize them? But I don't ask these things.

"Yeh," he says. He waits for a second, for me to say something else. I don't. So he presses the "play" button again.


I don't know when I close my eyes, what scenes I miss or if I just keep playing through the movie in my head when I fall asleep.

I must be waking up when I feel Wes beside me, when I know my hip's fallen into the trench against him and his warmth seems to be coming straight through my body.

I recognize the noises from the last scene, the circus around Anne and Wentworth when they're together in the middle of the street, finally sure of each other.

I register the sound of Wes's feet landing on the cork, too, and his breath against my cheek.

I don't know why I don't move, why I flush here in the darkness. I keep my eyes closed and listen to my bedroom door close softly behind him.

When I open them again, I can barely make out the outlines of my furniture. The laptop's closed on my desk, and the stadium lights seem far away tonight.

I sit up. The duvet's resting at my shoulders now.

My cheek feels warm. I put my hand over it and watch Wes's lights flicker through the trees as he pulls out onto the road.

# Chapter 13

*A cuttlefish can decide exactly how buoyant it wants to be by adjusting the levels of water and gas in its cuttlebone. Humans have tried to mimic this ability with hundreds of chemicals but comparatively little success.*

Sunday flies by in an IMRI-editing frenzy, and the Monday before Thanksgiving hits me like it does everyone, with that funny way time seems to condense just before a major holiday. This week's always planned chaos, from the undergrads cutting classes and jump-starting their cars in the parking lots to the Earthfare freezers lined with turkeys and my macaronis wedged in next to the pizza rolls.

I spend Monday afternoon in my lab. The building's quiet—there aren't any undergrads milling around, and Kyle and Milner don't come in. Storm clouds darken the windows.

My application feels foreign today, like there's a plot twist at the end of each section. It's the energy of these pre-holiday days, I think. There are always some little backslides, some details gone wrong.

I read and re-read, edit and shift things around, and read again. Somewhere in the middle of the morning, a storm rolls in, thunder shaking the walls until, finally, the clouds run out of rain early in the afternoon.

Around three, my application hangs together well enough to take a break for an early dinner at home and plan for more edits tonight.

I have the house to myself when I get back. Heather's doing some last-minute barn work before the break, and Lillie's at the office dealing with a retail company's data breach in time for black Friday. I haven't been able to catch her alone since Matt was here on Saturday. And she hasn't offered any explanation, hasn't said it was a work thing or a stealing-Heather's-boyfriend thing or something else, whatever else it could be.

I finish my macaroni in the gray, leaving the orange pendant lights off for now, and head out for a walk before it's fully dark. This is to clear my head, I tell myself, so I can look at my application again with fresh eyes when I get back, but maybe Wes is at the complex, too.

The sun's low by the time I make it to the tennis courts, leaving streaks of purple and pink through the clouds that lingered after the storm. I hear the *pop* before I see him. There's a kind of *chunk* before it this time, a machine shooting the little yellow balls at him.

I watch for a while before he sees me, note his hoodie and his shorts, the way he shifts back and forth like he doesn't know which direction the ball's going to come. He's training for real, you can tell, the difference between just trying and being so serious about something that you can get lost in it.

He stops when he sees me, then goes over to the other side of the court and turns off the machine.

"You want company?" he asks when he gets to the gate.

I tell him I would, and it surprises me how easily this comes. I think of all the times I haven't wanted company, of these holiday weeks when I was a kid hiding in the little nook under the staircase whenever my cousins would come over. I can still hear loud, always pregnant Aunt Judy and her squealing kids who trampled the hardwoods like a stampede of awkward bison in their dress-up shoes at Thanksgivings and nicked cookies from the cooling sheets on Christmas Eves.

But here I am, socializing around a tennis court in the late November cold as the stadium lights come on and the sun sinks lower into the clouds.

I wonder if Wes was like me, if he locked himself in a favorite bathroom, maybe, during the holidays, or spent recesses on top of the monkey bars with headphones and recorded NPR on a cassette player to help tune out the kickball. I ask him.

He tells me he wasn't very into holiday stuff. He had loud cousins, too. He asks about mine, and I tell him about Ethan and his Teenage Mutant Ninja Turtles that provided some of the cues for my cuttlefish mazes. My older cousins are all spread out now, at colleges or selling makeup or insurance and not useful for research purposes.

"You're goin home?" he asks.

"Wednesday afternoon until Friday."

"You have a big dinner?"

I think about Australia and about how different where he lived in Florida is, with its palm trees and its sequined sweatsuits and its manatees. So I tell him about the way Ohioians do Thanksgiving, how a parade of pies and gravy turn into turkey sandwiches for days and frozen stuffing you keep on defrosting until Christmas ham and eggnog and a fresh selection of simple carbs.

"Nice," he says. "How's your application?"

"Almost there," I tell him, and hope this is true. "I should get back to it soon. Have you heard from your doctor yet?"

He pulls his hood back up. It's getting windier, colder with the light fading.

"Earlier," he says. "I'm goin in tomorrow to see her."

I want to say something encouraging, like that doctors sometimes insist on in-person appointments to share good news instead of bad, like those people who pop confetti-filled balloons at fetal gender reveals. Maybe the fact that the doctor wants to see him at least means there are options for helping his knee, things to talk about.

I only have Heather's vets to compare. There are some things they won't tell her over the phone, about neurodegenerative diseases and arthritic joints in show horses, but also once about just a hoof abscess that healed in a couple weeks. So I tell Wes about the abscess, about how worried Heather was when she got the message saying she needed to meet the vet at the barn and about how it finally popped one day, after hours of soaking in warm water, and drained a bunch of green pus into a bucket.

"The waiting was the hardest," I say.

"Yeh," he says, kicking a stick off the path. "I am goin a

little stir crazy. I can't really run or make any quick moves til it's better."

Of course the same went for the Morgan on stall rest. He dug a hole in his stall and had to be given a special ball to play with. I don't think there's anything like this for Wes, though, any way to dull the pain of this pause in his career.

We finish another loop around the court, the sun gone now, and I say I should head back.

He nods and stays beside me when I turn towards the house. His head's down, his hair blowing out of his hood. There are some leaves the storms shook loose scattered around the concrete paths now. This is how it always is, after all the others have been taken away, little clumps that eventually break down under the snow. Some cling to the trees still, too, and will hold on through the winter. It's like they think they're needles.

Wes's shoulder brushes against mine when the path narrows through the timothy grass that seems to keep growing in defiance of the season. It's dark away from the stadium lights, that sweet, starry way it gets in July with the fireflies all over the fields and cars chugging by on the freeway, only cold now, and quiet.

We're quiet, too, when we get to the clearing behind the house.

"Will you text after your appointment?" I ask when we stop.

"Yeh," he says.

I can only see half of his face side-lit by the back porch light.

"And your IMRI? You've got to mail it tomorrow?"

I nod. There's the sound of a car driving by, splashing

through a puddle in the dip at the end of our driveway.

"I hope your appointment goes well," I tell him. "Fingers crossed for good news."

"For you, too," he says, but then we still don't move.

I watch his breath blow away and follow it up into the sky, like I have time, like this is one of those moments that's supposed to pause. The stars are hidden tonight by a hazy cloud that seems to stretch out like the milky way.

Then Wes's hand brushes against mine.

I pull mine back, out of habit. Then my fingers go to his chest, not out of habit.

For a second, I don't move. I don't think he moves, either, but then our breaths are together, our lips together. I press up against his hoodie, into him.

His hands are light on my waist, and this isn't like Saturday, with his breath on my cheek when I could have just imagined it, or like Franklin grabbing my wrist and his shins about to be bruised for a month, or like Cam with his spearmint and the sway in my back that always gave me sciatica pain afterwards.

This is like Wes, and I'm leaning into him with my eyes open. I can see the North star when the cloud over us breaks apart, but I don't feel the wind.

*      *

Tuesday morning, I wake up like a sailfish on the hunt. The final hours before I have to send the IMRI application wash over me with a surge of auspicious energy like Lillie's stay-awake-through-a-date tea and greasy breadstick ends and the best Thanksgiving stuffing from the inn all at once. I get out of bed at five and head straight to the lab.

The hallway lights are all off, and my tennis shoes make little squeaks on the terrazzo. I follow the glow of the exit signs to my lab and turn on a Tiffany lamp over my desk.

I work for a while with just this little circle of light warming my shoulders, reading through my application, moving things around, and fixing citations. Eventually, the first rays of sun break through the windows, making the glass sparkle with frost.

I take a quick break around eleven to jog over to the engineering building's cafe. There are only a handful of students there today. Down the hallway, the faculty offices are mostly dark except for the few unlucky ones with Tuesday morning gen eds to teach.

Since everything's closing at noon, the cafe only has some yogurt dishes out, all low on berry, and a spattering of donuts from yesterday. I order their rooibos and the biscotti I used to eat as an undergrad.

When I get back, I move my laptop into the bathroom, dropping crumbs from the biscotti into the trash can I've positioned next to my chair and letting the light from the window be enough. There's no orange cleaner this week, and the air smells fresh even with the window closed. The strip of rubber weatherproofing is starting to peel off the side, flipping around every now and then when the wind rattles the pane.

My editing comes with confidence today, not like I'm still

shooting in the dark. It feels like I'm finally on a roll and have been preparing for wild cuttles all this time, almost like I'm someone else, a Richard Olunsten or a Frederick Kikner instead of an N.A. Novak. By two, I've convinced myself the stumpy cuttlefish is about as magnificent as a blue whale in a healthy coral reef.

When I leave, I fold up my bathroom chair and take it with me, and I don't check the status of Milner's trash pile on my way out.

There's not much traffic and almost no line at the post office, so I mail my application with twenty minutes to spare before the last pickup of the day.

I'm thinking of Wes when I start my car again, and I text him while it's warming up. It's the endorphins, I think, the lack of sleep, and possibly some gut rebalancing from the biscotti that hasn't been part of my diet for so long.

*Do you want to get dinner sometime?* I ask, high on this feeling. Because dinner is a date, incontrovertibly, and it seems like if I can write an IMRI fellowship application in ten days, I should be able to do almost anything else.

I read the text a few times before I put my phone away. It sounds more like me each time.

The long day still hasn't hit me yet when I get back to the house, the orange pendant lights clashing with the dark cloud bank rolling in from the West. I check my text messages as I eat a macaroni. There's nothing from Wes. I check the clock. It's almost three. His green dot's missing from Social, too, when I open my laptop on the sofa.

By three-thirty, he still hasn't texted, and I wonder if he's out playing, if he got good news today, too, maybe, and now he's running around endorphin-high with his phone forgotten somewhere in his bag as he tries to beat the storm.

The sun's gone down, and everything's shaded in blue by the time I'm dressed to walk in my thermal yoga pants and a sweater.

Lillie and Heather are out grocery shopping, so I leave a note for them on the white board in the kitchen. It just says *walking*, but it means #FOMOing with the confidence today of a thousand bunny supreme users.

The sky's lower by the time I get outside, barely lit with purple, and night's pushing down on the horizon. It could break any minute in a downpour, that humid kind of cold that goes deep into your bones, the kind you need one of Lillie's oatmeal baths to chase away. The wind chimes Heather hung on the sycamore clang together as I jog through the yard.

It takes my eyes a while to adjust to the darkness, to follow the dirt path now that the timothy grass has been mown down. They must have done it today while the rain was holding out. I smell dead grass, and the cold stings my nose. I shove my hands deeper into my pockets.

I hear the *pop, chunk, pop* when I get to edge of the tennis courts and know right away that it's Wes.

It seems like the balls are coming faster tonight, or maybe the machine's just louder in the dark. The rest of the complex is empty. Wind rattles the fence.

I stop by the gate. Wes swings too hard, and the next ball flies into the net. There are a bunch of others around the court, spots of neon yellow glowing against the blue. His hoodie's fallen down, and there's a line of blood on one of his legs that catches the light.

He doesn't turn, doesn't even pause when I call his name.

Heather and Lillie get home a little before five, when I've just started *Frasier* and opened a half gallon of coffee ice cream.

I shouldn't need either, of course. This should be like any other disappointment if it's like anything at all, no different than rejected papers or having to give up whipped cream mochas that one time when I was an undergrad and my blood sugar came back a little high. This feeling will pass like those did. I remind myself that something simple will fix it if the ice cream isn't enough, something like the discovery of stevia ginger snaps or another journal acceptance after my first paper rejection. Tomorrow, I won't feel like all the oceans have just drained down into middle earth.

Heather and Lillie are in pre-Thanksgiving mode tonight, hurrying. They shuffle inside with our Whole Foods bags full of ingredients for Lillie's marshmallow pie and some other things to take with us to Cuyahoga.

While they're unpacking, I hear my phone ding from the pocket of my thermal leggings. The screen's on Wes's text chain when I unlock it. There's nothing new there; he hasn't responded. I look out the window, at the lights that are still on over the tennis courts.

"Something's wrong," Heather says as soon as she sees me. She plunks her pumpkin kefir on the counter and comes around to the sofa.

I shake my head.

Lillie drops into a lotus, still holding a bag of rice flour. This feeling isn't one I can hide, I guess. It's one of the things my face shows before I can convince it not to. Or maybe it's the ice cream that gives me away.

"I'm not sure," I tell them. I don't have to say anything else.

"Shit," Heather says.

Lillie pops up, scurrying for the tea kettle, and Heather digs out her phone to order us pizza with extra greasy breadsticks.

I remind her she's supposed to be going on a date with Matt tonight. It's important, their last-date-before-a-major-holiday. So this would probably be a high-stakes dinner for them even if he weren't sneaking around to meet Lillie behind her back.

"Canceled," she tells me as she searches for the pizza delivery number in her phone.

I look at Lillie. Lillie avoids eye contact as she gets out the mugs and starts the electric kettle.

"*He* canceled," Heather clarifies. "He's leaving town, apparently."

I wait. This "apparently" means it's good there's plenty of ice cream to go around. So when Lillie's ready with the lavender tea, I request an offgassing extension, and we gently prod Heather to share her Matt relationship-such-as-it-is.

These are just disappointed hopes, she tells us, I guess like mine. This afternoon, Matt decided to go to Tennessee with some friends for Thanksgiving.

It's one of those holidays that it's too early for her to spend with him, of course, but they'd planned a suitable substitute, an intermediary step in the direction she wanted to go. They were supposed to have dinner tonight at Amero's, and then they'd planned to get together for lunch tomorrow at the house before we go to Cuyahoga, for roast chicken and microwave stuffing and Heather's homemade mashed potatoes so Matt, from Oregon, could get an idea of how real Ohioans eat mashed potatoes, with a brick of cream cheese and a handful of rock salt.

But now there won't be any mashed potatoes, and she'll just have to eat the roast chicken and microwave stuffing herself.

"It'll be okay," she says at the end of this story, like these partially-coupled holidays are ever *okay* and we don't all know this is just an in-between time before a breakup's official, a transition like mine.

So when the pizza comes early, Lillie and I say the things you do about how there are so many men in the world and so much ice cream and so many bunny supremes.

I point out that winter tournaments are coming up and that Heather wouldn't want a Matt bogging her down into breeding and foaling season. Matt strikes me as someone who would be put off by placenta.

She nods and snorts in agreement, but it's a half-hearted, Morgan-with-a-cold snort.

"He's not worth this," Lillie adds, fully contorted now into her bendy-twisty with her spine bent over the pizza box.

I stare, but she deftly avoids eye contact.

Heather sniffs in. "You're not eating, Nora," she says, handing me the greasiest breadstick from the bag.

I take a bite and let it sit on my tongue, but even this doesn't taste good. Maybe I should have had protein first. Or maybe the biscotti I ate this morning was just too big of a change. I've only had that and the macaroni today.

"Your application didn't finish out well?" Heather asks.

"It did," I say, because my application came out like unicorn poop—to be discarded the way you might throw away unicorn poop if you weren't a fantasy biologist and had applications like Olunsen's and Kirkner's to read. But still, it felt like it should have been a greasy breadstick-eating, celebratory kind of night with the good *Frasier* episodes. With Wes.

"Wes," Lillie says.

"Wes," I confirm.

Heather sits forward. "What'd he do?"

"Nothing." I have to remind myself this is the truth. And that there are so many men in the world, and so many bunny supremes, and so many...there are not so many fellowships and teaching positions. I look out the window again. The lights over the tennis court are still on. Is he still playing?

"He didn't tell me how his doctor's appointment went," I say, finally. Which isn't a crime. It sounds whiny, petty, *silly*.

Lillie removes one foot from her bendy-twisty and nudges the pizza box a little closer to me. "Maybe he got bad news," she says. "Maybe he's still processing it."

"And he didn't respond when I saw him playing this afternoon."

Heather spits out her crust. "He ignored you?"

"Yes."

"That bastard," she says.

I swallow some dry breadstick. "And I texted earlier to ask him if he wanted to have dinner sometime. He didn't respond to that, either."

"Fuck," Heather says.

Lillie hastily refolds into a lotus.

Then they ask the questions you do, say all the platitudes I know already, and encourage me to eat. Heather takes over my phone to scroll through my messages and evaluate either just how much of a misunderstanding this was or, alternatively, how much of a scumbag Wes is.

"At least *your* love life's going smoothly," she says to Lillie as she reads, then to me, "Lillie's started seeing someone."

I look at Lillie. Lillie looks at her pizza. And maybe she's about to tell me about this someone. Maybe, I think, all of this isn't so bleak and she's actually going to tell me about someone who's *not* Heather's soon-to-be-ex-boyfriend. But my phone dings before she gets the chance.

"Jarod," Heather says. She jumps up and shows me the phone. "You missed a text from him over an hour ago. He's in town."

*Just got in,* the first text says. *I'd love to see you before you head home if you have time.*

The next one's a picture from his hotel, with the same fake pothos as the place where we stayed in Cincinnati. It probably has a sign somewhere nearby for a breakfast buffet with juevos rancheros. I scroll down.

*Dinner?* he asks.

The bite of breadstick sits heavy in my stomach. Jarod's visit should have been easy for me to remember; he flew in the same day my application had to be mailed.

But this is no time for evaluation. Heather's already clearing away the pizza. "Take our reservation," she says. "Amero's, eight. I was just about to call to cancel."

I don't move. I feel rooted to the sofa now, committed to breadsticks and ice cream.

"Go," Heather tells me, taking back my phone.

As she makes these arrangements with Jarod, I hover by the kitchen island. I don't know what to do next. Remove thermal yoga pants? Keep thermal yoga pants?

"He's picking you up in fifteen minutes," Heather says, then, "Nora, you can do this. You just have to change."

# Chapter 14

*When two male cuttlefish challenge each other over a female, they don't like to cause a scene. So they just look at each other menacingly until one of them swims away.*

Amero's is all heavy tablecloths and candlelight, smelly seafood dishes and fancy pastas. The lights have been turned down by the time Jarod and I get there, and a pianist is playing soft arpeggios in the corner.

I partition myself off behind my menu in an attempt to reset my brain and Heather's smoothing underwear that's migrating up my butt.

"Did you see the eggplant dish?" Jarod asks.

Jarod, who I remember likes eggplant and makes magical hummus. Jarod, who I forgot was coming into town. I have no excuse for this. I haven't been in a coma or anything. Maybe this is what Lillie would call a stress reaction.

I make a kind of affirmative but non-linear hum in my throat like a three-spined toadfish. This feels like all I can muster tonight, toadfish-level interaction. Jarod doesn't deserve this. Jarod deserves porpoise-level interaction at least.

I try to correct with my humpback song, but it comes out scratchy.

"It was nice of your roommate to give us her reservation," he says.

"Yes." I set my menu down on the table. My boobs—they must be mine, attached to me—are squished together in Heather's dress, peeking out of some dark blue lace at the top. It's amazing what shapewear can do, I think, how our bodies can go all viscous and change without us having to evolve internally at all.

Jarod asks me a couple more questions about the menu—how I order my noodles, what else I've heard was good here—as I take inventory of my new #freakingtiredofFOMOing body. My toes are pinched in Heather's heels. An underwire digs into my ribcage. My stomach twinges. And Jarod isn't the cause of any of this.

I try to refocus on him. "What did you think of Case?" I ask.

"I just got in," he tells me, "but the area seems nice. I was thinking about driving around town a little tomorrow. Any suggestions?"

"The aquarium."

"Of course," he says, because he's Jarod, someone who's like me. I don't have to ask if he enjoys rock and roll or goes to sports games. So I tell him about the spotted turtles— famous spotted turtles, special Ohio spotted turtles, something you really should see if you come to Cleveland.

"Your roommate mentioned you'd had a stressful day,"

he says when I finish. "But you got the application out all right?"

"Yes." Is it possible this was all one day, I wonder, since I woke up at five and finished my application and ate undergrad biscotti and asked someone on a date for the first time and he ignored me and Lillie almost admitted to dating Heather's now almost-ex-boyfriend and I forgot about Jarod coming into town?

But this is something that happens around the holidays; time condenses like my spandexed midsection and then balloons out in the end like Heather's add-two-cups bra. It's now, apparently, the Tuesday night before Thanksgiving, that I lose my mind and my memory and possibly my coffee ice cream and the bite of breadstick I had if Heather's underwear puts any more pressure on my esophageal sphincter.

"You must be relieved," Jarod says.

"Yes," I agree. Of course I should be relieved. My application's over. Humans aren't supposed to need projects like this constantly. We're supposed to have periods of rest, of transition. And how lucky mine's been so far; when the person I was trying to date ignored me, the person I'd forgotten I had possibly already dated showed up from across the country just in time for dinner.

Jarod and I talk easily for a while about a single-celled protist that was found recently on some coral in the South Pacific. I watch him over my noodles. His faces are all right, consistent. His speech patterns are what I remember, what I understand. There aren't any questions in his voice, any pauses that are off.

"This is nice," he says when he sets down his eggplant

fork.

I agree, because this *is* nice—this easiness, this responding to text messages consistently and eating olive oil noodles to lazy piano music, this way I think dating's supposed to go. We talk about things that make sense, like protists and gila monsters and bacteria frozen in glaciers.

"What about Penn?" he asks when the waiter brings us a dessert menu.

"Penn?" My stomach's finally working again, and I'm eyeing the caramel gelato. Maybe I just need more ice cream, like you do after a real breakup. Maybe this will start to feel better with more sugar in my blood.

"I was thinking you might still have time to apply," Jarod says. "I know you haven't taught before, so I was going to ask if you wanted to check out my teaching statement and some of my syllabi."

I thank him. Of course this would be helpful, and Penn's deadline is far enough off that I could presumably do this. And what else am I going to do while I wait for Olunsen and Kirkner to be announced for the fellowship and for their papers on penguins and evolving river dolphins to come out? Not sit in my empty lab. Not without the cuttles. Not play tennis.

"You know it's really great you did the IMRI," Jarod says.

I nod. Because this is great experience, practice...all the platitudes I know.

"It's not that you don't deserve it," he adds.

I hope I say the right thing then before I set down my dessert menu and excuse myself, retreating to the women's restroom like I have so many times when I've been too tired or been around too many people at loud family dinners and graduation parties and all the other occasions I've gotten through that weren't dates.

Amero's bathroom has textured black walls with glowing orange lights under the sinks. It's quiet here, but it feels like the floor's vibrating, the way old marble does, like everything's moving even when I'm just standing by the little chaise in the corner. I think the chaise is meant for these moments when you might feel like fainting. Not swooning, but real, vasovagal syncope.

I check my phone, stalling, breathing. There's still no response from Wes.

It's as I'm sinking into the chaise that I see I have a missed voicemail. I click.

"Nora, this is Dave. I'm sorry," he says. "I know you don't want to hear from me. But Nora, I...I think you might want to come down here."

It takes a short eternity to get to the aquarium—not the highway or the lunchtime way, but the GPS-on-Jarod's phone way, probably longer than all of my mapped routes. I wasn't thinking. His GPS is from Seattle.

I don't recognize anything on this route until we get to the back parking lot. When Jarod stops the car, I jump out and rush inside through the open door, past the shark tunnel and the Arctic and into the Caribbean room, where my cuttles are obviously—so obviously they could be fiddler crabs or frat boys—preparing to mate.

Dave's up on the platform saying the things I guess you do when you're trying to deflect blame.

My mitral valve starts to sizzle, the result of cold-induced asthma from running and the kind of panic that can only come from the petering out of innocent cuttle hearts.

There are so many questions and no satisfactory answers. Was it their diet change? The overhead lights? Do the cuttles feel like they're aging? How long has this been going on, right under Dave's nose? It's been four days since I visited last—too long. There were no harems then. So there are about eighty hours unaccounted for that they could have been in harems without someone noticing. *Fully-formed* harems.

Pulling crab from their shells was too much for their little hearts, and now he plans to just stand by and let them *mate*. He even has the nerve, at one point, to tell me this is a natural part of their life cycle, all Lillie-like with drawn-out vowel sounds that make me want to punch him in his shellfish-greased mouth.

When I get ahold of my thoughts, I send him for emergency crab, the best he has—something new, something distracting, anything that might stop this. Then all I can do is watch, helpless, as Bitty rebounds off the substrate in the far corner of the tank.

"This is amazing," Jarod says when Dave's gone.

I turn to look at him, then back at the tank. Dot does a zig-zag dangerously close to some staghorn coral.

"You seem stressed," Jarod says then.

Stressed? Is that what I seem? Yes, I tell him, that's what I am, *stressed.* Because of their hearts—Didn't he know about their hearts? How could he have *not* known about their hearts? There are three. You can't miss them.

In the storeroom, something crashes to the floor. The

cuttles don't come up, don't even act like they notice. I identify Franklin's girth hovering over a smaller group of females like a rotund alien hovercraft. One of the other males guards the harem with Dot over the cauliflower coral.

My head starts without me then. *Nurse, angel, frilled, cookie cutter...*

I hiss out a fire breath. It's always sharks in emergencies.

"It's really exciting, though, isn't it?" Jarod asks. "I mean, it's not very often you get to..."

*Zebra, bull, tiger...*

"You're doing great with this," he says. "You must be really..."

I let out a noise like a farting herring.

"Look at that," he says when Zedo, one of the smaller males with a distinctive torpedo shape, sneaks by Franklin, displaying bilateral coloring.

*Goblin, porbeagle...*

Jarod it calls it a dance, what they're doing, like my cuttles are engaging in a slow Viennese waltz.

*Blue, gray...*

Zedo maintains bilateral coloration, fooling Franklin. This is happening. Right now. I look back at the supply room. Apparently Dave's having to hunt the crabs himself.

*Lemon, dusky, spinner, sharpnose, broadnose sevengill...*

Bitty, who's been looking into the empty tank behind us, drops down beside Zedo, and my mitral valve settles into a steady burping rhythm as I watch my most brilliant cuttle quite intentionally being courted by the second smartest. Bitty's direct like that. She always knows what she wants. Bitty is not like me. I yell for the crabs again.

*Bizant River, Galapagos...*

I exhale another fire breath. Zedo's a little yellow for my liking, but even so, there's some tiny aspect of this that's right, at least, in Bitty refusing to settle for any of the larger models with less memory data converging in their hippocampi.

Finally, Dave opens the door.

*Whale, basking...*

I stand and take the crab bucket. Then I see it. Behind Dave in the next tank, a tall dorsal fin cuts through the water, heading straight for us.

*SANDBAR.*

The crab goes flying into the water.

A few minutes later, most of the crab's at the bottom of the cuttles' tank, and Dave's telling me about a sandbar shark with social anxiety.

She had to be moved from the tunnel, he explains, because she wasn't assertive enough. The other sharks were picking on her. She suffers from low shark-esteem. A sandbar shark, he means, also known as the *thick-skinned* shark.

"She wasn't getting enough to eat," Dave says. But he's losing height again, like in the ER room.

I lean over the water. The sandbar shark with social anxiety hasn't lost any apparent girth or mass. I thought at first that Dave might try to tell me it was something else, like George the friendly horn shark just over for a visit, like somehow I might not recognize this dorsal fin.

I open my mouth and try to corral my tongue. It feels like when I was kissing him, like it's stuck somehow and three times its normal size, but from rage this time instead of from anaphylaxis.

"Sandbar. Sharks eat. Cuttlefish." I swallow. My voice comes out high. Rhythm's beyond me. "They're mating because. They think they're the last."—gasp—"Cuttlefish in. The ocean and that—that…" I jab a finger at the water.

"Barbara," Dave supplies, because the sandbar shark's name is *Barbara*.

"…is about to. Eat them!" I'm out of fire breaths.

Dave avoids eye contact and clutches the empty crab bucket to his chest. Then he launches into a speech you might hear in the shark tunnel about the ecological importance of the sandbar shark, what with their flexible seasonal migrations when food sources change. Like how Barbara's migrated over here, obviously hoping to eat my cuttles.

"You can tell she's underfed?" Jarod asks at one point, leaning over the water of the monster's tank. It's separated from my cuttles only by a narrow access hallway and a couple glass windows. "She looks so…"

"We need to turn. Off the lights," I say, grasping at other variables to change. "Now. I don't know what. You were thinking putting them…Their circadian…" I hiccup.

Maybe the cuttles will dream of mating, I tell myself, and they'll wake up tomorrow and think it's already happened.

But Dave's in the middle of a speech about how sandbar sharks bear live young, and Jarod appears to be listening, learning about how the embryos eat something that comes from their uterine wall.

I reach for Heather's heels I abandoned a few feet away and consider throwing them at either Barbara or Dave.

Dave stops talking when I pick them up. "You're right, Nora," he says. "I'll get the lights."

Jarod grabs my jacket from where it's dangling over the edge of the platform, almost into Barbara's water. "We should go out to, uh..." He glances at Barbara, then at me again. "You could probably use something to drink," he says.

What I need, I decide, is tea—valerian, specifically, Lillie's, if pharmacological intervention's not immediately available. What Jarod thinks this means is that we should go to that neat-looking place he drove by on the way to pick me up.

I wasn't paying attention when we took the highway, wasn't watching when we turned, didn't realize I was even here until the probably mostly psychosomatic stench of crème brulee hit me.

Indigo Dreams isn't crowded the Tuesday before Thanksgiving coming up on closing time, but it still seems louder than usual. I order chamomile tea and two chocolate chip cookies.

Once we have our drinks, Jarod pauses at a table in the middle of the room. I keep walking and settle into the booth in the corner. It's the one where I sat with Wes until the Scribbles emergency what feels now like so long ago. Was it only a few weeks?

But this isn't Wes in a hoodie across from me. This is Jarod in a sports coat. Only the chamomile's the same. My heart's finally run out of bubbles. I think Heather's shaping underwear has started to remold my organs. I've been awake for over seventeen hours.

Jarod gets me to recount the beginning of my day, the application that was going so smoothly this morning in the quiet bathroom with the rooibos and the biscotti I should have left in my past. Then he asks how I met Dave and about the crème brulee and my ER visit.

I devour the first cookie as he tells me how much the cuttles impressed him—not their harems, of course, but their...cuttlehood, their focus, the speed with which Franklin moved to get that piece of crab and then returned to guard his harem, their...colors. Because cuttlefish are always impressive, always startling, even when you've seen them every day for years.

"I really liked Itty? Was that her name?"

"Bitty," I say, and tell him about Bitty's maze times, how she averaged over three seconds faster than any of the others and the pretty purple shade she takes on when she's concentrating. A bit of cookie gets lodged in my esophagus, and I take a swig of too-hot chamomile. It's the same purple shade she had tonight, concentrating on Zedo.

"And it seems like such a great place you found for them," Jarod says. "And this means—I know it's not necessarily good for their hearts, but maybe they'll be really...careful about it, I mean, since they're used to the university environment—"

I spit up some tea. Does he think the university's teaching safe sex to my cephalopods?

"—The eggs, I mean, could mean, you know, more of them. If there's any other research you wanted to do, maybe on the embryonic stage..."

I start to recite whales as I tell Jarod what's known about cuttles in the embryonic stage—a lot, it turns out, because they're the most brilliant embryos. They learn in the egg, starting to pick out their favorite foods based on what they're exposed to as they're developing. They watch, listen, and bide their time. This is something we'll have to account for, a protocol we'll have to develop to expose the eggs to different kinds of prey.

"And you never know what the future might hold," Jarod says. "We should toast to that."

"To what?" My inner voice screams that my cuttles are dying, like my career. My head-mom reminds me to reapply my vegan lipstick.

"I'm sorry," Jarod says, then, "You're handling this really well."

I look down at the table. I'm almost finished with my second cookie.

"I'm really glad I got to meet them," he tries.

I attempt my humpback noise, but it comes out like a seagull with a cold. Of course I'm glad, too. Of course I should have thought of sharing the cuttles with Jarod intentionally. This is how interest looks, I imagine, asking a person to dinner, expressing a desire to share your brownie—did I eat all of his brownie, too, with my first cookie?—complimenting their pets. It doesn't look like ignoring someone. This is human mating 101.

Jarod's leaning towards me, both feet pointed in my direction, maintaining a nonthreatening but small personal bubble at all times, and considering getting a second brownie to feed me in this personal crisis—*trying*, I realize.

And I'm sure I appreciate this. I'm thinking about it, anyway, later, when I get in his car and see Wes's hoodie walking away from us along the curb.

I call his name, and he turns. He must see me, but then he just keeps walking.

I can't sleep, even after all the chamomile and two cups of Lillie's valerian tea. Maybe it was the chocolate in my two cookies or in the one and a half brownies of Jarod's I ate.

I blame the chocolate for keeping me up, for making me want to look at Wes's text messages again.

There's one I missed at 8:54. I was at the aquarium then, before he saw me outside Indigo Dreams.

*Damn it, today was awful. I'm sorry for earlier, and I do wanna have dinner with u.*

# Chapter 15

The next morning, I sleep in until almost eleven. It doesn't feel like the Wednesday before Thanksgiving at first, with the quiet and the gray. It feels like January after all the holiday craziness is over and well before the first shoots of spring climb up through the grasses and the trees start to bud out.

Bits of yesterday intrude as I eat my oatmeal and take a shower, fresh memories swirling around in my head like diatoms in the Chuckchi Sea when the Arctic ice starts to melt each April. It should be pretty, incandescent, but it feels more like a waking coma.

I think about my application first, about whether I pressed "save" before "print" at the lab when I changed the font for the footnotes. Then about undergrad biscotti. Then about yelling Wes's name by the tennis court—How many times? I don't remember. I was hoarse from the cold. I think about my cuttles in harems, then about Jarod. And about Wes again, walking away from us down Lincoln Avenue.

My gut's heavy by the time I'm dressed, and I go through whale species as I drive into the lab to pick up my recommendation letter for Penn. Little drops of rain stick to the windows. The gray's uniform these days, and you can never tell what time it is until it's too late, when all the light's gone.

I sit in my car for a while reading through texts.

Dave's message is first, to inform me the harems had broken as of six-thirty this morning.

In the interest of self-preservation, I ignore Dave for the time being. I tell myself last night was just an anomaly and that my cuttles have, in all likelihood, totally forgotten about mating by now. Maybe I'll write a paper about this, about the first documented example of cuttlefish who were in harems and then collectively, spontaneously changed their minds.

The rain picks up, fat drops splattering my windshield. I turn off the car, and a chill sets in at my ankles as soon as the hot air from the floor vent stops.

I click on Jarod's message next. *Any cuttle updates? Had such a good time meeting them and spending the evening with you.*

I'm about to respond that I had a good time last night, too—never mind the breakdown—and that my cuttles are fine now that they're born again virgins. But then I click out of Jarod's message and read Wes's again.

*Damn it, today was awful. I'm sorry for earlier, and I do wanna have dinner with u.*

*Sorry about your day,* I write him. *Are you free Friday or*

*Saturday night? I hope your doctor went all right.*

I watch for the little check mark to show this has been read as I respond to the others, telling Dave to keep feeding the pre-pulled crabs and thanking Jarod for the ongoing cuttle support.

I flinch when my phone dings at full volume.

It's Jarod. *I hope you have a good Thanksgiving with your family*, he says. *I'd love to see you when you get back into town.*

I respond that I'd like this, too. I'm sure I'd be more enthusiastic had there been more time to evaluate before he showed up last night and if my head weren't still swimming with everything else.

I click on Wes's text message again before I go into the lab.

When I jog through the courtyard, the rain beads on my jacket, and the cold goes straight through my thermal yoga pants. I have to use my key fob to get in through the double doors and am surprised the lights in the hallway are already on. The rest of the building's empty, the university shut down until Monday.

As promised, there's an envelope with my name on Milner's door. He's put a letter each addressed to Mason and Penn inside, about my research and all the years he's known me and my paper and my conference presentation and my love of teaching, even though the latter's entirely speculative.

I put the pages back into the envelope, being careful not to crease the corners. I should go home now, I know, rest before the holiday, throw a suitcase together and have a leisurely lunch before Lillie, Heather, and I drive to Cuyahoga. I obviously need this pre-social peace.

But there's a little rumble through the wall and a light on in Kyle's office next door.

He doesn't seem to notice me knocking, the music from his laptop booming with something electronic and jarring.

I open the door. He's standing over his desk and emptying drawers into a plastic bag. His clownfish are all at the other side of their tank.

When I ask him what's going on, he shuts down his laptop and then turns to me with the most genuine smile I've seen on him, a kind of gerbil-that-swallowed-the-canary look.

He's packing, he tells me, since he's expecting to be doing something different next semester. Something he's more than happy to tell me about. Do I know the IMRI?

I squeeze the envelope to my chest. "IMRI? You mean the fellowship?"

Kyle nods. "Milner's gonna get it," he says.

"Milner..."

"Or he's a finalist, anyway. They emailed him this morning."

"Milner," I repeat.

"I guess he still has to interview," Kyle says, "but I'm gonna go with him, as his assistant, when he's..."

I don't hear the rest. It's just Kyle's voice bouncing between the walls of my skull then and a too-bright haze of red behind my eyelids that clashes with all the gray when I get to my car, still holding the freaking envelope.

A handful of hours later, Lillie's purring with her drawn-out vowel sounds like a spotted sea trout as she drives us through the rain.

Heather lounges in the back seat with her phone, cursing everything with a Y chromosome, from Milner to Matt to Wes to her too-aggressive two-year-old stallion and back to Milner again. Jarod seems to be left out for now. *Maybe I should be thinking more about Jarod.*

She's still reading Milner's paper online and looking up complaints against faculty for similar issues. *Because he discouraged me from applying for the IMRI. Because he got in my head. Because he's exactly like all the other faculty who have "borrowed" their grad students' work since the dawn of higher education.*

Heather thinks I'm looking at Milner's paper, too, as I re-read Wes's last text over and over like it might tell me something different each time I look. There's a check mark now by my reply asking about dinner this weekend. He read it over four hours ago.

*Damn it, today was awful. I'm sorry for earlier, and I do wanna have dinner with u.*

I evaluate for content and syntax this time. He said he was sorry, presumably for ignoring me the first time at the tennis courts, signifying the expectation of a continued relationship. He couldn't have meant at Indigo Dreams, since that was after he sent the text. He punctuated the contraction, a break in his usual pattern, and used a comma, but there was that "wanna" in the middle and the "u" at the end as per his usual. He did say he wanted to have dinner with me. It seemed so clear, so easy to interpret. *He* seemed so clear just a couple days ago.

But now he isn't responding. Like he didn't respond last night when I called out to him on the street, like he didn't respond at the sports complex, like he didn't respond to the beluga-sounding woman a few weeks ago.

Maybe *this* is his pattern, not responding, and I just didn't want to see it. We always show our patterns, give some hint of them even in the tiniest interactions. Maybe there are dozens—hundreds, if Heather's guess is right—of these women Wes has ignored all over Cleveland, and now I'm one of them.

I look at the phone again, at the check mark. Before, he always wrote back too quickly for me to see a check mark. He didn't read his messages when he didn't have time to respond, didn't ever take time to think about what he was going to say. But this sample size is small; I've only known him for a little over a month. Beluga woman probably knew him longer.

Scribbles bites at the bars of his travel cage as we cross 271 and Lillie takes the exit onto Wheatley, where soggy leaves line the ramp.

"You're going to be okay," Heather repeats. "And you're going to file a complaint about Milner being such a loser asshat, and we're going to have a fucking great Thanksgiving."

"The best," Lillie agrees, turning off her blinker.

I look back at my phone.

"And you're going to forget all about this when you go out with Jarod again," Heather adds.

I should be looking forward to Jarod. Jarod, with his extensive list of pros. Jarod, with his hummus and his publications and his soft voice and his symmetrical face.

Lillie ruins this reflection with, "Has Wes written you back yet? About dinner?"

"No."

"Fuck him," Heather says.

I point Lillie onto Riverview, then onto Bath.

"Think how pretty the park'll look," she says, "with the leaves. Maybe we could go for a walk Friday before we drive home."

"You should text Jarod about this weekend," Heather tells me, "and don't even think about Milner or Wes again until Monday."

I nod. I guess I can avoid thinking about Milner or Wes this week like we're avoiding talking about Matt for Heather's sake. I've agreed not to even mention his name, not even to Lillie, not even to ask whether *she's* seeing him now.

When we get to the house, I hug Scribbles' travel cage to my chest and make a beeline for my room, pretending not to see Cam standing in the kitchen with my vegetarian stuffing.

*      *

Thanksgiving doesn't hit me until almost eleven, when I roll over in my old bed and smell turkey. These are patterns I know, smells I recognize—the turkey and the stuffing and the pies. Normally, I'd already be in the social isolation room with my mom before company arrives. We stay there, brooding like octopi until either the agreed-upon start time or a persistent fire alarm.

So it's ironic that my phone's the first thing I reach for when I wake up. There's one new message this morning, a hopeful little red mark on my text app.

*Can I bring you anything today?* It's Cam.

I ignore this, practicing denial. It's not just me, though; there's a solid anthropological reason that this is the season of alcohol and suicides and perpetually-silenced phones. Probably for most people it's more their families than their exes, but I imagine the past holds pretty much the same dangers for all of us. It's so easy to revert.

When I come out of my room, Heather and Lillie are already busy in the kitchen, Lillie mixing her marshmallow pie batter and Heather ripping apart a head of iceberg lettuce in a way that suggests she's thinking about Matt again.

She starts to vent as I get my oatmeal. He finally called her this morning and left a message. He apologized for his last-minute trip and indicated that there's someone else he's not over. But he still wants to talk to her, suggesting there's something left for them to talk about.

I look at Lillie, wondering if this is the moment she tells Heather *she's* the someone else, right here in my parents' kitchen on Thanksgiving morning. Maybe she's been in some kind of quiet crisis since Ned, since she never got to explode. Maybe I should have noticed, should have said something.

Lillie doesn't look up from her marshmallow pie batter.

Heather keeps going, explaining that this is the last straw, the last shred of hope for whatever-might-have-been with Matt squashed like a Thanksgiving potato.

When she's gone back to quietly ripping apart the lettuce, Lillie asks if I've seen the sweet potatoes my mom made this morning. So sweet, you know, so *ooorange*.

"And it's fine," Heather adds, in a way that lets you know it's definitely *not* fine. "I didn't have the time coming up, anyway, like you said, and..." She sucks in air, then focuses back on the iceberg lettuce. "I'm fine," she repeats.

"*Fiine,*" Lillie echoes, and I add a "great" for good measure before we go through the *his losses* about Matt. They'll say the same thing about Wes if I don't hear from him soon, that this was all his loss, not mine. Because this is what you say; it doesn't matter if it's true.

"You're doing okay?" Heather asks me, "with Cam here?"

I look down at my oatmeal. "Fine," I say, but I feel like a swellshark who's swallowed her tail.

Of course there isn't a reason for me to be anything other than fine with Cam. He brought dinner for everyone last night along with the vegetarian stuffing I eat from the inn. He remembered all of our favorite dishes, because he's spent the last nine Thanksgivings in this house and the last six with Heather and Lillie here, too. It was so much easier than using that food delivery app, Dad told me; he just texted that we were ready to eat, and then, like magic, there Cam was.

I look around at the gourds, the candles lined up on the mantle, and the bits of sterilized straw in little tied-up tufts around the island. These are things I'm used to. The cranberry and vegetables from Earthfare are ready to be uncovered in the warmer, and the china's been set out on the dining room table. There's a smaller kids' table in the living room outfitted with biodegradable plates with pumpkins on them.

Heather and Lillie take this opportunity to muster some goodwill towards other men, mainly Jarod, because they don't know what to say to me about Cam yet. At the end of this talk, Lillie sets down her mixing apparatus and pushes a ginger cookie my way, promising it will go down easier than the oatmeal.

Later, when I'm brushing my teeth, I work on another text to Wes, because this is how holidays work; we repeat old patterns ad nauseum and expect different results. So I tell myself maybe he thought he responded to my last message and just forgot to send it, or maybe he's having trouble settling his calendar for this weekend.

*Happy Thanksgiving,* I write, even though it doesn't sound like me at all. *Dinner this weekend?*

I take a shower and get dressed, my phone quiet on my nightstand, and then, suddenly, it's noon, less than an hour until everyone will get here. So I hurry to the big storage closet we soundproofed sometime in the late eighties for pre-social quiet. Since I've seen it last, Mom's added a little monitor that shows the doorbell camera and reupholstered the chaises.

She's already marinating there under her new red light. I sit on the chaise next to hers and suck in the peace like a whale shark with copepods.

"You're doing okay?" she asks, the way everyone is today.

"Okay," I confirm. I can feel the red light warming the left side of my body through my leggings and sweater.

She shifts. I can tell she wants to ask me about Cam and the extra stuffing he'll bring me today and say something about #FOMOing, but she's probably not sure if Cam's something I could still be missing out on, after all those years I wasn't.

"Heather mentioned you saw the ecologist again," she says instead. "So he's in town?"

"Yes."

"You could have brought him here."

"I didn't think about it." But would it have helped? Could

Jarod have made this less difficult? I'm not sure. Mom will say something about fun next, I think, the theoretical version.

"You seemed okay with Cam last night," she says.

I guess she's going in the not fun direction.

"Yes, okay," I tell her, because Cam and I have always been okay. Probably very few people have had more practice at being *okay* than we have.

We sit in the quiet for a little while then, rejuvenating, preparing. I think about how much of our lives we spend preparing like this, then recuperating, then preparing again.

I'm just starting to drift off when the monitor beeps. It's the doorbell, at least fifteen minutes early. This is how it starts, when we enter the Bermuda triangle of holiday time warps. Now it will go slowly, ages condensed into a few hours.

Mom sits up and looks at the camera.

"Nina?" I ask.

Mom closes her eyes and makes a long exhale, then retracts her lips into her non-xygomatic holiday smile.

"Cam," she says. "Remember, Thanksgiving is *fun*."

# Chapter 16

I let the water run hot over my face, my head buzzing and my stomach distended like a black swallower. I'm trying to steam the holiday out, to let the day rinse away as I evaluate in the quiet of my old bathroom with its pale pink tile and the ocean waves in the towels. These are relics of a simpler time, an easier time, pre-#FOMOing.

Dinner went well, or at least it wasn't any of the disasters it could have been. It was a usual Thanksgiving, I guess, the same volume as always, the same conversations, everything you'd think I might have ruined when I crawled through Cam's window.

He never let on that anything was wrong between us. He sat across from me, with Ethan, and then after dinner, they threw a football back and forth in the freezing afternoon wind like they've been doing since Ethan got that jersey for

Christmas when he was five. There was football-watching, as usual, in the den after dinner. American football. Not football. Tomorrow, Cam and my dad will have more American football to watch with a bunch of turkey sandwiches soaked in gravy.

When I turn off the shower, the house is quiet. Nina must have finally gone home. I guess I've been in here a while.

My phone's gone dead again, steamed over and exhausted like I am. I plug it in on the sink once I've dried off.

I find my pajamas—real adult pajamas I brought with me, the kind with buttons on the shirt and a drawstring waist on the pants, not the Peptol Bismol-colored nightgown with the rosettes—and walk around my room a couple times just digesting, stalling.

I must miss the chime when my phone restarts. I don't notice the little red mark on my text messages until the screen goes blue. When I click, I'm surprised to see Wes's name at the top of the list.

*Busy*, he says, and that's all.

I sit down on my bed and read through this exchange one more time. But there's nothing else, no pattern other than the one I can't help but recognize. An explanation isn't required, of course, when a relationship's this short, when there's been just one kiss and not even an attempted dinner.

So I won't know if it's something wrong with him, like Lillie and Heather will inevitably tell me, or if it's something wrong with me, which is more likely, since there wasn't really an *us* for it to have been. Maybe I'll pretend later that it's at least partly the holidays and that new relationships don't stand a chance this time of year. There are too many patterns of each other's to learn too quickly, too many traditions to try to meld together. Nothing ever just fits.

When I come out to the kitchen, Cam's there like he has been through nine other Thanksgivings and Christmases. He fits here. He's drying the last of my mom's china and stacking it up on the counter. The rest of the house is still as moonlight settles over the lawn.

"Lillie and Heather?" I ask.

"Shopping," he says as he drains some soapy water from the sink. "They're at a thing at Summit with your mom."

"My mom's shopping?"

"She'll probably stay in the car," he says, because he knows us.

"My dad?"

"Went to bed."

I nod. I'm not sure what to say next. Gratitude's probably the right thing, for him doing the dishes, for him doing all the things he does over Thanksgiving every year, for my stuffing and for Ethan's football-throwing and for not announcing to my cousins and aunts and uncles who love him that we're separate and have been for however long it's been now.

And he makes this easy for me, like he always has. "It was a long day," he says, putting the stack of dishes in their cabinet. "You're overwhelmed."

I agree I am, a little.

He hands me a couple DVD's that were sitting on the counter. "I thought you might want these tonight. I figured you left yours at home."

The top one's *Frasier*, Season 4, the one with "A Lillith Thanksgiving."

"There's Gatsby, too," he says.

I look at the other DVD. *The Great Gatsby* was on my passenger seat when I met Cam. I was reading it for a lit class I'd taken to fill an interdisciplinary requirement when I started grad school. I remember how he asked me about it when we had our first acai sorbet and peanut butter fudge split at the Dip the next week. I told him I liked the image of the eyes of Doctor T.J Eckleburg watching over the city, seeing everything. I'd always jotted in the margins when someone's eyes were mentioned and wondered how much they saw, if this was intentional on Fitzgerald's part, a piece of some puzzle he was making, some pattern he was trying to establish. My whole end-of-term paper was about eyes, from Fitzgerald to Austen. My professor gave me credit for effort, I think, even though he didn't see a pattern. But he was more concerned with God and sex and Hemingway. So maybe he missed it.

Cam's standing in front of me when I look up from the DVD. "I'll put it on?" he asks.

"Yes," I say, because this comes so easy.

We start with *Frasier*, how I always unwind from a holiday. Cam positions himself with our standard six inches of sofa cushion between us.

I think about *Frasier* instead of about my failed #FOMOing then, cataloging my favorite Niles lines and my list of Lilith episodes, cross-referencing this with my list of Frederick episodes, cross-referencing this with holidays.

Cam starts to talk to me once *Gatsby's* in and taking its time with music and close-ups of faces. He mutes the loud parts like always.

He asks about my cuttles and my applications, and I ask

about his winter menus and new suppliers, his holiday specials and the old cafe he's interested in buying on Market Street, the one across from the steakhouse. We used to take these easy conversations for granted, like crossing the Atlantic every year for blackpoll warblers or finding our natal beaches for loggerhead sea turtles, always sure of where we were going.

I see him watching me at one point in the middle of the movie like I'm someone new, like I might have turned into a different person over these months I haven't seen him.

I drink my water and consider whether I *am* different as Daisy runs down Myrtle like this isn't who she's been all along and everything spirals into tragedy. *Gatsby's* one of those stories that almost ended differently, that came close to being something else, something better.

The green light at the end of the dock's there again for the credits, bright and calling. It reminds me of the green dot next to Wes's name on my Social chat, this thing I never even noticed before late night epinephrine and misspellings and him.

Cam's leaning towards me when the screen goes dark, and I look at him with the green light a blind spot in the middle of my vision. This is the end of something, I think as he comes into my bubble.

I duck and put my forehead to his chest. For a breath, I don't move. I can still see the green dot behind my eyelids when I pull away.

*      *

I can finally eat again by brunch on Friday morning, scarfing down some uneventful pumpkin pancakes with Lillie and Heather before we drive home with our usual cooler full of leftovers. I leave the rest of my vegetarian stuffing in Mom's compost heap.

When we get home, I drop my bag in the hall and am jogging down the path between the timothy as the sun starts to drop lower into the clouds. There's a kind of orange tint to the light tonight that makes the locker rooms glow against all the gray like a threefin blenny.

The tennis courts are empty. Wes isn't here. He's changed his mind about me. But then, I've changed, too.

*          *

Saturday, I meet up with Jarod and show him as much of the city as I can in one day.

You can never see all of Cleveland in a single trip, can never really get a sense of what it is from just a handful of neighborhoods or even a bustling downtown festival. Cleveland's *A Christmas Story* and corned beef and fashion week, the Clinic and the museums of art and national history and the botanical garden, the Rapid and the metro parks and the garlic celebration Jarod's just missed. It's offshore turbines and sports, scientists and rock and rollers and sailors and doctors and upstarts of every kind.

We walk through the warehouse district to the flats, where there's revelry and fresh roots in the ruins of the old steel mills. Afterwards, I take him to a chic eatery Heather recommended on the East bank, where he tries the corned beef and I have some kind of artisanal salad. We watch people hurry by in the cold as we talk about the snow projections for this year and the things we like about estuaries.

"You know Florida has that center," Jarod says between bites of his sandwich. "They could be interested in a fellow."

I thank him and say something about the manatee populations in Silver River, because I've reached that point in my life when estuary desalination's a real concern. But I've already had a postdoc, already gone down this path. And I can only muster so much enthusiasm for desalination, for Milner's sea shrimp and Kikner's evolving river dolphin and all the other work that isn't mine.

"You'll apply to Penn?" Jarod asks, wiping some corned beef from the corner of his lip.

A perfect lip, I think, a perfect smile. It's what I saw the first time I met him, almost at the same time as the hummus, how perfect he was.

"Their department head's probably retiring soon," he says.

I nod, because this is my next step, Penn, another application, something else to throw myself into at least for the next week and a half.

"To fruit flies," I say, and raise my carrot juice in a toast.

He smiles, clinking his glass with mine.

Afterwards, we catch a water taxi to the West bank, huddled on deck with a crowd bracing against the wind.

"You know this place well," Jarod says as I settle onto a bench, and I agree. I don't know exactly when Cleveland became home to me, when I got to know all its rhythms. It's one of those cities that sucks you in, that makes you a local before you've really thought about it.

We're like Cleveland, though, always moving on, always going somewhere, growing or shrinking or becoming something else altogether. I'm not sure which of these I'm doing now or where I'll end up next.

We spend the afternoon walking around the West bank. We talk about the biggest controversies in ecology and biology in a friendly way there, unhindered by philosophy department linguistic concerns or the awkwardness that comes with romantic entanglements. We're two of a kind, I think, members of a noncompetitive species.

I remember he has an early flight tomorrow and probably not enough time for dinner. He should be full, anyway, from the corned beef, and a traditional Cleveland Polish boy would give him heartburn all the way over the prairie states. So I suggest we head home.

At his recommendation, we stop in at the aquarium on our way back. It's busy this weekend, full of children and exhausted parents and blue-vested employees with fake smiles speed-walking between the rooms.

We visit the penguins this time and sit for a little while watching a stationary spotted turtle before we settle in with the cuttles. They're acting normal today, like they weren't just considering mating on Tuesday night, like they really know what they're doing with the ends of their lives.

Bitty does a graceful dive with a loop at the end like a marine park dolphin, and a boy on the other side of the tank claps for her. She stops and flutters at him, her kind of bow. Are her mouth packets full of cuttle semen? Is she weighed down by these biological imperatives, weakened but ready to greet the last stage of her life with the same enthusiasm she shows for New Zealand green mussels and the most complicated mazes? There's noise on the platform overhead—almost time for their four pm feeding—and she zooms up to the surface.

We leave the room before Dave can see us, and Jarod drives me home and walks me to the door.

We exchange the usual niceties there, his thanks for the city tour and my interest in his job dilemma and his support for my applications. I think we mean these things.

When he leans towards me, I duck and wrap my arms around him to hug, instead, butt-neutral, and tell him this has been nice.

*          *

Sunday night, Heather goes straight to Matt's place once he gets back from Tennessee. When she comes home an hour later, she looks like she does in the trenches of breeding season when the mares are all foaling at once and her vets are off delivering calves, instead, and her undergrads are making out in the tack room and not paying attention to the monitors.

"I need to talk to you," she says as soon as the front door closes behind her. She flips on the orange pendant lights and pulls out a barstool, dropping her purse on the floor.

Since Lillie's out—somewhere—I've prepared to facilitate the ice cream and *that bastarding* myself.

"It's definitely over," Heather says.

I go for the freezer. I already have the bowls and spoons

out.

"I don't need ice cream. He apologized."

"That bastard," I say.

"About the someone else thing. I knew before, but I thought he'd get past it. It's why he was so distracted, so wishy-washy."

I look towards Lillie's room, where her constant harp music's on Christmas songs now. This is a post-Thanksgiving tradition. We always listen to the Christmas station on the drive home.

"But you still broke up with him?" I ask.

Heather nods. "Because you don't want somebody you're a second choice for," she says. She bends over the island, and I wonder for a second if she's about to transition into Lillie's sacred bendy-twisty.

I start to take up the ice cream.

"Nora, with your...I gave you bad advice," she says.

"You did?"

"With the walking," she says, "and the clothes, and..."

I pause, still holding the scooping spoon.

"We were talking about stingrays," she reminds me.

"Stingrays?"

She waves a hand. It's bare, like she's just come from the barn, free of all the rings and bracelets she usually puts on for dating armor. "The swaying. It's not your thing. And you shouldn't do *not* your thing for...You're not a stingray, Nora. You're like...a tiger shark. So next time Wes, or..." Her voice trails off.

"Jarod?"

"Jarod, or Milner or anybody else...next time you feel like

you have to change something so they'll act a certain way, remember they're just little fish, and you're a big, toothy tiger shark. You don't have to waste your energy trying to make them feel comfortable."

I evaluate, looking between the ice cream and her.

"Screw being a sexy stingray. They have to show up for *you*, and if they don't..."

"I destroy them," I guess, with my twenty-four identical incisors.

Heather opens her mouth, then closes it again, then looks at the ice cream tub.

"Yes," she says, when she gets up to get her bowl, "because they're...tilapia. And you're a fucking tiger shark."

*       *

Monday afternoon, I feel like I really am a tiger shark on my way to confront Milner—not because Milner will change something about his behavior or because I need an apology, but because I'm ending a decade of taking out his trash.

When I got a sore throat last night, Lillie had me write down everything I was holding inside me as an exercise, a letter of grievances to open my throat chakra. I was supposed to email it to myself but not to send it to Milner. So here I am, just before his two pm seminar, ready to deliver it verbally. And I feel, for the first time in this building, maybe one of the last times I'll ever have a reason to be in this hallway, like this space beyond the women's restroom really could be mine.

Milner's not in his office, where trash has piled up all

around the perimeter. I leave it and dodge a herd of undergrads as I make my way to the classrooms on the other side of the building. One of his teaching assistants is standing outside the lecture hall.

The TA turns away when he sees me. He's one of the ones in his fourth year. He plays ping pong with Milner and Kyle sometimes and doesn't talk to me.

"Milner?" I ask.

"Not here." He avoids eye contact, looking at a bulletin taped to the wall about free STD testing.

"Where is he?"

The TA's face reddens. Maybe I sound like a tiger shark now, too.

"He's getting ready. For his interview. For the IMRI fellowship," he says. "At home. Because it's tomorrow."

So I leave the TA and Milner's overflowing trash and rush through the double doors and out into the wind. I jog through the courtyard without putting on my coat, and my heart's racing when I get to my car and open my email. Because I can copy and paste my letter and get this out of my system one way or the other.

But there's an email in bold at the top of my list. It's from an address I don't recognize. I have to read it twice, check the domain name and then read it again. It's from the chair of the IMRI board congratulating me on being a finalist for the fellowship and saying I have an interview a week from Thursday.

# Chapter 17

*At some point in its evolution, the flamboyant cuttlefish got tired of reefs and predators and moved to the ocean floor. Now, it uses its tentacles to walk around and a potent neurotoxin to destroy anything that disturbs its peace.*

While I wait for my IMRI interview, I dig a new rut with the Penn application. This isn't a transition, isn't gradual or careful or smooth. This is a full reset.

My internet window's sparsely populated with tabs now, no more Academic-A lists or journals. I spend my time reading teaching philosophies and sample syllabi, instead. Jarod texts me every now and then with tips on how to write my own.

I avoid my lab this week, working in different places. This is how you establish a new pattern, like how you'd overcome an addiction, changing everything to change the thing that matters. My first workspace is our living room, listening to Lillie's *Pride and Prejudice* DVD on repeat in the background.

I swap my macaroni for butternut squash ravioli before

heading to the aquarium for quick visits with the cuttles over Dave's lunch breaks, when I tell them not to die, always trying to ignore Barbara and waving at George on my way out.

I spend afternoons in the engineering building's cafe. You can tell the semester's winding down there, students spreading out with books and caffeine and late-term effort. The baristas hand out to-go mugs, steaming lattes and mochas that make that distinctive finals week smell that wafts all the way down to the lecture halls. By the middle of the week, there are paper snowflakes hanging from the ceiling and red and gold tinsel wound around the support beams.

I don't cross the courtyard anymore. Milner hasn't emailed me since his IMRI interview, and only Heather and Lillie know about mine next week. I try not to think about this like I try not to think about my lamps yet, and my books, and all the other things I'll have to clear out of my lab before the break.

I tell myself the Penn application is in the #FOMOing spirit, too, trying something different, losing myself in new work. By Friday, it's at least starting to feel familiar. I've worked some neuroscience into my sample syllabus for freshmen biology and cuttlefish cognition into my teaching philosophy.

In the evenings, I walk across the sports complex and sit in my favorite booth at Indigo Dreams with a cup of chamomile tea. I breathe in the crème brulee and wear my headphones and pretend I'm not looking for anyone as I make edits. It helps to keep working, to not think too much.

When I start to think, I read the affirmations app Lillie put on my phone, instead. These are increasingly unhelpful.

Like today's, *I wait patiently for the future.*

*          *

December doesn't really hit me until Saturday, when I finally have a solid draft of my Penn application and it's time to decorate our Christmas tree. This is a house tradition, a flash of brightness in the darkness of early December.

We start, as always, by gorging on the last of the frozen Thanksgiving leftovers and whipped cream from the can. Then we go through the traditions we wanted to keep from our childhood holidays—the old choral Christmas music of Heather's that plays through the TV's speakers and Lillie's giant, multi-colored string lights she brought with her from California that we worry each year won't turn on. My contribution is a Frasier Fir likeness that looks like the ones my family used to get before my mom and I were able to recognize contact dermatitis. This one lives in the hall closet and is PVC-free.

While we untangle the lights, conversation comes easily, like it always does. This is one of those sacred, peaceful nights when we avoid talk about things like men and wayward Morgans.

Before we start decorating, we trade ornaments in our usual circle. Heather gives Lillie another crystal pendant—chrysoprase this year for fresh beginnings in love—and I give Heather her traditional blown glass horse, this one wearing a bikini.

Lillie's gotten me a new sea creature, a tiger shark with glitter on its fins. I lay out the shark with all my other ornaments—the cuttlefish, the vampire squid, the blue whale, the dumbo octopus, the frilled shark, and the narwhal.

As we decorate the tree, I hum along to the music and think about all the Christmases I've spent in this house. I remember that first cuttlefish year, with bubbly grape juice and Heather's new position, and the frilled shark year, with Lillie's appendicitis and our ornament exchange in the emergency room. I think of the new, non-buzzy lights just as I was moving in, of all the cork flooring going in my second year, of the orange pendants we installed ourselves over the course of a long, snowed-in weekend just before my dissertation defense, and countless pizza nights and ice cream emergencies in between. Seven Christmases go by quickly.

Before we put on the star, Heather hands me a little red bag. This is a break in our usual pattern; we don't unwrap gifts until the 23rd.

"We thought you might want it early," she tells me. "It's to replace the card on your door."

I move some tissue paper aside and pull out a long gold bar like the one outside Milner's office. This one says *Dr. Nora Novak* in a simple script. Not *N.A. Novak,* like the disintegrating paper card outside my lab and my paper submissions, "not applicable," as Heather always said. The colored lights shimmer on the gold when I hold it up to the tree.

I thank them, running my fingers over the inscription as Lillie climbs up on the sofa and secures the star to the top branch. We turn off all the other lights then and sip hot chocolate in the glow of the tree, laughing about the oddities of this year as we share a tray of Lillie's homemade marshmallows.

The sports complex is dark now, and the window just shows the colored beads of light from the tree. When I catch my reflection in it, I wonder if the person I was seven years ago would recognize me now.

A couple hours later, I'm sitting up in bed reading through my cover letter to Penn again as the stadium lights start to flicker across the park. Maybe the university's having an event of some kind, like a finals week frisbee tournament, but I think of Wes out playing in the cold instead, of his breath clouding in front of his face and the steady progression of pops echoing off the locker rooms.

I'm still looking out the window when Lillie knocks on my door.

"I'm heading out," she tells me. "I thought you might want the rest of the marshmallows." She has them on a little snowman plate with a few dark chocolate pieces like the ones I used to eat in grad school.

I take it and thank her. "You're going out?" I ask.

She nods and bends into partial *plié*.

"With Matt?"

"Matt," Lillie says, dropping straight into a lotus in my doorway. "Matt?"

So I remind her about the messages he left on her phone and tell her I saw guilt on his face that first time I met him, wrapped up in her blue chenille blanket and supposedly waiting for Heather, and then again the night of Heather's sister's wedding.

Meanwhile, she appears fascinated by the seam in a cork

floorboard.

"You're going to tell Heather?" I ask.

Her face crinkles into a frown like a walrus. "I already told Heather," she says. "I'm going out with Gregg."

"Gregg," I echo.

"Gregg," Lillie confirms. "You remember him, don't you? From the vet's office?"

*Gregg*, I remember—Gregg the vet tech, the non-programmer, the stranger Lillie almost destroyed with her karmic death ray when he tried to touch my rat. "*Gregg* is the guy you're seeing?" I ask it like this is possible, like rat boogers could provide fertile ground for romance.

Lillie nods. "He's stopping in to see Scribbles first."

I look between her and the bunny supreme that sits fully erect on my nightstand. *Gregg*. Then I think of the multiple antibiotic flavors, the rat echinacea, and her continued insistence on keeping Scribbles in her room. I missed all of it. I never even considered Gregg.

"Matt did ask me out," she offers after a few seconds. "He'd had a...a thing for me, I guess, for a while, and he came here after Ned told him about the breakup that night you were watching a movie with Wes. I told Heather right away."

"You turned him down?"

Lillie folds inward and flattens herself against my doorframe like an offended sunfish. "Of course I did."

"Because of Heather?"

"Because of both of them," she says. Then she turns pink as she tells me about Gregg, about how the piña colada flavoring was all his idea and how much Scribbles likes him now, about how different he is than Ned and Matt and all the others.

Of course it's expected that he would be different than the programmers. He's not Lillie's type. I want to ask her how this feels, if it strikes her as wrong, breaking a pattern she spent so many years establishing. Until tonight, I thought Lillie's patterns were incorruptible, that she was unchangeable like the blockchain.

But when she finishes telling me about Gregg, she's smiling a dreamy kind of xygomatic smile, looking up at my bunny supreme from her lotus. I think about my own patterns, about my own kind, then, for not very long before I think about *not* my kind again, about Wes.

The stadium lights are still on half an hour later. It's too cold to go out and run. My phone says the high tomorrow's only twelve. So I read through my cover letter to Penn again before I print and sign it. I write out "Nora" for the first time and feel like "N.A." is someone else.

*     *

The next couple days of the Penn application are monotonous, and my teaching philosophy and syllabus come along steady like the constant gray that waxes and wanes through the windows. The university's in its last days of final exams, and the buildings are all clearing out for winter break. Most of the hallways are quiet, and the cafe keeps running out of cookies.

Tuesday, I print out what's left of my application in the engineering department. After I mail it, I head back to the house and bundle up in my warmest thermal leggings and the jacket Heather says looks like it was a flotation device on the Love Boat.

My lungs hurt, and it's almost dark by the time I've gotten to the tennis courts. I've been jogging at odd hours lately and haven't seen Wes at all. There are no signs of life at the soccer fields, either, no more of his Sunday games until spring.

The cold goes straight through me, stinging my cheeks when I pass the locker rooms. I loop the whole complex twice before my phone beeps with another affirmation, *I follow my heart in all things.* When I get home, I silence the app.

*       *

Wednesday, with Penn out of the way, I switch gears again. I get up early and go back to my IMRI notes, to blind hope and stumpy cuttlefish. My google calendar has a bar lit up in red for my interview at one tomorrow, ominous and dark like a scorpionfish. I've checked and double-checked the video-chatting service on my laptop, and there's a constant, subtle pressure around my chest like a too-tight bra.

It's icing, a steady pattering against my bedroom window as I study more cuttle distribution maps through the afternoon. I don't know how else to get ready for the interview; there's no research to know, nothing to have memorized but my own qualifications and what I've learned about maze-navigating cuttlefish that probably have very different goals than the ones off Eastern Australia. I wonder how many other careers ever come down to this, to hour-long interviews and perceived competence about lesser-known species in far-away places.

I ignore my phone when Jarod calls in the middle of the afternoon, too busy to muster the extra social reserve. He tries again just before I eat dinner and leaves a voicemail this time.

I listen to it as I wait for the kettle to brew with my nighttime tea. I've been going through a new blend of vanilla rooibos Lillie found, another pattern I'm changing. There are enough things that are different now, it's almost hard to keep track, to remember what I was doing before.

I put the voicemail on speaker when the blue light of the kettle kicks off. Jarod says he was hoping to talk to me. Northwestern's just offered him an incredible opportunity, a project studying subarctic ecosystems he's been after for a long time. So he'll be there instead of at Case next year. He'd really like to keep in touch, he says, and trusts I'll be doing something great, too.

When I listen again, I note how the ends of his sentences slow down, what sounds like disappointment in his voice. Probably I should feel the same way. But there's no disappointment in me; I'm happy for him.

As I'm eating my ravioli, I text my congratulations and say the project sounds perfect for him.

He responds right away. *Thanks a lot, Nora. You're ready for Penn?*

*I sent it yesterday,* I tell him, then, *I interview for IMRI tomorrow.*

The dots barely undulate. *Holy shit,* he says, *that's incredible!*

*Thanks.*

*You've got to put that on your CV right away,* he tells me, *that you were a finalist. It'll give you a huge boost at Penn.*

I thank him, but this doesn't do much for me, Penn and the prospect of taking over as the reigning fruit fly queen. I walk back to my room and watch the cuttle maps load up again, splashes of various shades of purple across my screen.

And as I go through them, I think of my dad's backup plans, of all the flat tire warnings and forwarded emails, all the platitudes for when the thing you want doesn't pan out. I've taken the career precautions now, and I have a plan B, but all the eggs I really want are still in one basket. I want to ace this interview more than I want all of my routines—because of blind hope and wild cuttles, and not because of my CV and everyone it might impress. I haven't thought about Olunsen and Kikner, or even about Milner, for days.

*You have to tell me what it's like*, Jarod says, and then I think he's as excited as I am as he starts talking about all the people on the board, the kinds of questions they might ask, and how great it will be to video chat with all of them at once.

*I'll text you after*, I promise.

The dots undulate for a while this time as I zoom in on the giant cuttlefish populations off Brisbane.

*I was disappointed we won't be in the same area next year*, he says. *I'd really like to keep in touch, Nora.*

*I'd like that, too*, I write, and mean it. My heart bubbler doesn't weigh in.

*I'll be thinking about you tomorrow*, he says. *You know there's a chance that Stark'll even be there.*

I think about Lillian Stark and about whales then, about long odds and wild cuttles as I stare into the maps, leaving Jarod with a thumbs up.

Late that evening, when the purples of my maps are starting to blur together in a kind of blue light filter sunset, Lillie and Heather come for a pre-interview pep talk.

They've already thought of everything that could go wrong. They're worried about my lack of sleep, of course, and about my digestion that might be affected by nerves. I should wear a dark shirt, they tell me, that's loose and can breathe, and a bra I'm comfortable in, probably that neither Heather nor my mom would approve of for any other occasion. Lillie's spritzing a soothing lavender mist all over my room.

"Remember, you're a tiger shark," Heather says.

"And don't apologize," Lillie adds. "You know more about cuttles than any of the people interviewing you."

I nod.

"You're gonna do it from here?" Heather asks. "Not the lab?"

"Yes," I tell her, because this environment can be controlled, can be guaranteed Kyle-free. I show them my desk, clear now that I've stacked all my journals up against the far wall.

Lillie nods. "I'll be home by two," she says. "I'm going to take Scribbles' wheel out before I go into work so it doesn't squeak."

I thank her and show her my new headphones, because I've already thought of this. They have a little microphone on the cord and should cancel out everything I don't need to hear, helping me focus ahead like those hoods the Morgans wear when they go driving so they don't see the cart chasing them.

"Perfect," Lillie says.

Then there's a pause. Heather looks at Lillie. Lillie looks at the floor.

"Lillie?" I ask.

Lillie lotuses in my doorway, and Heather gives a half-hearted snort.

"Scribbles is okay," Lillie says first.

"We wanted to tell you in case you get online tomorrow," Heather says.

I wait. Heather climbs onto my desk chair, crossing her legs and leaning forward over a knee like she does when her hamstrings get stuck after too long in the saddle. Lillie remains lotused but avoids eye contact. I think she picked this up from my rat.

"It's Wes," Heather tells me. "He was on the radio. I caught it a couple hours ago. I'll email you a link with the recording I took, but I think you probably don't want to listen to it until after your interview, okay?"

"It's nothing bad," Lillie adds.

They're both looking at me how we looked at Lillie when we thought she might have her post-Ned meltdown. I guess we must be close to my breakdown, if it hasn't happened already. Or maybe it's a slow leak. Maybe waves of these will just keep coming until I'm a puddle of patternless postgraduate goo.

Lillie weaves her fingers together the way she does before her upside-down-bendy-flippy. "It's just that he's going to be staying in town," she tells me, "doing a community program thing. He had some kind of chronic injury with his knee..."

"...that doesn't make him any less of an asshole," Heather adds. "It's not an excuse, and you still don't have to talk to him."

"We just thought you should know," Lillie finishes.

I thank them, but they don't move. I look back at my window. There aren't any lights over the sports complex tonight. It's damp out, well below freezing, dropping some snowflakes every now and then. They're the sneaky kind you don't notice until they start to stick to the grass.

I talk to my reflection for a bit, reassuring my roommates that Wes's choice to stay in town won't impact my emotional state, interview confidence, or digestive motility, which apparently Lillie has a separate tea for, and eventually, they leave me with a big mug of valerian on my nightstand and several assurances that I don't need it.

I only stay up a little while after, sipping the valerian and looking out the window. Jarod texts just before I go to bed with encouragement and a squid emoji, and then there's an email from my mom with a link to a makeup tutorial on youtube.

I don't click on the email from Heather with Wes's interview, and I tell myself this is right, that I can face the end of this #FOMO alone.

# Chapter 18

*Whether it's the end of a maze or shrimp in a jar or a diver's gloves, if a cuttlefish wants something enough, it will <u>always</u> find a way.*

I sleep in until after eight. When I wake up, the sun's breaking through the clouds and pooling over my comforter. The sky's a brilliant blue like deep ocean in the South Pacific.

I rush for no reason at the beginning, dumping too many flax seeds into my morning oatmeal and pulling on mismatched socks. I'm wrapped up in my big orange parka and outside by nine.

The cold doesn't sting today, and the complex is empty, no scuffling of shoes or pops of tennis balls or shouts from the soccer fields. It reminds me of how it used to be when I'd run in the evenings, the wind buzzing through the fences and my head full of maze times.

I run a few extra laps at a pace I'm not thinking about, then take a shower with the oatmeal scrub Lillie left out for me. I guess this is a time I could be itchy, that big interviews are like first dates, something you have to shed your outer skin before or it pulls and tugs at you like a too-tight sweater all the time you're trying to grow.

Afterwards, I get dressed and open the cuttle distribution maps, but I know these by heart . So I go through turtle and whale species in my head as I re-check the view from my computer camera, the bunny supreme now hidden under my bed.

Around eleven, when I'm pacing circles in the kitchen, I turn on *Frasier* and eat a butternut squash ravioli with some ginger tea Lillie's already put in the strainer for me. She left a note out on the counter saying I should add ginkgo for concentration, but it feels like I might actually be *too* concentrated now, like I need to spread out like algal bloom and settle into myself somehow.

I turn off *Frasier* after a couple episodes. Outside my window, some cumulus clouds are rolling in, starting to turn over each other like the ravioli in my stomach.

I check my Social, where there aren't any green dots, and my email. The university's sent out a few messages, updates about holiday hours and closing times for the food services and parking lots that need to be cleared out over the break. There are always these disruptions around the end of the year, little delays and changed patterns.

Heather's email's just below the first one from the university. I look up at the clock. It's only 11:52.

When I click on her link, it's Wes' voice that comes through my speakers. I recognize it before the end of his second word, his diphthongs and his funny vowels.

I press the space bar to pause and then find the button to rewind. The same line plays again.

"'s a good opportunity."

Heather must have started recording somewhere in the middle of the interview. Like how I found him, in the middle of something, while I was in the middle of something else.

"And does that mean you'll be staying in the area?" a voice asks, one of those deep, boomy ones that makes my laptop speakers buzz. "For the foreseeable?"

There's a pause. "For the foreseeable," Wes says.

"Well," the voice says, "young ladies of Cleveland, I hope you're listening."

There's no response, a longer pause this time.

"Can you tell us a little about what brought this on? It came as, you know, a surprise to a lot of us, I have to tell you, that we're not gonna be seeing you out there playing next year."

Wes takes "a little" the literal way I knew he would, with something vague about his knee injury.

"So maybe next year?" the voice presses, because he can't hear that the rhythm of Wes's voice is off, doesn't recognize the breaks at the wrong times. "If there's a change in your knee, you'll get back to playing?"

"Don't think so."

"So you're done, then? Are you saying...Is this the end of your career?"

Wes doesn't respond right away, and I can hear his shrug more clearly than the early thunder that rattles my window.

"You've got to move on sometime, yeh?"

"Yeah?" the voice asks. "Well, *yeah*, then, and our gain, too." He sounds like the men in commercials talking about vehicle overstock or free products with only extra shipping and handling or unprecedented opportunities in the gold market.

"Now, you'll be running this with Frank Brooks, is that right? Who was your coach in...what year was it?"

"Yeh," Wes says.

"And it sounds like this is gonna be a very different kinda program than we've seen here, something modeled after one you had growing up in Melbourne. Is that right? Can you tell me more about that?"

"'s for everybody," Wes says. "You don't separate out the men and the women, kids and older people or people with special needs, people playin for fun or for exercise or to compete."

The other voice elaborates more on the program, reading through some subsides for low-income players and opportunities connected with the university's sports camps and a club downtown for disadvantaged youth.

"And what a treat for our community," he says at the end of this, "to have you and Frank here spearheading this."

Wes doesn't respond.

The voice keeps going. "We're really glad you agreed to talk to us today, Wesley. Now our live feed's really piling up here. If you'll take a look at all these questions...like will you personally be coaching?"

"Yeh."

"Wow, great. And the private lessons, are those just for competitive players?"

"No."

"And there are all these questions you see coming in about you personally. Can I ask you about that? Are you seeing somebody special?"

There's a pause, a breath. Maybe it's my breath.

"Somebody at all?" the voice asks. "Like this post from Brittany says..."

"Yeh," Wes says, then, just when I don't expect him to, "I was."

I miss what the voice says next, listening to slow thunder and the blood rushing between my ears. My energy has a pulse now. It starts in my feet tapping on the cork and pushes up through the rest of me.

"...we tell our listeners you're ready to get back out there and..."

"No." It's a hard stop at the end of Wes's voice this time, no long *o* sound that almost turns into an *r* like they usually do.

The voice makes a kind of throat-clearing grunt like a *Haemulon plumierii*. "No?" he asks. "Well, then, she must have been somebody special, huh?"

There's a long pause this time. Outside, it starts to rain.

I think he's finished talking when he says, "Yeh."

"You want to give her a shout out? Maybe she's listening."

It's like the sound's died for a second then, just the rain hitting my window, before Wes comes back through my speakers. "I fucked up."

"Well, that's..." the voice trails off, losing its boom.

I hear it in my chest then like a bass drum, steady now, strong and bubble-free.

Wes doesn't say anything, and it's louder somehow than everything else, than all the noises inside me or outside my window or coming through my speakers.

"So it's complicated," the voice says eventually,

recovering, like this voice could possibly know complicated, like this voice could possibly know Wes.

I don't hear the rest of the conversation, the boomy voice that keeps on going or the heating system or the cars chugging by outside my window, splashing through the puddles along the sides of the road. I just sit and watch the recording run out of its sound lines and listen to my heart keep beating.

My heart's a steady, driving rhythm by the time the interview starts, and I forget about Lillie's tea as I focus on my screen.

A new box appears with a face each time one of the IMRI board members asks a question. It's a kind of pop-up game like those pastel groundhogs at the arcade my dad took me to for my eighth birthday—one face, one question after another. I aim for speed, watching the foreheads as they appear and ignoring eyebrows, wrinkles, and oddly-shaped hairlines.

The questions come at steady rhythm, about my data pool and how I'd document the cuttles I encountered in Australia, how many species I'd expect to track and how long it might take me in each coastal area.

I'm the last person they're interviewing, so they know all the questions. And I know all these answers. I can respond quickly. My legs pump under the desk, my running shoes tapping on the cork, ready to go somewhere.

A balding man with a thick German accent pops up. "You'd need a small team of divers," he says. "You would be comfortable with the management?"

"Yes." This is one of the rare times I know without having

to look in a mirror that my face matches my nod and my words.

"You'd expect to use the full three months," another head says—American, East Coast accent, receding hairline.

I explain why I might need this time for flexibility. We don't know what cuttles will be where, when it might be worthwhile to follow one population and when it will be better to move on. So I'd need accommodations with broad date ranges in several coastal towns, divers willing to travel, and no home base.

The man's lip twitches like my dad's when I finish.

Another head with blonde hair pops up. "And would you be comfortable staying in these arrangements, in places you haven't been before? As..." He clears his throat. "Is safety a concern for you?"

I tell him I'd make myself comfortable, spouting off some statistics Heather compiled about the lack of crime in Australia and their advanced healthcare system should I scrape myself on some pretty zonathid coral or swim into an irukandji.

The blonde guy's still up. "It's possible we'd need someone to take a look at accommodations and give some insight into safety," he says. He sounds British.

"I'd plan to collect a lot of information on each area ahead of time," I tell him. This isn't fear. I'm not blustering, not guessing, not afraid to travel on my own now that I've seen my cuttles about to mate and done a full-blown #FOMO. Today, even an irukandji wouldn't scare me. So I don't have to hide anything on my face. "I'd need to talk with local fisheries and tour companies to find the best dive locations, and I expect they'd be able to guide me with respect to accommodations, as well."

The head nods. "So there's nothing you can foresee that would prevent your being able to work there on your own."

"Nothing." I blink when no other heads pop up right away. Little light spots drift behind my eyelids like fluttering cuttles. This pause is long, and my legs stop pumping.

Then a woman's face appears in the box, and my jaw drops like a hungry whale shark.

"Nora, there's something here that complicates this a little, and I'd like to know what you think about it. Timothy Milner applied for this position, as well."

She waits. I nod. It takes me a few seconds, but I remember to close my mouth.

"I believe he was your advisor," she says.

My "yes" comes out softer this time, scratchy in my throat.

"He was also a finalist," she tells me. "You're familiar with his research on desalination, I think."

"Yes," I say, a little stronger. I'm more than familiar. And I wonder if she'll ask me about this next, if I'd be the person assisting on Milner's project like I did on the paper he applied with.

"Good," she says. "I'm wondering if this could potentially cause some discord in your relationship. Do you have any concerns about that should you receive a fellowship and he does not?"

I think of Wes, but it's my voice in my head that screams, with no apology at all, "*fuck him.*"

"No," I say, sure this time. "That wouldn't affect me." My

mitral valve holds steady, and I let my face say "fuck him" for me.

Then Lillian Stark—this woman who once shut down one of the best-funded military projects in history, this woman who single-handedly saved several species when women themselves were rare species even in the liberal arts departments—smiles at me.

"That's good to hear," she says, "and Nora, I'm very excited to see what you do with this."

Some time later, my screen saver's showing its endangered species, fading out on Hector's dolphin. I'm still in my chair, stunned like a cold loggerhead, except blood's rushing through me, pounding in my ears and shimmying along my limbs like I'm in the middle of my last loop around the soccer fields in the August heat.

It takes a while for me to catch my breath, to catch my thoughts. Then I'm waking up my laptop, closing the empty video chat window and starting up a browser. Social seems slow now, but there's a green dot next to Wes's name when messenger finally loads.

*Thank you*, I write him. And maybe I should explain why, before I text the people I promised to. Maybe I should tell him his advice was helpful or that he was the only one who told me I should do this, or that it meant a lot to me, this relationship-or-not, whatever it was, that changed me.

My hands hover over the keys, considering typing something without me. In the end, I just add, *I got the fellowship.*

I stare into the green dot until the check mark appears

next to it. *Read at 2:17*, it says.

I stick around until 2:20, watching it, but Wes doesn't type anything. The undulating dots never show up.

I'm about to run when Lillie catches me at the door.


I'm running fifteen minutes later, jogging past a tour of coughing kids in the shark tunnel and a new interactive screen by the stingray tank.

Around us, everyone else seems to be rushing, too, the way they do in December. There are too many voices in this room, too many smells, too many heartbeats.

*Black-tipped reef shark, white-tipped reef shark, mako, great white, hammerhead, bonnethead…*

My legs keep pumping when we get to the little staff-only hallway between Barbara's tank and the cuttles.

*Sandbar, Galapagos, Port Jackson, Bizant River…*

Around me, all the noises blur together as I lean into the tank. I have to squint to see them, the spattering of inky eggs clinging to the seagrass that dips and waves in the current.

*Blue, gray, lemon, dusky, silky…*

Dave's babbling the way he does—about their unexpected discovery, about the tank he's getting ready to move them to, about the things he's read on cuttle development—and when he says "nursery," it hits me. My cuttles are having babies. This is the end, another beginning, an appropriate time to hurl my butternut squash ravioli all the way to the stingray tank.

*Cookiecutter, frilled, nurse, angel…*

To my left, Lillie's devolved into a steady cooing, all vowel sounds like a plain midshipman fish with the diaphragmic endurance of an opera singer. Behind us, Barbara moves in slow circles, watching through her window, probably wondering what all the fuss is about. Steve's head peeks around the corner occasionally like a scrawny moray eel on the lookout for an octopus. Dave just keeps talking.

*Zebra, goblin, porbeagle, bull, tiger...*

My heart bubbler continues its high-frequency buzzing in my chest until Bitty comes over and taps on the glass with a tentacle. She's telling me to focus, of course. I need to focus now.

*Spinner, sharpnose, broadnose sevengill...*

There's so much to be done, so much to be researched, so much to learn still. This is no time, I tell Bitty, or myself, for any kind of meltdown.

*Basking, whale, horned, pelagic thresher, bigeye thresher...*

"...so I was thinking by the jellyfish," Dave's saying now, about their hatching spot. "If you wanted to be here when..."

I stop the beginning of a recitation of the sharks at double-time, two species in time with each step. "I'll be here," I tell him. It's a good thing I don't leave for the fellowship until late August, the start of spring in Australia.

I think of everything there is to do before these eggs hatch, of everything Dave can't be trusted with, of how I can't fit *white-tipped reef shark* and *black-tipped reef shark* back to back without slowing down my feet.

Dave keeps talking, and Lillie turns her cooing on Barbara, who she's designated an "auntie."

I survey the cuttle tank and take a quick inventory of parental health, slowing down my feet. Dot flutters around some anemones. Franklin burrows deeper into the sand in his favorite spot, where he's built up a little mound. They're acting like this kind of thing happens every day. It takes me a while to process this, to take a full breath and shut up Dave and get control of my voice.

When I do, I order the cuttles mussels (de-shelled, obviously) and pre-pulled crab. Now—*right now*, because of course they'll need more protein. And the skimmer, an extra of those, and the bubblers, and...

I stop thinking on *bonnethead* when Heather rounds the corner with Steve trailing behind her. Steve's flailing like when I met him, pointing at a "staff only" sign, obviously unaware he's no match for someone who's used to handling horny Morgans.

Wes pushes past him, and it's Wes my eyes settle on then, Wes who gets to me first.

I forget *sandbar* even as Barbara swims by, and then everything else around me slows down, too—Barbara, Lillie and Heather, Dave's voice. These moments barely move, like waking up in bed with a yogurt-smeared stranger or kissing in the late November cold. There are voices still, all half time now, talking about eggs and ink and life cycles.

I don't say anything, because I don't know what to say, and time doesn't go back to normal until Heather pulls me away. The others school together like hammerheads then, leaving Wes standing alone.

Heather tugs me past the seagrass, where Dot's swimming in circles.

"He came to the house," she tells me. It's a hiss like a whisper, but it pounds in my head, loud. "He was looking for you, and your phone was off for your interview still, and Lillie had just texted after Dave..."

I look back at Wes. Wes is looking at me.

Heather taps me on the shoulder. Her eyes are Morgan-breach-birth wide. "Is that...okay?" she asks. "That he's here? He wouldn't..."

My feet stop. I must have been holding my breath. I forgot *spinner*. "Okay," I tell Heather. "I'm okay."

She stares. Probably I don't look very okay. Then she nods and squares her shoulders like she does on the Tuesday night each March when she has to teach her students how to peel the dead skin off a horse penis.

When Barbara drifts by again, Heather's voice joins the others in a kind of hushed blur I can't differentiate anymore.

Only Wes is quiet. I walk up to him, and we both turn to face the cuttle tank. I think first of tiger sharks and all the things I should be asking him now, about why he didn't respond to me before and why he decided to come to the house today.

He has things to say, too, I can tell. But these words can come later, if they still matter now that he's here.

My head voices all quiet down when Bitty flutters over. She looks at Wes, then at me. I can smell him over all the fish and the carpet shampoo and the people and the butternut squash ravioli turning over in my stomach. But I can't hear anything except for my heart in my ears.

Bitty does a back flip and touches the glass with one of her tentacles.

I'm out of sharks now. Wes's hand brushes against mine. This time, I don't pull away.

# Epilogue

*As soon as they hatch, cuttlefish know how to make good choices. When given a chance to go through a door with four shrimp, for instance, or one with five, they'll always choose the right direction.*

February comes on a Sunday with a blanket of fresh snow. A blizzard blows through in the early hours of the morning just ahead of the unexpected arrival of Heather's first foal of the season.

I used to think we'd get used to surprises like this, by some age, but they seem to just keep coming, always catching us at least a little off guard.

The filly's wrapped up in a blanket now in a straw pen, and we're in the middle of a breakfast to celebrate her arrival. Maybe this will turn into a pattern, too, pancakes in the early dark of February mornings. Like Wes, beside me, is part of my pattern now.

It took us a while to establish this, to sort through how close we came to not knowing each other at all. Like how upset he was after his doctor's visit and how he saw me with Jarod afterwards, when he was coming over to apologize for not responding at the tennis courts, and the way we both used to think that some things—complicated things like human relationships—are too much work to unravel.

Apparently humans couple a lot like sea shrimp; there's more than one variable that matters. But Wes and I both do more choosing than falling, so our environmental conditions didn't make as much of a difference as they might have.

It's 7:26 when Dave calls my phone. Then everything's abandoned, maple syrup left congealing on blueberry pancakes and a bowl of batter dribbling over the edge of the counter. We all move slowly, it seems like, but we must be rushing. These are moments that pause, that freeze everything else going on around them.

Outside, it's that lake effect cold that doesn't hit you right away, the kind that gradually squeezes in through the crevices in your bones and pools in your abdomen and your toes. We pile into Heather's SUV and blast the defrosters.

The drive to the aquarium's long on back roads that have just been drizzled with beet juice. Little bits of pink dot the plow lines at the curbs. The rest of the snow's still pristine in the headlights. In a few hours, the church traffic will pepper it with exhaust. In a few hours, the cuttles' eggs will all be empty.

I note the street signs as we pass, not recognizing Gardenia or Brookhurst. I'll remember them next time. Our brains are funny like that, going on high alert, zeroing in on little things, on too many things at once in these important times, looking for a saber-toothed tiger or a stampede of bison when all there is are street signs and headlights and softly falling snow.

We use my key fob to get in the front door of the aquarium and rush by some dark displays and through the shark tunnel, George trailing behind us. I don't look at the cuttles' empty tank this time when we pass by.

On the other side of a heavy door at the back of the jellyfish cave, the nursery's quiet. Barbara looks in on us through her window, drifting soundlessly through the darkness.

Dave starts saying things, the way he does when silence would be better, but these words aren't what I need to process.

I lean into the glass and don't see them at first. Then my eye catches movement over one of the blades of seagrass, a tiny cuttlefish climbing out of its inky egg and buzzing up to the surface. Some other egg casings are already drifting in the current, empty.

Once I focus on one baby, I can see all the others. It alters my field of vision, like when von Leeuwenhoek looked through his microscope and saw bacteria for the first time and suddenly, everything changed.

There are too many cuttles to count, miniature versions of their parents that flutter and buzz and float along in a current like the lazy river at the amusement park. Some walk on the bottom, the way they might in the ocean to evade predators, little specs already blending in with the sand. Others weave between the seagrass, making themselves into leafy appendages. One faces the current bar head on, pushing against the water with all its might, like van Leeuwenhoek— fearless, determined, even with all the odds stacked against him.

There are things about odds I can't help but think now. Like how it's the wrong season for cuttlefish to be hatching, like the end of November was the wrong time for their parents to mate before they passed on to the great, unbleached reef in the sky. But these cuttles don't know their arrival wasn't perfect, that the world's anything but theirs to discover.

One stops just in front of my face, turning a light pink to match my flush. I think it looks at me with Bitty's expression, raising little purple bumps like she used to in the maze.

My eyes refocus on the room then, and there's everything to do at once. There are water samples to take, another tank to prepare. The newborns will need to have something to eat—as many options as we can give them, I tell Dave. You never know what will make a difference, what will stick. They'll have ideas about what they want from the shrimp and eel and crab I had him wheel by their eggs on rotation, but they can always change their minds.

I take a breath. Bitty II flutters closer to the glass, where the current's weaker. She flashes pink and peach in lazy waves.

Lillie coos at Barbara. Heather and Gregg watch Dave get the food ready. Beside me, Wes is quiet.

My head's quiet, too. I don't have sharks running through it now, like I thought I would.

I listen to the lights then, and the filters and the little fragments of quiet in these slow moments. They remind me of a handful of months ago, before all my daily patterns were overturned and I started #FOMOing and falling asleep with tennis players and changing my signature, back when I was still taking out Milner's trash and had a three-month plan for adding flax seeds into my morning oatmeal. Everything was simple then.

But my mitral valve doesn't even flutter, and I feel my heartbeat strong and steady in my chest. When I lean into Wes, I know *this* is what I want—not easy, not simple, and I smile at Bitty II as I reach out to touch the glass.

# Discussion

Book clubs: Please reach out at info@bleaupress.com.

1) Nora's on the autism spectrum. In what ways do you think this affects her relationships (her friendships, her interactions with her colleagues, and her potential romantic interests)?

2) Nora's professional ecosystem is diverse and complicated. There are big differences between Milner's experience in academia and his wife's, for instance, and between how Nora and Kyle work. What advantages and disadvantages do Nora's unique circumstances (her narrow research focus, her gender, her goals, and her spectrum "powers" and challenges) provide her in this context? Where do you think these leave her professionally?

3) Whether voluntarily or involuntarily, several characters in *Cuttle* are going through major life transitions. Some, like Nora, make conscious changes. In Chapter 18, she references needing to shed her past like a too-tight skin that "pulls and tugs at you all the time you're trying to grow." Which changes do you see being effective in the long run? Do you value any of the characters' decisions *not* to change?

4) In spite of her successes, Nora doubts herself on a daily basis. Do you think this is a feature of her personality, her life experiences on the autism spectrum, or a common experience of her age group?

5) In chapter 7, Nora says that INTJ's choose rather than fall in love. Have you ever had a similar experience? Do you think this choosing affects relationship satisfaction?

6) Nora has a lot of influences in her life, from her mom's blush and emergency hoops and her dad's well-intended cautions to Milner's career advice, Heather's date-coaching, and Lillie's soothing affirmations. Heather eventually regrets her advice to Nora in the blending and swaying departments. Is there a way to know which influences in our lives are positive, or at least helpful, and which hold us back?

7) Wes shares some of Nora's relational challenges and has vastly different interests, which she acknowledges are likely to complicate their ongoing relationship. How do you think this will turn out?

8) Nora also considers the relative safety of personalities and life trajectories she understands. When she imagines relationships with Jarod and Cam, she's confident she could have a good, or at least an "okay" life with either of them. Do you think she's missing something in devaluing this stability?

9) *Cuttle*'s characters mirror the diversity and flux of Cleveland, as Nora says in Chapter 16, "always moving on, always going somewhere, growing or shrinking or becoming something else altogether." What's next for them?

Thanks for reading *Cuttle*!

I'd love to hear from you. Say hello on Goodreads or Bluesky or through my website, chelseabritainauthor.com. (Unfortunately, like Nora's, my internet competence stalled sometime in the mid-nineties, so if I respond like a sea cucumber, please try again.)

I'd also appreciate it if you'd consider leaving a review where you purchased the book to help other readers decide if *Cuttle* is for them.

Happy reading!

Chelsea Britain

www.ingramcontent.com/pod-product-compliance
Lightning Source LLC
Chambersburg PA
CBHW051653180726
48284CB00006B/1975